A Spirited Mother-In-Law . . .

What's wrong, Lindley? Isadora asked with mocking concern. *Is your precious Ash Park harboring ghosts and ghoulies?* She opened her fan, passed it in front of her face, then smiled saucily at Iain over the top.

How can I resist?

With malicious glee, she stepped up behind him and waved the fan at the nape of his neck. The ebony locks fluttered back and forth and Iain yanked his head up from his hands.

He turned to look behind him while one gloved palm patted searchingly at the back of his head. He spun around, frowning first in the direction of an unopened window, then to the closed French doors.

Isadora drifted backward toward the door, waving the fan at him once more. The hair on his forehead wafted with the current.

Breezy, isn't it? she cheerfully called before floating away through the study wall.

Praise for the novels of Casey Claybourne . . .

"This engaging tale brims with wonderfully vibrant characters and piquant originality."
—*Romantic Times*

"The characters sparkled; the plot shines, making this one gem of a book . . . a real treasure."
—*Affaire de Coeur*

Don't miss the Haunting Hearts Romances,
Stardust of Yesterday and *Spring Enchantment*

Turn to the back of this book
for a special sneak preview of
Heaven Above
the next Haunting Hearts romance!

A GHOST OF A CHANCE

CASEY CLAYBOURNE

JOVE BOOKS, NEW YORK

A GHOST OF A CHANCE

A Jove Book/ published by arrangement with
the author

PRINTING HISTORY
Jove edition / August 1996

The Putnam Berkley World Wide Web site address is
http://www.berkley.com

ISBN: 0-515-11857-5

A JOVE BOOK®
Jove Books are published by The Berkley Publishing Group
200 Madison Avenue, New York, New York 10016.
JOVE and the "J" design
are trademarks belonging to Jove Publications, Inc.

PRINTED IN THE UNITED STATES OF AMERICA

10 9 8 7 6 5 4 3 2 1

For Andrew Walter Stroud,
my "cowboy concubine"

With thanks to Candice Hern,
Judith Reuss, Susan Krinard,
and Shelley Blanton-Stroud

Prologue

"Dearly beloved . . ."

Daphne crossed her fingers in a plea for luck and hid them in the folds of her wedding gown. *Luck*. Dear heavens, she would need more than mere luck to survive this next hour. She would need an honest-to-God miracle. She glanced to the back of the altar, where the morning sun shone through the stained-glass window. At least she was in the right place.

Pleated through the gown's shimmering white fabric, her gloved fingers shook with cold. The church felt as icy as a crypt, belying the droplets of sweat trickling down the vicar's jowls. Poor Reverend Lenox. Daphne experienced a twinge of pity for the cleric, wondering if he might not be even more nervous than she was. The vicar was one of the few people aware of the tempest that could explode at any moment in this remote country chapel. A redheaded tempest by the name of Isadora Harkwell.

Reverend Lenox swallowed hard as he turned the page of his prayer book and Daphne bit down on her lip. Now was the time for that miracle. And she did believe. She did believe in miracles.

Please God, don't let her say anything. Oh, please . . .

"Into this holy union, Daphne Eloise Harkwell and Iain Frances Edward Ashingford now come to be joined. If a—" The reverend's voice cracked and he noisily cleared his throat. "If any of you can show just cause why they may not lawfully be married, speak now; or else forever hold your peace."

Daphne knew it wasn't so, but to her ears, it seemed as if all the occupants of the church held their collective breaths.

Then, from behind her, Daphne heard her mother sniff and her heart sank. Mother's snorts and snuffles were more eloquent than the most lauded poet's verses. The wealth of meaning conveyed in that single sniff from Isadora Harkwell would have put both Byron and Blake to shame. It was a disdainful sniff, a preamble to the fiery denunciation that Daphne was certain would follow.

But just as she thought that all might be lost, the vicar proved himself to be truly of divine inspiration. He did not permit any expounding on that expressive sniff, nor did he even acknowledge Lady Harkwell with a glance in her direction, but launched into the service with a speed and loudness of voice that was awe-inspiring. If one could be said to bellow swiftly, Reverend Lenox did so, setting his jowls to swinging with his vigor.

Daphne breathed a silent sigh of relief, but did not uncross her twined fingers. She dared a sidelong peek at her groom to note his reaction to the vicar's bellows and abruptly felt that sigh catch in her throat.

The Marquess Lindley. It really was a good thing,

Daphne thought, that she was a sensible girl or else she might be feeling a bit weak in the knees. She, Daphne Harkwell, a well-bred lady of modest fortune and even more modest beauty, was marrying the most elusive bachelor ever to be born to English soil. And although she'd had three weeks to prepare herself for this event, she still found it incredible that this day should actually come to pass. Her wedding day.

Daphne felt herself flush with embarrassment at the direction of her thoughts. She was a modern young woman, not some milk-and-water miss who swooned at the sight of a pair of broad shoulders. An educated woman, a free-thinker, *Isadora Harkwell's daughter . . .*

However, as her gaze slid over her soon-to-be-husband's profile, she knew that she—like every other woman save her mother—was not proof against Iain Ashingford's striking good looks. From the moment she had first seen him, over four years earlier at a neighbor's summer house party, Daphne had been captivated.

Fifteen years old, gangly and uncomfortable with her dawning womanhood, she had been at an impressionable age. Their gazes had clashed for no more than a second, but that was enough for Daphne to lose her heart. She had returned to the seclusion of Harkwell House, where she had passed many lonely hours weaving girlish fantasies around the dark-haired stranger with the haunted gray eyes.

Although she had outgrown gawky adolescence, she'd never quite abandoned her dreams of white knights on destriers. A romantic and an optimist, Daphne had clung to her dreams with a steadfastness worthy even of the tenacious Isadora.

Therefore, when her father had called her to his study a few weeks earlier to inform her of the betrothal, Daphne had, for the space of a heartbeat, believed her fantasies had come true. But she had allowed herself only that momentary delusion before logic had stepped in.

Despite her romantic tendencies, Daphne possessed a fair measure of common sense, and as her father had explained it, she could hardly have hoped for a better match. The wealthy and handsome Marquess Lindley was the catch of the *ton* and she had seen no reason to object to the marriage. Her mother, however . . .

"Ahem."

Reverend Lenox discreetly called Daphne back to the business at hand. With a wiggle of his bushy gray brow, he signaled for Daphne to offer her fingers to Lord Lindley. She did so, raising her gaze to her groom then hastily lowering it to hide her disappointment.

Honestly, she scolded herself, 'twas foolishness itself to expect more than a smiling politeness. She should be glad that he spoke his vows easily, with no hint of reluctance or uncertainty. His deep voice resonated with a confidence that bolstered her spirits and she reminded herself that it had been Lord Lindley who had approached her father with the offer of marriage. Iain Ashingford could have chosen any woman in the kingdom and he had chosen her. Daphne was human enough to feel flattered, if honest enough to recognize that nothing so banal an emotion as love had prompted the proposal.

"In the name of God, I, Daphne . . ."

She spoke her vows softly, in marked contrast to the booming cleric. When Lord Lindley slipped the diamond-and-gold band onto her finger, she did not meet his gaze again but only stared at the brass buttons on his coat.

Reverend Lenox then joined their hands, and with the ceremony nearing completion, Daphne sensed that the vicar grew bold with his success.

"Those whom God hath joined together, let no man"—the reverend paused for effect before fixing a quelling look in the direction of Lady Harkwell—"or *woman* put asunder."

"Hmmph," Daphne heard her mother retort, but at this point the indignant sound carried little weight. It was done.

"Amen," the witnesses echoed.

Daphne had wed the Marquess Lindley.

Strangely enough, as her new husband led her out of the church, Daphne could not identify any of the faces that blurred before her. She was simply too shocked. The wedding had taken place in spite of her mother's opposition.

As far back as she could remember, Daphne could not recall her mother ever not settling matters exactly as she pleased. If Isadora wanted the withdrawing room decorated in the Egyptian style while Percival Harkwell preferred the Greek, Egyptian it would be. If Daphne's mother desired veal for dinner while her father had a hankering for lamb, most assuredly veal would be presented at the evening table.

Thus it had been Daphne's entire life and she had never known her father's will to prevail over that of her mother. Once or twice in the past, her father had tried to overrule the headstrong Isadora. When her mother announced last year that she would not send Daphne to London for a Season, both Daphne and her father had hotly protested the decision. But to no avail. Isadora Harkwell had adamantly refused to auction off her daughter "as if she were nothing more than a prize heifer." No amount of logic could sway Isadora and Daphne was too proud to resort to tears. Tucked away as they were in the remote Cotswolds, Daphne had nearly resigned herself to spinsterhood until her father's startling announcement.

Stumbling on the single step leading away from the church, Daphne felt Lord Lindley's grip tighten on her arm. She looked up at him, then followed his gaze higher to where ominous, black thunderclouds threatened to let loose their stores. The wind gusted around them, pulling at Daphne's veil and flattening the dark curls on her husband's forehead.

Daphne frowned, remembering how clear the skies had been that morning.

"I wager Mother arranged this," she muttered beneath her breath.

"I beg your pardon?"

Daphne looked up to find her husband's face very near hers, and her pulse accelerated.

"Oh, nothing, my lord. I was thinking of the breakfast arrangements."

He smiled briefly into her eyes, then turned away to watch the wedding guests file from the church.

Shame on you, Daphne's conscience chided. It would only make matters worse if Lord Lindley was to learn of her mother's aversion to him. Then again, *aversion* might be too faint a term for her mother's sentiments, Daphne conceded as the Baroness came into view.

On the bright side, Mother had not worn black. And despite threats to the contrary, she had attended the ceremony even if that outlandish scarlet gown with dyed-to-match boa was raising a few eyebrows. But as always, she carried herself like a queen, her crown a feathered turban that looked as if it might topple with each windy gust.

Daphne smiled. The turban would not dare fall from Isadora Harkwell's head. She would never permit it. She stood there tall and proud and Daphne thought she did not look too cowed by her defeat. No, not at all. Not in the slightest. Apprehension caused Daphne's smile to grow stiff. Oh dear, Mother was looking calm. Determined. And that glint in her eyes. *Oh, no.*

A shiver raced through Daphne that the Marquess must have attributed to the cold.

"Come, we should go," he said.

Daphne turned back to him, swallowing her trepidation and forcing warmth back to her frozen smile.

"Yes," she answered. The distant rumble of thunder shuddered across the valley, urging them to make haste.

Daphne was just settling herself on the seat when the first raindrops began to fall. She heard the guests' cries as they raced for their vehicles and the delicate *ping-ping* of the rain bouncing off the hood of the carriage. The Marquess took his place beside her and the coach set off with a bounce, jostling them together. Daphne realized that she was alone with the Marquess for the first time.

Although he'd spent this past week at Harkwell House with the intention of getting to know her, her mother had succeeded in limiting their time together to but a few hours and not once had they been without a chaperon.

"You handled yourself well."

Daphne started, squeezing her hands together. "Thank you, my lord. So did you."

A spark of amusement flashed in his generally sober gaze. "Yes. Considering how neither of us has been married before, we did quite well, I think." He leaned back, stretching out his legs as far as he could in the coach's narrow confines.

Pale gray breeches hugged the muscled contours of his thighs and Daphne followed their length to the tips of his black patent-leather shoes. He had unusually large feet, prompting her to recall some nonsense her abigail had whispered to her about a man's parts. Daphne hadn't understood a word of it, but Rose had giggled breathlessly in such a way that Daphne had felt as if she ought to have known what her maid found so titillating. She had a feeling that it had something to do with the wedding night.

Her gaze skirted upward past his lean waist and his wide chest, over that authoritarian jaw and firm mouth to . . . to find him watching her. Watching her look at him.

Heat washed into her cheeks, and as she scrambled for an excuse to be staring at him, he asked, "I hope that you were satisfied with the ceremony?"

Daphne nearly laughed in her nervousness. How collected he was. Evidently he was accustomed to women gawking at him like lovesick virgins—which, of course, was exactly what she was.

"The ceremony?" she repeated. "Well, the guests didn't have to strain to hear, which must have been a comfort for Uncle Gideon. He's eighty-four and neither seeing nor hearing well these days. But he is an old dear. I only wish my friends could have been here, but, of course, they're in London for the Season." Daphne consciously subdued any wistfulness that might have crept into her words. "Did you miss having your friends and family here, my lord?"

To her surprise, he did not immediately answer but reached up and tucked a curl behind her ear. His finger traced the curve of her lobe before he pulled his hand away and said, "I believe we can do away with the formalities, Daphne. You may either call me Lindley, as my friends do, or if you choose, Iain."

Her ear felt as if it had suddenly caught fire and her fingers clenched spasmodically around the small bouquet she held in her lap. "I think I prefer Iain."

"Iain it is." He shrugged and crossed his legs at the ankles. "No, I concur with Lady Harkwell that a wedding is a private affair. As the Baroness said, we wouldn't want to do it up common with banns or a showy display."

Daphne frowned. Was that irony she heard in his tone? Did he perhaps know how her mother felt about their union?

She fidgeted with a button on her glove. "Father did insist on inviting the Harkwell relations. He had his own ideas, you understand, and wanted a grander celebration, so he and Mother had to compromise."

"And what of your wishes? What did you want?"

Daphne raised her eyes to find his glittering gray gaze boring into her and she blurted out the truth. "I wanted to marry you."

His brows veed together then smoothed straight again. "Your father told me you were a sensible girl and I see he was right. It's not every day a young lady has the opportunity to be a Marchioness, is it?"

His tone was light and easy, neither malicious nor taunting, yet Daphne wanted to protest, to deny that she was marrying him for his title. But what could she say? That she had agreed to marry him because she had once held a youthful *tendre* for him? That counter to every rational, sensible part of her, she was already half in love with this man with whom she had shared no more than a few dozen words?

After she had given her father her consent, she had worried that she had allowed her daydreams to carry her away. She knew almost nothing of the real man behind her fantasies.

But then, she had seen him again and he had lived up to every inflated quality her imagination had accorded him these past four years. She had remembered him as suave; Iain Ashingford personified flesh-and-blood poetry. Her memories had told her he was handsome; Daphne thought the angels must weep when they looked upon his perfection. Heavens, *she* felt like weeping. Dampness stung the corners of her eyes and she blinked hard.

Suddenly warm fingers wrapped around hers and she glanced down to their joined hands.

"I'm glad you've common sense, Daphne, or you wouldn't have agreed to marry me."

She looked up. "Really?"

"Really," he answered, his expression solemn. He looked

so sincere that Daphne heard herself ask the question that she had not allowed herself even to think these past weeks.

"And why did you wish to marry me?"

He smiled then, a smile that seemed almost bittersweet. "I would imagine that my reasons were very similar to your own."

Baffled, Daphne could make no response. He was an enigma, this new husband of hers. This past week he had proved himself to be courteous, intelligent, well-read, and charming. But she knew that the few hours she had spent in his company were not adequate to fully reveal his character. He had been polite, yet reserved. And on more than one occasion, when he thought no one to be looking, Daphne had caught a spark of heated emotion flare in his gaze, its identity or origins a mystery.

She was curious. Very curious.

Daphne could still hear her mother's scream echoing through the house when her father informed Isadora of the betrothal. Daphne had been in her room but she'd crept downstairs to listen outside the study doors.

"He's a rake!" Isadora had shrieked. Her father had countered that all young men sowed their wild oats.

"A womanizing drunkard! I won't allow it!" her mother had declared.

"You will allow it," her father had retorted in a tone of voice that Daphne had never heard before. More cries had followed, accompanied by the tinkle of shattering glass, and then the butler, Jansen, had discovered Daphne and shooed her away.

The arguments had continued day after day, and although neither parent had confided in her, Daphne had wondered whom she should believe. Her father, who wished to see her marry the Marquess, or her mother, who had been heard to cry that she'd "rather see Daphne enter a convent"?

The Marquess's arrival had put her fears to rest. The tall, dark man who stepped from the crested coach was every bit as charismatic as Daphne remembered. And to her credit, Isadora did not shoot him on sight, but treated him with a chilled civility that could have been attributed to her reputation as an eccentric. As a precaution, Daphne enlisted the help of her maid to make sure that her mother had no plans to poison or otherwise dispose of her intended, and so the Marquess had survived to take his place at the altar.

And yet she continued to wonder why her mother despised him so. To her, he was all that was masculine and pleasing while Isadora depicted him as Satan in a top hat. Why?

The question made Daphne's toes curl in her slippers, as cool metal slid across the arch of her right foot. Her lucky sixpence.

She smiled softly, feeling somewhat relieved and comforted. Whatever ill fortune her mother might have wished upon this day—and upon the Marquess Lindley—at least Daphne had done all she could to ensure the day was a happy one. She had placed her lucky coin in her shoe, had wished on last night's first star, and had refrained from wearing red the entire week.

Perhaps it was silly superstition, but she had always believed in things magical. Fairies, birthday wishes and . . . marrying the man of your dreams.

The coach lurched along as the rain began to fall more heavily, and soon they pulled up in front of Harkwell House.

Of Dutch inspiration, the house's tall, narrow proportions were atypical for country design, but lovely when set against the background of the Cotswolds peaks. Its mellowed butternut exterior looked warm and inviting, and in spite of her excitement, Daphne felt a small sadness knowing she would no longer call it home.

A footman carrying an umbrella hurried forward to greet them and to accompany them into the manor.

In the entrance hall, Daphne paused and ran a hand over her mist-dampened curls. "If you'll excuse me, my lord, I need to refresh myself before we sit down for breakfast."

"Of course." He bowed over her hand, hesitated, then turned her fingers and pressed a kiss to her palm. The heat of his mouth seared right through the glove, causing Daphne to suppress a shudder of delight.

Iain righted himself, smiling one of those devastating smiles. "Have a care, my dear, for you seem to be taking a chill."

Daphne blinked, but did not answer as wedding guests began to filter through the doorway, complaining of the wet.

"Excuse me," she whispered again before pivoting away to hurry up the stairs.

At the top of the first landing, Daphne rounded the corner into an open doorway, then leaned against the wall to catch her breath. Her palm still tingled from Iain's caress and she hugged it tightly to her bosom.

So this was passion. She had secretly read of it in novels that were deemed unsuitable for young ladies, never understanding what "ecstasies of the flesh" entailed. She had wanted to ask her mother, especially once she knew she was to be wed, but her mother's distaste for the Marquess made her reluctant to bring up the subject of the marriage bed. Thanks to Rose, she had an extremely vague idea of what to expect this evening, although the maid's description of passion sounded to Daphne more like endurance than the ecstasy she had read about.

She splayed her fingers across her chest and wondered if tonight—

"Daphne."

Father. Daphne peeked around the corner and saw the

good Baron huffing as he reached the top of the long, winding staircase, his face ruddy with exertion.

"Here, Papa," she called.

"Faith, girl, what are you doing in there?"

"Catching my breath."

Her father threw a glance behind him before stepping into the room. "We could all do with that, I suppose." His voice was rough as he asked, "And how are you, my pet? Holding up?"

"Any regrets, is that what you're asking?"

"I suppose I am," he conceded with a nod of his head. Tight white curls clung to his pate like hardy snowflakes.

"No. No regrets. Should I have any?"

Her father's expression softened. "No, I think he's a good man, Daphne, or else I would never have accepted his suit. I believe he can make you happy."

She laid her hand on his arm. "I know, Papa."

"About your mother . . ." He clumsily patted her hand where it rested on his coat sleeve. "I suppose you've heard some of what's been said but I don't want you to worry. Your mother's a proud woman—too proud if you ask me— and she refuses to see Lindley for who he is."

Daphne waited for an explanation, but finally had to ask, "Why?"

A sigh rose and fell in her father's chest. "Many years back, a dispute arose between the Ashingfords and your mother's family, the Whitings. The feud has stood for decades and your mother will not put it aside. It's that cursed pride of hers, Daphne. It's truly a curse."

"A feud?" Daphne shook her head. "I cannot believe that Mother would take a family rift so personally."

"For her, it is personal, my dear. She has taken this alliance with the Ashingford name very badly and I doubt whether she'll ever forgive me for my part in it."

Daphne emitted a weak half-laugh. "Father, now you sound like Mother with your dramatic declarations."

"I suppose I do, but I fear 'tis so. She would have done anything to keep an Ashingford from marrying into the family. Absolutely anything."

Alarm weaved its way up Daphne's spine as her mother's determined expression outside the church resurfaced in her mind's eye.

Anything? she silently echoed.

Down below, Isadora Harkwell had finally found the Marquess Lindley in the Baron's study, where he was in the process of downing a jigger of gin. Disgust rolled through her with the knowledge of how correctly she had read this degenerate Ashingford upstart. How could Percival have given their precious daughter to this reprobate?

"At the bottle already?" she asked from the threshold.

Lord Lindley turned from the sideboard and raised the crystal decanter in invitation. "May I pour you one, Lady Harkwell?"

Isadora pursed her lips. "You may not." She closed the door behind her with a decisive click and marched into the room. "You and I must talk."

Lindley waved his arm invitingly toward a pair of club chairs as if he were the host and she the guest. Isadora bristled at the man's effrontery.

"I will stand and so will you," she ordered.

The Marquess set down his glass, then lazily propped an arm atop the sideboard.

With deliberate slowness, she reached for the quizzing glass hanging from the gold chain around her neck and raised it to her right eye. Ah, but he was the very image of his father; all that bloody charm wrapped in an attractive package to boot.

"As I thought," she drawled, before dropping the glass with a disdainful sneer. "You are an Ashingford."

"I beg your pardon, Lady Harkwell, but I had thought that fact had already been established."

"Save your cocky grins, young man, for one who might appreciate them," Isadora snapped. "I know why you've stolen my daughter and I'm here to tell you your plan will not succeed!"

Now she had his attention. He'd straightened from the sideboard and was moving to stand in front of her. Tall like his father, he towered above her turbaned head.

"It's not Daphne you want, but Ash Park, and I swear to you, Lindley, you'll never have it." She sniffed meaningfully. "Oh, your father tried the same tactic, wooing me with pretty words in his hopeless attempt to secure Ash Park, but I saw past his ploys. I sent him on his way, as did my father."

"Your father stole Ash Park from my grandfather."

"How dare you! Your grandfather lost the estate in a wager. It's common knowledge."

"But is it common knowledge that your father, an inveterate gambler, fixed such games of chance?"

Isadora took a deep, steadying breath, feeling the blood begin to pound in her head. "Poppycock. Pure and utter nonsense."

"I'm not here to argue your father's gaming practices, Lady Harkwell. My only concern is seeing the Ashingford ancestral home returned to its rightful owners."

"Don't play the high-and-mighty with me, boy. I've crushed greater men than you in my day, I assure you."

"My father for one?"

Isadora glanced to the hearth, but it lay cold and she wondered why she felt so insufferably hot. Rallying her nerve, she leveled on him her sternest glare. "I don't care to discuss your father. I only want to make clear to you that you will have neither Ash Park nor my daughter."

She saw him tense.

"What are you saying?"

With feigned indifference, she withdrew a handkerchief from her pocket and dabbed lightly at her temples.

"You do not love Daphne and my daughter deserves more than you can give her." She fluttered her handkerchief in front of his face. "You needn't raise a superior brow at me, you young pup. I've heard all about your mistresses and affairs and your numerous bedroom conquests. Daphne is too good for you."

"But she is mine," he answered in a carefully controlled voice.

"She is not," Isadora countered. "Her father insisted that the marriage take place. Well, it has. But that doesn't mean I will hand over my only child to a man who married her solely for her marriage settlement."

Isadora actually heard his teeth snap as the muscles in his jaw worked. "I see no reason to continue this discussion, Lady Harkwell. Your husband and I have already reached an agreement."

He took a step toward the door before Isadora stopped him with her next words.

"You may think you have, but you have not."

He stilled but did not turn around. It was time to play her trump card.

"The estate is held in trust and Percival does *not* act as trustee."

Charged silence held them both.

He then slowly pivoted on his heel, fixing her with a glacial stare. "Lord Harkwell gave me his word."

"Hmmph. It was his word, not mine."

"Are you saying that you would repudiate your husband's promise?"

With a swipe of her hand, she adjusted her turban. "I would and I shall. And don't think for an instant that Percival can bend me to his will. The trust is held for me in the same manner that I hold it for Daphne. Ash Park becomes hers when I instruct the trustee to transfer the property or upon my death. No sooner."

Fists clenched, he accused, "I've been duped."

"No, my lord, you've been outfoxed. You had thought to swindle both the estate and my daughter and now you've been tripped up in your own game."

"And Daphne?"

Isadora stiffened defensively. "She, at least, has your title. If you can care for her, understanding that Ash Park will never be yours, then I wish you happy. Otherwise, we can immediately set about arranging an annulment."

Lindley's balled fists unfurled, and with mocking precision, he bent over and bowed. "My congratulations. Yet again, your family has succeeded in playing an Ashingford for a fool."

Isadora nodded, acknowledging his damning praise. She had forced his hand and Lindley would have to show his true colors now. She glanced to the mantel clock.

"We'll be going in to breakfast in fifteen minutes. Why don't you compose yourself before joining us so that Daphne isn't overset by your poor humor?"

With one final adjustment to her turban, Isadora sailed out of the room like a conqueror born.

A full thirty minutes later the fourteen wedding guests, the bride, the host and hostess milled about the dining room, awaiting the groom's arrival to the wedding breakfast. The table had been decorated with satin ribbon and white flowers, the crystal sparkled, and the silver gleamed. The chef hovered at the door to the kitchen, evidently concerned about the delay in serving his culinary creations.

Isadora toyed impatiently with the chain to her quizzing

glass while maintaining a watchful eye on the entrance to the dining room.

So Lindley seeks his petty revenge by making us wait while the breakfast grows cold. How terribly childish of him, she thought with a sniff.

Her gaze skipped to her husband, who chatted amiably with a Harkwell cousin while shooting worried looks toward the empty threshold. Her darling Daphne was putting on a brave face, smiling and laughing, but Isadora could see the tension in the set of her slim shoulders.

"Marsh." She loudly summoned a footman. "Kindly inform Lord Lindley that we await his pleasure in the dining room."

"Yes, m'lady."

All eyes followed the footman as he departed. The minutes crept by. Three, four, five, six. *Faith, what on earth was keeping that nincompoop Marsh?*

At last Marsh reappeared at the doorway, panting as if he'd run a footrace around the estate. His face flushed, he stood clutching the door frame with one hand while tugging at the tails of his liveried coat with the other.

"Well?" Isadora demanded.

"He's gone, m'lady."

A murmur ran through the room and Isadora experienced a sudden tightness in her chest.

"What do you mean *gone*?"

"The Marquess is gone, m'lady. He packed his bags and left with his man near twenty minutes ago."

Oh, dear God. Isadora felt the blood drain from her head in a sickening rush. She had committed the cardinal sin; she had overplayed her hand and the Marquess had called her bluff.

Her eyes flew to Daphne, who was looking at her questioningly, the pain in her daughter's green gaze almost too much to bear. Percy's expression, both sad and accusing, was also one of disappointment, disappointment in her.

What had she done? All she had wanted was Daphne's happiness and instead she had brought on this agonizing humiliation for her daughter. To be deserted by your husband of only a few minutes in front of family and friends . . . Oh, her poor, sweet Daphne! And she was responsible.

The tightness in her chest increased and her head suddenly flooded with an incredible pain. She jerked. Everything before her became a blur. The pain intensified and then she knew.

Dear God, she was dying.

She could not draw a breath, but how she wanted to. She had to tell Daphne how sorry she was. She had to explain that it wasn't supposed to have happened this way, damn that wretched man! Her vision swam in colors and shapes and she felt herself floating. Floating. Then all grew dark as she crashed to the floor.

Chapter One

Three months later

Ash Park.

Iain's fingers trembled on the reins as he brought his winded mount to a standstill. The horse lowered its head and pulled deeply for air while Iain's own breath rasped shallow and shaky with keen anticipation.

He had done it. He'd finally come home.

An unfamiliar knot of emotion swelled in his throat and he swallowed hard, surprised by the depth of his reaction. Pride and regret—and anger—warred within him as his possessive gaze swept over the land that he now called his own.

Yes, he was proud, damn it! He'd done as he'd promised; he'd fulfilled the vow made to his father. Although it had cost him a great deal—his freedom and a measure of his principles—he'd righted the wrong done to his family. Ash Park was theirs once again.

But what should have been a moment of great joy was shadowed with regret; regret that his father hadn't seen the promise brought to fruition. James Ashingford had been dead nearly two years now.

Iain's hands tightened reflexively around the leather ribbons. His father should have been here. He should have shared this victory with him.

The mare sidestepped restlessly beneath him, sensing his sudden anger, and Iain leaned forward to pat the animal's neck.

"Easy, girl," he soothed. "Easy."

The words proved calming for the both of them. Iain straightened in the saddle, his eyes narrowing with conviction as he deliberately let go of his frustration. This was a day he'd worked for many months and he would not allow bitterness to mar his triumph. This moment was his and his alone.

He had not sent word ahead of his arrival because he hadn't wanted a footman or valet to precede him. He wanted to be the first to see Ash Park again. The Marquess Lindley reclaiming his lost heritage.

Staring out onto the valley, Iain thought he might, at last, understand his father's obsession for this land. There was something magical about the rolling fields, dappled with summer color, waving their long grasses in a rippling, emerald welcome. The crystal-blue waters of the River Derwill seemed to bubble their own greeting as they spilled over boulders polished smooth through the centuries. Perhaps it was only the emotion that held him, but Ash Park did seem to possess a mystical beauty, a beauty that enchanted.

Over a century ago Iain's great-grandfather had built Ash Park, investing a sizable share of the Ashingford fortune into the construction of the lavish manor house. Situated in the most beautiful of Dorset's valleys, the estate had become the crown jewel of the family's holdings, coveted and admired by the wealthy and titled.

Unfortunately, the Earl of Whiting had been among those who had coveted Ash Park, and fifty years ago Iain's grandfather had lost the property to the Earl under suspicious circumstances. Iain's father had been but a child at the time, yet had never forgotten the ignominy of being evicted from his home.

Emerging from the copse of trees, Iain slowed his horse to a walk. There she was, to the west, her magnificent domed turrets rising above the treetops, flags dipping back and forth in the fitful breeze.

She was a noble house, her gray stone facade softened by weather, her mullioned windows arching beneath the turrets, reflecting the morning sun.

Iain squinted as he drew closer. Something was not right here. Annoyance kicked through him when his gaze settled again on the flags. The Earl of Whiting's crest flew above Ash Park instead of his own. Dammit, why hadn't the Whiting flags been removed? He should have sent someone ahead if only to ensure that the Lindley banner was flying over Ash Park when he arrived. The sight of the red-and-black Whiting dragons brought a foul taste to his mouth and he vowed to see the cursed flags burned before the day was through.

But for the distant barking of a keen-eared hound, the grounds were quiet as Iain approached the manor's front. A fountain, in the shape of a phoenix, dominated the entrance and Iain recalled the story of how his grandfather had waited until the fountain was completed before building the house that was to surround it. Representing the beauty and strength that can arise from tragedy, the phoenix had symbolized for Iain's family the Ashingford spirit.

Iain jumped down from his horse, then looped the reins over the hitching post. Slowly he ascended the stairs to the great double doors, the feeling of completion—of having come full circle—increasing with each step. He did not have to use the knocker, for the footman swung open the door before he reached it.

"May I help you, milord?"

With deliberate calm, Iain yanked at each finger of his gloves and peeled them from his hands before responding.

"You may. I am the Marquess Lindley. The master of Ash Park."

Well, it was about time.

Perched amid the branches of the brass chandelier, Isadora Harkwell—or rather, the spirit of Isadora Harkwell—gazed down at her loathsome son-in-law as he sipped at his brandy.

His brandy. *Hmmph.* Three months ago it had been *her* brandy, but that fact didn't appear to sour Lord Lindley's palate overmuch. The wretch actually smacked his lips as he drained his glass, then, in a triumphant gesture, he flung the crystal—*her* lovely Irish crystal—into the hearth, where it shattered noisily into a thousand sparkling shards.

Isadora's brows snapped together and she inhaled angrily, although no air entered her lungs. This was going to be even more difficult than she had imagined. After three months of prowling around Ash Park, waiting for Lindley to make an appearance, her patience had begun to wear woefully thin. Not that patience had ever been one of her strongest virtues, but waiting in this vacuum of existence called purgatory had truly begun to prey on her nerves.

The Lord knew—or, at least, she'd been told He knew—how she'd blustered and fussed and carried on about her sentence; she'd kicked up quite a spectral stink. She'd tried everything, using every trick she'd ever employed on earth, but had been unable to budge the celestial powers. In no uncertain terms, they'd informed her that she would not be allowed to move on to the next heavenly plane until she had fixed the mess she'd created here on earth. Not until Daphne and Lindley were reunited would she be freed from her ghostly state.

Isadora adjusted her turban with a huff. She still had not completely reconciled herself to her odious mission. Granted, the prospect of haunting Lindley was not so very disagreeable, she conceded as she flashed his bent head a malicious grin. Not too disagreeable in the least. However, the thought of having to play Cupid between Daphne and this pillaging pup . . .

Her lips puckered with distaste and she smoothed the feather draping from her headpiece. It wasn't as if she was solely to blame, after all. Lindley had heartlessly deserted her daughter and thus was every bit as responsible as she—if not more so—for the current estrangement. What he had done to Daphne—

Some of the starch went out of Isadora's spine as pictures of that fateful morning returned unbidden to her memory. Tears coursing down Daphne's parchment-white cheeks. Percy's keening moan of despair.

After her death, as Isadora had hovered above her body and witnessed her family's grief, she had known a pain greater than any she had ever known while earthbound. Helpless to comfort them, she could but watch as they grappled feebly with their mortal anguish. If only she could go to them now and console them, but she could not. She had been sentenced to Ash Park. And to the Marquess Lindley.

She glared down at him where he sat behind the desk, flipping through a stack of papers. So unconcerned, so unaware. So damned secure in his position of wealth and power. Oh, the boy deserved a comeuppance! And she was just the ghost to give him one.

A speculative gleam sparked her gaze as she eyed him from her perch. Just how much progress, she wondered, had she made with her supernatural skills? Enough to create some entertainment for her arrogant son-in-law?

Admittedly, she hadn't had an easy time of it at first, crashing into walls when she was supposed to have floated easily through and slipping from moldings when her powers of levitation had wavered. But she was slowly getting the hang of this haunting business, even if she still had much to learn.

A wicked chuckle escaped her. Oh, the fun—

Here now, what's this?

Lindley had raised his head and was looking around the room with a frown between his eyes. He couldn't possibly have heard her laugh. Or could he have?

Isadora toyed thoughtfully with her quizzing glass, watching his gaze travel the length of the study. No one else had heard her during these past months at Ash Park, even when she'd flown into a temper at finding the silver improperly stored. To her knowledge, her presence had gone wholly unnoticed. Until now. Could Lindley hear her or had some other sound caught his attention?

Lindley, she called imperiously.

He didn't look up.

She tried a little louder. *Lindley.*

He lowered his gaze back to the paperwork and Isadora grumbled disappointedly. Perhaps, with practice, she might learn to breach the void between her world and his. Certainly it bore trying as the possibilities for diversion were simply too delightful to ignore.

Suddenly Lindley slammed shut the ledger he'd been studying and laid his head back against the chair. With a disgusted sigh, he closed his eyes.

Isadora inched forward and peered down at the face
tilted up to her. She snorted contemptuously. Aristocratic
nose, intelligent brow, too-proud jaw. The resemblance between Lindley and his father was remarkable—and remark-
ably disturbing. She brushed aside a guilty fluttering in the
vicinity of her heart, refusing to allow her thoughts to follow the direction that they so frequently had since her arrival at Ash Park.

Lindley snapped open his eyes and sat forward. Purposefully he snatched up a pen and began to whittle it to a fine
point. His movements were brusque, yet sure. He shoved
aside the pile of papers with a careless sweep of his arm,
then withdrew a note card from the desk. He dipped the pen
into the inkwell. Once. Twice. His expression grave, he
poised the pen over the parchment for a long moment.

Curiosity got the better of Isadora. Cautiously she
stepped off the chandelier, wobbled momentarily, then
floated toward the floor.

She landed with a thump, flat on her derriere.

Blast it!

Lindley glanced up, brows drawn together. He gave his
dark head a quick, ear-cleansing shake before returning his
attention once again to the blank card.

So, he could hear her, if not regularly, at least on occasion.

Isadora pondered that point as she picked herself up off
the cold marble with as much dignity as she could muster.
She regally shook out her taffeta skirts, then tucked a stray
red lock beneath her turban. Resettling her shawl about her
shoulders, she walked around the desk to stand behind
Lindley as he slashed the quill across the card. She squinted
to where amorphous ink blots ran together in an indecipher-
able blur.

Fustian, where's my glass? she muttered impatiently, tugging at the gold chain around her neck. She settled the

quizzing glass against her right eye and leaned over the
Marquess's shoulder. The note card, imprinted with the Ash
Park phoenix, read:

Madame—

> *After much consideration, I have concluded that it*
> *would be best for you not to join me at Ash Park. This*
> *decision is solely mine and is no reflection whatsoever*
> *on your many charms. Perhaps we might further our*
> *acquaintance at a later date.*

—Lindley

The scoundrel! Never say he'd invited his fancy-piece to
Ash Park! Without thinking, and in a purely impulsive gesture, Isadora rapped the back of his head with the edge of
her quizzing glass. But the glass passed through his jet-
black hair like fog passing through a dense forest. He didn't
feel a thing.

He then withdrew an envelope from the desk drawer and
Isadora was surprised to see that he planned to send the letter by messenger instead of by post. She wondered at his
urgency and his reasons for revoking the invitation, then
stiffened as an idea occurred to her. Botheration, what if he
weren't planning to remain at Ash Park? What if he
planned to leave after but a cursory examination of the
property? Oh dear, that wouldn't suit. Wouldn't suit at all.

Isadora practically draped herself over his shoulder as
she leaned over to read the name he penned on the envelope.

The Comtesse deCheval, Durham Place, Chelsea.

She cocked a disdainful eyebrow. Not the most presti-
gious of addresses, but probably suitable for a widow hunt-

ing for a wealthy protector. *Disgraceful*. Although she had expected no less from an Ashingford.

Isadora fell back a pace as Lindley pushed to his feet. He stalked across the room and, instead of ringing, called for the butler. "Wilkinson."

The servant appeared instantly.

"I've left a note on my desk that I want delivered as soon as possible. See to it, won't you?"

"Certainly, milord. I'll send straightaway to the stables for a messenger."

The butler turned in one direction while Lindley headed in the other, toward the entrance.

Isadora heard the footman bid the Marquess good day as the front door closed with a muted thud.

She tapped her quizzing glass contemplatively against her chin while frowning down at the letter. Now, how might she turn this situation to her advantage? Indeed, she would find herself in very difficult circumstances if Lindley did not stay on at Ash Park. How could she possibly be expected to reunite the pair if neither Daphne nor Lindley was in residence?

She suddenly narrowed her eyes and smiled. *Isadora, my dear, you are a dashedly clever woman!* she congratulated herself. However, the exuberant smile dimmed somewhat as her gaze fell uncertainly on the pen.

Although her skills had improved with each passing day, Isadora had not yet had much success in manipulating objects of the material world. She'd managed to levitate a handful of light items, but to wield a pen deftly enough to form words . . .

She glared ferociously at the quill the way one might stare down an enemy. She'd do it, by goodness, or die in the trying! Oh, well . . . of course, she couldn't really die again, but she knew precisely what she meant.

Marshaling her abilities, she first broke open the wax

seal and removed the note from the envelope. She then crumpled the envelope and hid it at the back of the drawer before selecting a clean one. By the time she laid the new envelope upon the desk, she was puffing with her efforts. From her gown's pocket, she withdrew a handkerchief and dabbed daintily at her ghostly brow.

Hmmph, she muttered. *The exertion involved in the most minor of spectral labors!*

With renewed determination, Isadora tucked the silk square back into her pocket and reached for the quill. Her grip faltered and the pen fell to the table, trickling ink. She did not give up, but reached again for the implement and this time succeeded in dipping it into the inkwell.

She focused every ounce of her concentration on the pen, and painstakingly began to write. . . .

Chapter Two

The Most Hon. the Marchioness Lindley.

Daphne stared at the envelope lying upon the silver tray, her heart thumping erratically in her breast. She had not previously seen her married name in print and the sight of it brought a hot, indignant flush to her cheeks. It looked so false. And it made her feel false, like a charlatan, a pretender. A pretend wife and a pretend Marchioness.

Reluctantly her gaze drifted to the finger of her left hand. The diamond-and-gold band that had adorned it only a few days was hidden beneath a pile of childhood memorabilia in her room. Like her memories of her wedding day, Daphne had buried the ring where it would not serve as a constant reminder of her girlish folly. Of a time when she believed in happily ever after and gallant suitors with limb-melting smiles.

She lowered her teacup to its saucer, dismayed by the

tremors that caused the porcelain to rattle loudly in the
drawing room's quiet. Amber liquid sloshed into the
saucer, spilling over onto the white damask cloth, and
Daphne jerked her gaze away from the clear evidence of
her agitation.

She clenched her fists in her lap. She would not think of
him. She would not allow Iain Ashingford to take posses-
sion of her thoughts, not now, after she'd spent these past
months ruthlessly driving his image from her mind.

Daphne leaped to her feet and began to circle the small
tea table, her black bombazine gown rustling with each
angry switch of her hips. The outrage felt safe and good,
the same familiar companion that had sustained her these
many weeks. After many tear-filled, sleepless nights,
Daphne had learned that the anger was much easier to live
with than the humiliation had been.

Not that the humiliation had ever truly left her. Rather,
more powerful emotions had repressed the more trivial.
The embarrassment of being discarded by a husband she
had never known now seemed petty when contrasted with
the heartbreaking loss of her mother.

Daphne strode to the window and pushed aside the heavy
silk hangings. The picturesque Cotswolds peaks stretched
across the west, their limestone hills covered with the pale-
barked beech and deep green of summer lichen. To the far
end of the vale, the escarpment broke away at a steep cliff,
revealing bands of rock in every shade from ivory to
smoke. The beautifully striated limestone held Daphne's
gaze as she unconsciously sought a particular hue. A silvery gray that both held and reflected light, a color she'd
seen only once before. The color of Iain Ashingford's eyes.

Daphne's fingers curled into the curtain fabric when she
realized what she sought. She cursed softly, feeling justified in doing so.

Blast it, the man warranted the occasional oath! After all,

he had abandoned her on her wedding day, shaming her before her family; he'd hied off to London, leaving her to face
the consequences; and, then, upon the death of her mother,
he hadn't even had the decency to send a note of condolence.

Not that she would have read any message from him had
he sent one. During those first horrible, grief-filled days,
Daphne had held Iain responsible for her mother's passing.
Her sorrow and her anger had become intertwined, one in-
distinguishable from the other. She'd blamed him. If he
hadn't left her, Mother wouldn't have died.

In time, however, Daphne's innate fairness had rejected
the idea. No matter how bitter she might feel toward him,
she could not hold Iain accountable for her mother dying.
He was guilty of many sins, but not that.

Truthfully, to her mind, his gravest offense had been the
destruction of her dreams. In one fell swoop, Iain Ashingford had crushed every bit of romantic optimism with
which Daphne Harkwell had viewed life. She had entered
into their marriage with sentimental hopes, born of the
naïveté of youth and a sheltered existence. He had, in one
cruel act, ripped away that rosy veil of illusion and substi-
tuted it with a somber shroud of reality.

Reality. Daphne tossed aside the curtain and turned
around, her eyes drawn again to the envelope.

Curious, she sidled slowly toward the table to gaze down
at the mysterious note. Scrawled in a shaky, unpracticed
hand, the handwriting looked to be that of a child. She
frowned. The Marquess's penmanship could not be so poor,
she assured herself.

The letter must be from one of the Harkwell relations
who knew of the marriage, for no one else had been apprised of the union. No notices had been sent to the papers,
no announcements posted to friends and family. Once Lord
Lindley had fled Harkwell House, it was as if he had never

been. Not once had his name been mentioned since her mother's death.

"Don't be a goose, Daphne," she whispered.

She reached over and picked up the note and the silver letter opener. A crest she did not recognize, a phoenix rising from the ashes, embellished the upper left corner of the envelope. She wedged the blade beneath the plain wax seal and tugged it open with a sharp twist.

Immediately, she noticed that the handwriting on the envelope did not match that on the card. Then her eyes scanned over the page's few lines and the opener fell from her suddenly limp fingers to the floor with a clatter.

"I—I . . ." Daphne felt as if she were choking on her fury. "H-how dare he?" She read the lines again as her eyes began to burn with angry tears.

She raised her head, her gaze darting around the room for something to throw. She snatched up the first item she found, a brass candle stand, and drew back her arm . . . when, abruptly, she stilled.

What had possessed her? The spirit of her mother?

Slowly she lowered the candle stand back to the table, nonplussed by her uncharacteristic outburst. Never had she felt the urge to throw an object in anger; tantrums of that nature had been Isadora's way, not hers. But then again, Daphne had never known such a violent fury as she did in this moment. For him to forbid her to go to Ash Park . . .

She looked back to the card and two words loomed from the page.

Her charms. She snorted in a fair imitation of her mother. Did the Marquess think her some mongrel to be satisfied with that meager complimentary bone? Did he believe her so shallow that she would accept his edict simply because he offered her sham praise?

Flinging the letter onto the tray, she began to pace, arms

folded across her chest, where they rose and fell in a sporadic cadence with each impassioned breath.

"He asks Father for my hand—"

Daphne's pacing brought her to the far wall and she pivoted smartly on her heel.

"Marries me, deserts and humiliates me—"

Her long-legged gait carried her to the window, where she spun around again with enough speed to experience a moment of vertigo. She steadied herself and continued her pacing.

"And then—" She raised her arm, forefinger extended as if making a point to a judge. "*And then* prohibits me from visiting my mother's home! Why, the gall of the man is simply not to be believed!"

In her agitated state, Daphne failed to take note of where her steps were leading until she practically bumped noses with the butler standing in the open doorway.

"Jansen!" she cried, flushing as she tripped clumsily over her feet. *How much had he overheard?*

But she had nothing to fear from the starched, stiff-necked butler for he frowned ever so slightly and said, "I beg your pardon, Miss Daphne, were you speaking to me? I do apologize but I could not hear what you were saying."

Daphne smiled weakly, grateful for his discretion. "No, I was but talking to myself. What is it, Jansen?"

"Sir Roger is calling. Shall I send him up or inform him you're not receiving?"

"Roger," Daphne breathed.

She hadn't seen her childhood friend since long before her betrothal, for Roger had gone to London in early spring. She had written him shortly after her mother's death and had informed him in one stark sentence of her marriage; his answering letter had expressed sorrow at Isadora's passing, but had made no mention of her surprising alliance.

Daphne knew that he wouldn't have been pleased to

learn of her marriage in such an offhand manner, but she had known of no other way to tell him.

"Miss Daphne?" Jansen prodded.

Daphne shook herself. "Yes, please send him up and ask Gertrude to bring in a fresh pot of tea, won't you?"

The butler departed and Daphne clasped her arms around her waist. How fortunate that Roger would come today when she so desperately needed his thoughtful and pragmatic advice.

Her gaze darted to the note. Without consciously asking herself why, she hurried over and grabbed up the missive, then crumpled it into a ball, which she shoved into her dress pocket. Her fingers tightened around the thick parchment, squeezing hard.

"Daphne."

The familiar voice spun her around.

"Roger, how good it is to see you." She stepped forward as he removed his hat, then she eagerly clasped his hands in hers.

"Just look at you," she said, spreading their hands wide in a gesture of admiration. "You're the absolute pink of the *ton*."

He did look fine in his new London attire, his honey-blond hair cut shorter à la mode. The polish of his first Season had matured him, she thought, noting the air of confidence in his easy manner and gracious smile.

"And you, dear Daphne . . . you look well."

Releasing him, she laughed softly. "Roger, you've always been a poor liar. I know that black ill suits me, but I wear it for Father's sake. Come sit down."

As they took their seats on the divan Roger said, "Your mother would have hated to see you in mourning. As I recall, she despised the practice."

"Yes. When Grandfather died, Mother refused to follow custom, scandalizing some of our stuffier relations. But she did so love her vibrant colors." Melancholy touched her as she remembered the day two months ago when she had tearfully packed away her mother's wardrobe. Fuchsia, co-quelicot, bottle-green, turquoise. "Her garb reflected her character, don't you think, Roger?"

His soft smile warmed her. "Yes, I do. I'll never again see a feathered turban without thinking of her." His blue eyes saddened. "I wish I could have come home sooner, but I had to stay for Deborah's debut ball. Neither she nor Mother would have forgiven me had I missed my own sister's coming-out."

"Of course. I would not have expected you to cut short your time in Town."

"Has it been very difficult?"

Daphne looked to her lap. "To some degree, I have reconciled myself to her being gone, but Papa is inconsolable. He's hardly left his study since the day of the funeral. He even takes his meals in there . . . when he bothers to eat." She raised her troubled gaze to Roger's. "I worry about him, Roger, I truly do."

"And is that the reason you're still at Harkwell House?"

Daphne stiffened. She knew this question would arise, but she wasn't sure she was prepared to address it. Fortunately, Gertrude's arrival with fresh tea forestalled an immediate response. The maid left and Daphne tried to turn the subject.

"Tea?" she offered too cheerfully.

"No. Thank you."

Her hand lingered on the silver urn's handle as she heard the unspoken questions in Roger's voice. She knew that she owed him an explanation, but she allowed the silence to stretch out between them.

Finally, he spoke. "The postscript on your letter gave me quite a shock, Daphne."

She bit gently into her lower lip, torn by her need to

share her confusion and her reluctance to expose her shame. How much did she dare reveal to her old friend? Until now, she hadn't spoken of her bizarre marital situation with anyone. But this was Roger. Dear dependable Roger.

"Yes, I'm sorry about that."

"Sorry? 'P.S. On April twenty-seventh, I wed the Marquess Lindley,'" he quoted, shoving his gloved fingers through his hair. "Faith, the Marquess Lindley! The man's got the devil's own reputation, don't you know? 'Twas even rumored that he'd ruined a neighbor girl—"

"Roger!" She looked at him, aghast.

"By Jove, Daphne, I'm concerned for you. You always insist on seeing the best in people and sometimes you overlook their shortcomings."

"Well, I could hardly do so in this case," she said, promising herself she wouldn't cry.

Roger gentled his tone in the face of her obvious distress. "So the Marquess is not the white knight you'd dreamed of?"

"I had thought he was, I honestly had. But, it seems he's more dragon than knight."

"Lord, I wish you'd spoken to me first, Daphne. I don't know him well, but he's said to be a hard, bitter man."

She stood, nearly upsetting the teapot. Oddly enough, as infuriated as she was with the Marquess Lindley, it disturbed her to hear Roger speak ill of him.

"What might I do to help?"

"You cannot do anything, Roger. It's a mess, an awful, awful mess."

She began an agitated circuit of the room, feeling her earlier anger return.

"Legally, I am his wife as decreed by the church and the courts, but that's the extent of it. Nothing more. I daresay you won't believe it but, in reality, I'm no more married to him than I am to you, for heaven's sake! He's playing some game—he must have some purpose in all this nonsense—although for the life of me I cannot imagine what it might be."

Roger's blond brows met over his nose. "What are you saying, Daphne?"

She threw her hands into the air with an exasperated sigh. "I'm saying that I haven't spoken with nor seen my 'husband' since the day of our wedding."

Roger sat back with a thoughtful frown. "Might he be giving you time to grieve before making—ahem—his marital demands?"

"I think not," she dryly retorted.

"Have you tried to contact him?"

"No."

"And he's not contacted you once since the day of your wedding?"

Daphne curled her fingers around the note in her pocket. "No, not really."

Walking to the window, she leaned against the sill and stared unseeing into the afternoon.

"Are you pining for him?"

"Good heavens, no!" she answered, more vehemently than she'd needed to. An awkward silence followed, which Daphne hurried to fill.

"No, the worst of it, Rog, is the maddening sense that I no longer have control of my own life. This man, whom I know not at all, can dictate to me from a distance, and as his wife, I am expected to comply."

"Not the daughter of the proud and indomitable Isadora Harkwell?"

A strangled chuckle met Roger's attempt at humor. "Frightful, isn't it? Mother would—" Daphne stilled, her breath catching in her throat. What would Mother do?

She shoved away from the window and turned to stand in the center of the drawing room. "No!"

"No what?"

"No, I won't allow it," Daphne declared, her eyes rounding with the boldness of her inspiration. "I am going to seek an annulment!"

Roger sat forward, ever the voice of reason. "What of the scandal? You must consider your reputation."

She clenched her fists determinedly. True, her reputation might suffer, but then again, her standing in society would be severely compromised once the facts surrounding her marriage became public knowledge; once the polite world learned how the Marquess had cast her aside before the ink had even dried on the church register.

"I have to take that risk." She pressed her palm against her forehead, feeling overwhelmed by her decision. "Roger, I'll have to be away for a few days—most likely, three or four at the most. Could you keep a watch over Father, perhaps stop by each day to make certain he's eating and caring for himself?"

Roger rose to his feet, his curly-topped beaver in hand. "You know I'll do anything I can, Daphne, but I urge you to think this matter through carefully."

"Yes," she promised. "I shall." But her mind was elsewhere, forming a mental picture of Iain Ashingford's expression after opening such a letter from her solicitors. Would he feel tempted to wrathfully fling a candle stand as she had been? Or might he, instead, be relieved that she sought an annulment?

"I'll take my leave then." Roger's low-voiced announcement interrupted her thoughts and she turned to him just as he reached out and caught her gloved hand in his. "However, I want you to be assured that I will support you in whatever decision you make, Daphne."

She patted his cheek. "I know, Rog. You're the best friend I could ever hope for."

Something flickered at the back of his eyes. "Thank you," he said simply, then bowed and left her before she could wish him good day.

Daphne stood in the middle of the room, her mind drifting back to the questions she had just posed to herself. How would her husband react?

She realized that she could not guess at his reaction since she still had no explanation as to why he had bothered to marry her in the first place. Three months ago she had been too caught up in her own foolishness to seriously question his motives. But now . . .

Slowly, yet surely, something deep within Daphne began to harden until it coalesced as a hard knot at the bottom of her stomach. Resolve.

She had never had to take charge before, her mother had been only too willing to fight her battles for her, but now her time had come.

"No," she said. She wasn't going to remain hidden at Harkwell House like a frightened little mouse while her man of affairs liberated her from her marriage vows.

She wasn't going to go to London. Not yet, at least.

Before she had her solicitor arrange an annulment, she was going to go to Ash Park to get some answers to her questions. And—she smacked her fist into her palm—she was determined to make Iain Ashingford squirm while answering them.

Chapter Three

The morning was as peaceful as any Iain had ever known. All the elements of nature had conspired to set a scene of pastoral perfection that only the master hand of Rembrandt or Gainsborough could have reproduced.

Up with the dawn, Iain had passed a few hours poring over the ledgers before the song of a nightingale had lured him outside. As absorbed as he'd been with the estate accounts, he'd been surprised that the lilting notes had penetrated his concentration and he'd raised his head from his work with a puzzled frown.

A bird's song. When had been the last time he'd taken note of anything so ordinary? He'd thought back over the last years he'd spent with his father at their home in Sussex, but could not recollect any occasion when he'd been able to appreciate a pleasure as simple as a songbird's melody.

He'd tried to return to his work, but the sweet trilling had proved irresistible. Without even donning his coat, he'd followed the bird's call out the French doors of the study and across the wide field fronting the manor.

The morning air was crisp as Iain strolled toward the riverbank, his boots growing shiny and damp with dew. A lightness buoyed his steps, remarkable in its unfamiliarity.

The past three nights he'd slept the deep, dreamless sleep of a child, awaking with the sun more refreshed and energetic than he'd been in years. Nightmares that had plagued him since his father's death had not intruded here at Ash Park, and he wondered how much was due to the halcyon surroundings and how much to his own satisfaction in seeing his vow realized.

Heedless of the damp yet clinging to the grasses, Iain lowered himself to the sloping embankment, stretching out so that his boot heels dug into the mud at the water's edge. Sunshine wrapped around his shoulders like the warm, weighty caress of a friendly arm, while not a cloud marred the pristine sky nor a sound disturbed the quiet. Even the nightingale had hushed.

Propped up on his elbows, Iain felt a hint of something that he had not experienced for a very long time. A sense of peace. A feeling of calm. Just fluttering around the edges of his consciousness, he sensed the serenity that a day as beautiful as this one could bring.

What had he been thinking to invite the Comtesse here? Two bottles of champagne, and six months of celibacy, had caused him to issue that rash invitation when, in fact, he now questioned whether she held much attraction for him. Her overblown proportions and raucous laugh were not generally his style, and as soon as he'd arrived at Ash Park, he'd acknowledged his error. Like a garish hothouse flower amid a country garden, Winnifred would have disrupted Ash Park's subtle beauty. Although her pursuit of him had been vaguely flattering, Iain was glad that he'd sent the message and that she would not be intruding on his new home.

A breeze swept across the meadow, ruffling his hair and drawing a leaf from the oak tree that branched over the river. The leaf danced and dipped on the wind, finally landing in the water almost at Iain's feet. Its color struck an unpleasant chord of remembrance, bringing a scowl to his face when the association became clear.

Daphne Harkwell's eyes had been that color, that same lustrous olive green, rarely seen outside a forest setting. But no, Iain corrected himself, Daphne Harkwell no longer existed, did she? She was now Daphne Ashingford, his wife.

Resentment burst the fragile bubble of calm that had so briefly surrounded him as he watched the leaf swirl aimlessly along the swift current. He cursed beneath his breath. Why should this idyllic day be tarnished? He reminded himself that he had reclaimed Ash Park, that despite the underhanded machinations of the Harkwells, he had achieved everything that he had desired from the marriage. Well, almost everything—

With an embittered smile, Iain sat forward, resting his elbows on his knees. Downstream, the leaf responsible for stirring his unwelcome memories glistened with sunlight, mocking his sudden shift of mood. Impulsively, Iain picked out a stone from those along the bank and flung it in the leaf's direction. The rock missed to the right.

Yes, he might now own Ash Park, the truth of which eased a measure of his resentment toward his young bride, but Iain's pride continued to rankle with the knowledge that he'd been duped. As surely as Samson had succumbed to Delilah, he'd been deceived—not by a worldly woman or a great beauty skilled in the arts of seduction. Rather, Iain Ashingford had been taken by a chit of nineteen; a girl barely out of the schoolroom, armed with nothing more than a sweet, breathy voice and a straightforward gaze.

She'd had nothing outstanding to recommend her, nothing more than an indefinable charm. . . .

He sent another rock flying downriver. To think that she'd actually succeeded in making him feel guilty about his purpose in marrying her. Iain shook his head with disgust.

During that ride home after the wedding, when she'd questioned him so earnestly about his reasons for offering for her, he'd been ashamed. Truly ashamed. She had looked so hopeful in her virginal white dress, nervously mangling the blossoms of her bouquet. Her question had surprised him, catching him off guard, for he'd fully expected that Lady Harkwell would have advised her daughter of his mercenary motives.

But when confronted with Daphne's wide-eyed innocence—or a credible portrayal thereof—he'd discovered that, despite previous accusations to the contrary, he was not utterly heartless. He'd circumvented her question, unwilling to define their union for her in its starkest terms: a business exchange. His title for her property.

He'd felt chagrined. Unsettled enough that once they'd arrived at Harkwell House, he'd gone in search of a drink to pacify his censorious conscience. And then Lady Harkwell had found him and neatly turned the tables. Or so she had thought.

Iain's gaze flickered across the sun-kissed horizon. Lady Harkwell was probably spinning in her grave like a top. If not for her unexpected passing, Iain and his solicitors would still be wrangling over Ash Park, since he knew enough about Isadora Whiting Harkwell to know that she would not have surrendered the estate without a fight. A fight to the death.

Smiling faintly, he thought that she probably would only have wanted him to have Ash Park this way. Quite literally, over her dead body.

He rolled his weight onto his feet and stood with a languorous stretch. He had come to Ash Park to make peace with painful memories, to discover the tranquillity his father claimed this land could offer. Thoughts of Isadora Harkwell and her perfidious daughter did not suit that purpose and he shrugged them off with a deliberate roll of his shoulders.

As the nightingale resumed its warbling song Iain turned to retrace his path back to the manor, determined to finally put his ghosts to rest.

Isadora circled Iain's desk, restlessly snapping open her fan, then closing it with a click. *Snap, click, snap, click.* La, but how she hated to wait!

Heaving a gusty sigh, she dropped into the companion chair opposite Wilkinson, the butler, where he sat answering his master's queries about the manor house. Isadora listened with only half an ear, her thoughts occupied with Daphne's pending arrival.

She knew her daughter must be en route to Ash Park. She knew it. Daphne was her flesh and blood, raised in her own image. Perhaps not as tall, nor as stately. Hair a shade lighter than Isadora's own vivid red, and a spirit—

Isadora's gaze warmed with pride. In all respects, Daphne was a softened version of herself, but in no trait was that more obvious than in her daughter's disposition. Although compassionate and idealistic, Daphne was neither empty-headed nor weak-spined. The girl knew her mind. She would not care one whit for Lindley's dispatch; of that Isadora felt certain.

Of course, Daphne had not yet been tested. She had never been in a situation where she'd been sufficiently challenged, where she'd been forced to realize her full potential. The girl's spirit was strong, but even stronger than Daphne herself recognized.

If all went according to Isadora's plan, Daphne would come racing to Ash Park with daggers drawn and fire in her eyes. Oh, how splendid it would be to see her again! But then . . . then, she would have to set about putting things to rights between her darling Daphne and *him*.

Lindley leaned back in his chair, his heels casually propped on the desk corner. He'd loosened his cravat and rolled up the sleeves of his shirt nearly to his elbows. A blade of grass stood out among the black locks shoved haphazardly off his broad forehead.

She sniffed. *He looks like a common laborer.*

"Tell me, Wilkinson, how often does the steward travel to London?"

The butler frowned in concentration. "Mr. Thompson makes a trip every few months or so, milord. Since his lordship passed away, that is."

"And the Earl passed away . . .?"

"Eighteen months ago, milord. The Earl's daughter, Lady Harkwell, left the running of the estate to Bertie, er, Mr. Thompson."

Isadora snapped shut her fan, oddly unsettled to hear herself as the topic of conversation. More often than not, she had to remind herself that she was indeed dead, no longer living, caught in this curious place between heaven and earth.

"Did Lady Harkwell never personally oversee Ash Park?"

"No, milord. After Lady Isadora wed, she never returned to stay at Ash Park. Since the Earl's passing, Mr. Thompson has sent the estate's quarterly reports to the Baron." The butler lowered his voice. "I believe, milord, that some manner of rift had developed between Lady Isadora and her father, the Earl."

Isadora bristled, casting the butler a scornful look. *Wilkinson, you old prattle-box.* After nearly four decades in the Whiting family's employ, the man's allegiance seemed to swing with the wind.

"A rift?" Iain questioned.

Wilkinson bobbed his head. "For over thirty years her ladyship refused to come back to Ash Park. Some grudge she held with the Earl, they say, and if you knew Lady Isadora, you'd know she could hold a grudge better than most."

Iain levered an amused brow. "Not the forgiving sort?"

The servant smiled conspiratorially. "Not by a long shot."

Suddenly Iain cocked his head toward the French doors and, from a distance, the faint rumbling of hooves intruded on the afternoon.

"Perhaps that's Mr. Thompson, now, milord," the butler offered.

"No, Wilkinson." Annoyance sketched across Iain's brow as he turned back toward the servant. "It's not a single rider, but a coach. It appears we're to have guests."

The butler rose to his feet while Isadora clapped her hands.

Daphne, at last. Thank heavens.

The hoofbeats grew louder as Wilkinson excused himself to see to the visitors.

Iain, still frowning with apparent displeasure, stood up and walked over to a gilt-framed mirror to reknot his cravat. He botched his first attempt and jerked the linen free with a vicious tug.

"Devil take it!" he muttered.

Isadora smiled smugly at his reflection as he attempted another go at a Gordian knot. *Oh, what a delightful surprise I have in store for you, Lindley,* she taunted. *You'll not be rid of us so easily, you'll see.*

Her skirts swishing behind her, she sauntered over to the hearth, then fastidiously levitated to the mantel, where she alighted without incident. *Perfect.* She was in prime viewing position to witness Lindley's reaction when Daphne burst into the room like an avenging angel.

Iain was just slipping into his coat when a rap on the door preceded Wilkinson.

"Well, Wilkinson, which neighbor is doing the neighborly?" Iain asked, his query terse as he tugged at his coat sleeves.

"Milord." The servant craned his neck awkwardly. "The Comtesse deCheval."

The words were no sooner out of Wilkinson's mouth than a blur of mulberry muslin dashed past him and catapulted into the Marquess's arms.

Iain nearly tumbled to the floor.

Isadora nearly tumbled from the mantel.

"Lindley, darling," the Comtesse cooed, wrapping her plump arms around Iain's neck in a hold that any wrestler would have been proud of. "I thought I should never arrive. The horses were so wretchedly slow—oh, but I am here with you now and that's all that matters."

Incredulous, Isadora watched Wilkinson discreetly retreating and she slid from the mantel to chase after him.

Wilkinson, you get back here this instant! Don't you dare leave my son-in-law alone with this . . . this . . .

"Winnifred."

Isadora's attention swerved back to the center of the room. Iain had taken hold of the Comtesse's elbows and was gently disentangling himself from her headlock. The widow released his neck, only to press herself up against him so that her décolletage looked in danger of overflowing her bodice.

Isadora's eyebrows shot up to her hairline.

The widow deCheval was clearly bent on seduction. The pelisse of her traveling ensemble had been removed, no doubt to more prominently display her white arms and generous bosom. And her gown . . . Isadora had never seen a muslin so thin.

"Winnifred, I take it you didn't receive my missive?"

The widow pulled back slightly. "Oh dear, no, Lindley. Were you concerned about my delay? Is that why you'd written?"

Isadora spied the confusion that momentarily flitted across Iain's expression before he evenly answered, "It was not important."

Not important, Isadora choked, rapping her fan into the palm of her hand. Of all the plaguesome coils! She had never thought that the presumptuous baggage might arrive before Daphne. The woman would have had to leave London on Lindley's very heels—

"Truthfully, I hadn't expected you to arrive so soon," Iain commented, echoing her thoughts.

"Soon? But I haven't seen you in over a week, Lindley. Aren't you glad to see me?"

The Comtesse fluttered her lashes, and for a moment Isadora thought ash from the hearth had flown into the woman's eyes.

"It's always a pleasure, Winnifred," Iain answered, and gallantly raised her hand to his lips.

Isadora clenched her teeth, not caring for the manner in which Lindley's welcome had unexpectedly warmed. A spark had entered his gaze that spoke of intentions unbecoming a newly wedded groom.

"You must be parched. May I offer you a glass of sherry?" Iain crossed to the sideboard and held aloft a decanter.

"But, of course," Winnifred purred, coming up behind him. "Although champagne would more fittingly celebrate our reunion. Later perhaps?" Her suggestive tone could not be mistaken.

Later in the privacy of your boudoir, you mean?

The Comtesse accepted the sherry glass handed to her, then made a thoroughly disgusting show of tracing its rim with the tip of her pink tongue before taking a sip. She cradled the glass in her palms, pouting up at Iain.

"London has simply been an absolute bore without you, darling."

"The entire week?"

Isadora smirked at Lindley's subtle mockery. Too subtle, apparently, for the Comtesse.

"Oh, yes," she complained. "Half the *ton* has already gone off to their summer homes and only the dullest of the dull have remained in Town. Why, I don't think I attended even a half-dozen parties this past week."

"Shocking," Iain confirmed.

"Not that I could enjoy myself, since I was so very impatient for our"—she paused coyly—"friendship to finally commence."

With her free hand, the widow reached out and ran her finger up and down the buttons of Iain's coat. "I've been imagining every detail, wondering what it would be like to feel your—"

Why, I never! Isadora gasped, tossing her shawl as she crossed the room to stop mere inches from the widow's nose.

She scrutinized the woman with a critical eye.

Long, narrow face. Square jaw. A toothy smile like a horse eyeing a trough of oats. In fact, she quite reminded Isadora of a sorrel Percy had purchased last spring.

Hmmph, she sniffed. *Appropriate you married deCheval, Whinny, for the name aptly suits!*

Isadora then turned to Iain, and her eyes slitted in disapproval. Her son-in-law, seemingly indifferent to the Comtesse's equine likeness, had developed an unholy interest in the deep cleavage presented before him. His gray eyes had grown heavy-lidded, and he was bending forward, his lips on a direct course—

You cad!

In an instinctive reaction, Isadora jabbed her fan into his ribs.

He jerked upright, eyes wide.

"Lindley!" Winnifred protested.

Iain clasped his hand to his side and ran his palm up and down. "I . . . I apologize. It must have been a stray pin."

Isadora stared, first at Iain, then at her fan. Then a smile of pure delight stretched across her face.

Only a few days ago she'd struggled awfully with that blasted pen, and yet, just now she'd broken through to the physical world with nary a thought.

She looked back at Iain, who had recovered himself and was lowering his head again—

Isadora gleefully smacked him on his derriere.

"Bloody—" He swung around fast, his forearm catching the widow's cheek. Suddenly the Comtesse was wind-milling backward and Lindley was lunging forward, and the sherry glass was flying heavenward and . . . *thud.*

Oh, I say.

"Dear God, Winnifred, are you all right? I am so fright-fully sorry, I cannot imagine . . ."

Iain dropped to his knees beside the woman laid out flat as a board upon the thick Aubusson carpet while Isadora moved to stand over his shoulder.

How fortunate that Father believed in quality appoint-ments, she sardonically remarked.

The sherry glass had fared well, for it had landed upside down directly on one bountiful breast, soaking the thin muslin. Alas, the Comtesse's absurd little jockey hat had not been so fortunate, for it had been crushed in the fall and now lay cocked across one eye, so that when she raised her head—wobbly, yet still attached—the widow looked, and smelled, as if she'd been well and truly in her cups.

Isadora's lips pursed. No real harm had been done; the twit had merely knocked the wind from her sails.

"Winnifred, be still," Lindley ordered, and hoisted the Comtesse's considerable bulk into his arms.

Despite herself, Isadora had to admire his show of strength as he lifted the widow's deadweight straight up from the floor. The Comtesse was probably half again the size of her willowy Daphne.

Isadora trailed Iain across the room, noting wryly that the widow had appeared to lose consciousness, although her arms still clung to Iain's neck. At the study door, Iain juggled Winnifred to one arm and pushed open the door to discover Wilkinson immediately outside. Apparently, the ruckus had brought the servant running.

Seasoned retainer that he was, the butler did not so much as blink to find his master cradling a woman in his arms in plain view of God and everyone in the central hallway of his home.

"The Comtesse has taken a spill," Iain explained.

Wilkinson nodded with commendable aplomb. "I'll fetch Mrs. Emmitt, the cook's assistant. She's skilled in midwifery and doctoring, milord."

"Good, and tell her to hurry," Iain instructed.

Wilkinson bowed and turned toward the corridor, Iain headed across the vestibule to the staircase, and then the front door flew open without the aid of a footman. As a gust of evening air rushed through the opening, all eyes turned to the entrance.

Daphne had arrived.

Chapter Four

Daphne stepped through the threshold and froze.

During the arduous and nerve-racking eight-hour journey from home, she'd passed the time wondering what manner of reception she might expect from her estranged and enigmatic husband.

Fury. Penitence. Indifference. Her imagination had run the gamut. She'd envisioned him falling to his knees and begging her forgiveness, as well as pictured him literally throwing her from Ash Park. She had thought she had prepared herself for any eventuality. But no. None of her imaginings had suggested she might find this.

It took only moments for her gaze to encompass the scene. The agitated butler flushing guiltily; Lindley, with one foot planted on the staircase's first riser, his handsome features rigid with shock; and . . . the woman. Daphne's attention lingered a moment longer on the female whose head

lolled limply against Iain's chest. One white shoulder was
exposed where the woman's gown had slipped—or had
been slipped—from her arm. Her eyelids were closed, her
crushed hat was falling crookedly across her forehead.
Floating about, mixed with French perfume, was the spicy-
sweet scent of sherry.

She's foxed. The realization came to Daphne amid a
wave of revulsion.

Against her will, her gaze shifted to Iain's and their eyes
collided in a clash of emotions. His were dark with aston-
ishment and stony with hostility; flat, steel-gray eyes from
which Daphne did not flinch. She had anticipated his ani-
mosity and had readied herself for it. She had also anticipated his surprise, expecting to gloat over it, to savor the
knowledge that she had confounded the unflappable Marquess Lindley. She had so been looking forward to bringing
this very look to his face, but now she could not enjoy it.
Everything inside her had gone cold. Ice-cold.

Their gazes held. Daphne's mind reeled. Then Iain's full
lips quirked down in a sneer and he practically spat the
question at her: *"What are you doing here?"*

A heat, like the very fires of hell, rose to Daphne's
cheeks. Dear God, was this man's sole objective in life to
humiliate her at every opportunity? Would he not be content until he'd stripped her of the last shreds of her tattered
dignity?

A stirring behind her reminded Daphne that her abigail,
as well as the gray-faced butler, were observing her hum-
bling "welcome." Before the night was through all of Ash
Park would know how her husband paraded his trollops
through their home then greeted *her* as if she were the tres-
passer.

But she would not run from his scorn. Why should she?
This was her house as much as it was his. She'd come here

with a purpose and she'd see it through, no matter how Iain Ashingford attempted to belittle her.

Daphne held her voice to a derisive calm. "Perhaps it's escaped your memory, husband, but we *are* married. And this is *my* home."

She unlaced her bonnet with shaking fingers and handed it blindly to her maid behind her. Then, from her pelisse pocket, she pulled out his letter, still crumpled into a parchment ball, and extended it toward him flat on her gloved palm.

"Did you honestly believe your note would keep me away?"

His expression grew more severe, his ebony brows veeing tightly together. He stepped down from the staircase and half-turned toward her. "Dammit, now is neither the time nor place—"

"Not the time?" she interrupted. With a twist of her wrist, she dropped the note onto the marble floor. "Such a master of understatement, Lord Lindley. Why, even I can see that my timing is . . . inconvenient for you."

Her gaze flashed contemptuously over the woman he held in his arms before she raked him with the same look.

"The Comtesse is unwell," he answered her without apology.

"So I gather."

"If you believe—"

A loud moan cut off his words and both Daphne and Iain glanced to the woman whose eyelids fluttered but did not open.

"Shall I fetch Mrs. Emmitt, milord?"

The butler's hesitant query breached the tension as Daphne recalled that *she* was the mistress of this house. She'd best make that clear directly from the outset.

"Mrs. Emmitt?" she broke in, obliging the uneasy servant to address her.

"Yes, milady, she's the cook's first assistant—"

"Fetch her immediately, Wilkinson," Iain ordered.

Daphne's eyes narrowed but she forced herself to take a calming breath. If Lindley meant to demonstrate who would have the last word in this house, she would match him word for word.

"Please do, Wilkinson," she smoothly interjected, "and have her meet us in the Comtesse's chamber." Daphne took two determined steps toward the staircase, then paused, looking back at the aged retainer. "I trust the Comtesse is staying with us?"

The servant shot a questioning glance toward Iain, who responded in his place.

"Yes, the Comtesse is a houseguest."

Daphne coolly met his stare. He displayed absolutely no remorse; not even the slightest chagrin that he'd been caught red-handed with his lightskirt. His poise would be admirable if she did not despise him so very much this minute.

The butler cleared his throat. "Er, milord, the Comtesse has been placed in the Ivory Chamber in the east wing."

"Thank you, Wilkinson." And, as if Daphne were not even there, Iain turned his back on her and headed up the staircase.

For the briefest of moments, Daphne debated whether to follow, but then decided that she had no choice. She could not calmly wait downstairs while her husband tucked his paramour into bed.

Up the winding staircase and down a long hallway, Daphne followed Iain, glad for these minutes to compose herself. As they passed by gray stone walls, decorated with medieval armor and ancient weapons, Daphne felt her initial fury begin to subside to a smoldering anger. In one regard, she thought, she should be grateful for his indiscretion, for it would make it all the easier for her to demand an annulment. How could he deny the truth of what she had seen with her own two eyes?

Yet, while their footsteps echoed through the vast corridors, Daphne realized that gratitude was not the foremost emotion fluttering in her breast. Beneath the anger lay pain. The same pain of betrayal she had known on her wedding day.

Iain stopped outside a room where candlelight, and a quiet humming, seeped beneath the threshold into the dark hall. Daphne followed Iain into the room, where they surprised a young maid arranging clothes in an armoire.

"Lord 'a mercy," the girl breathed, dropping a handful of gowns onto the floor.

At the maid's feet, two half-empty trunks lay open, suggesting to Daphne that the Comtesse was only recently arrived. Perhaps that very day?

The chamber was luxurious, the furniture *en suite* ivory-painted woodwork, the bed curtains and upholstery an ivory-and-white striped silk.

As the abigail rushed forward to assist Iain in lowering the Comtesse to the mattress, Daphne wondered where Iain's bedchamber was located. Next door perhaps?

"Your mistress fell and struck her head," Iain told the maid.

Daphne jerked her gaze to his broad back, surprised by the lie. The fumes from the alcohol were even more overpowering in the warm room, so why would Iain bother with pretense?

Another groan came from the bed and Daphne approached to find the abigail placing a cool compress upon her mistress's brow. The maid stroked the Comtesse's chestnut hair away from her forehead and Daphne felt strangely relieved to note that the woman was not a great beauty. Her features were elongated, and she suffered from an overbite. She was not unattractive, but neither was she a diamond of the first water. Conscious of her own rather ordinary appearance, Daphne would have found it most hurtful if Iain's lover had proven to be unusually lovely.

Not that she should care, she told herself. It mattered not at all with whom her husband chose to break their marriage vows since she planned to see those vows nullified, and nullified soon. It was simply her own vanity that caused her to be grateful that the Comtesse was no raving beauty. Certainly not jealousy nor any sense of rivalry.

The maid stepped away to remoisten the cloth and the light from the candlestick drifted across the Comtesse's left cheek. A faint purpling had begun to color the skin along the woman's cheekbone and Daphne realized that Iain had been speaking the truth. It appeared that the Comtesse *had* fallen.

Perplexed, Daphne slanted a wary glance to where Iain stood at the other side of the bed. What in heaven's name had been going on here? Lindley might be a rogue, but she couldn't believe him capable of—

A knock rapped at the door and Iain's deep-timbred summons jarred Daphne from her thoughts. The butler entered, accompanied by an enormously rotund, middle-aged woman dressed in an apron and mobcap, and carrying a wicker basket.

"Mrs. Emmitt, milord, milady," Wilkinson introduced. Mrs. Emmitt curtsied as deeply as her girth would allow, then wobbled to the bed, where Iain stepped aside to make room for her.

"Ooh, fine, her color's good," Mrs. Emmitt commented in a broad country accent. "I'll mix up one of me powders and keep a watch on her, but I'll wager she'll be in fine twig tomorrow, if not the day after."

Daphne looked over at Iain and found his brooding gaze fixed to the Comtesse. Concern shadowed his gray eyes, the sight of which sent a pang of envy shooting through her. At one time—although it seemed a lifetime ago—Daphne would have sold her very soul for Iain Ashingford to look at her with such intensity. But that was so very long ago. . . .

The room had grown quiet while Mrs. Emmitt rummaged through her basket and Daphne suddenly recognized the awkwardness explicit in that silence. Wilkinson, standing as stiff as a dandy's collar, maintained an impassive demeanor, although a tic in his left eye revealed his discomfort. The Comtesse's maid was twisting her fingers into knots, her face so pale that Daphne feared the girl might swoon.

Daphne felt her own color rise with irritation. Ludicrous. The entire situation was ludicrous. Like children caught in a naughty escapade, no one dared breathe a word, waiting to see how she might resolve this most uncomfortable dilemma. *How was one supposed to conduct one's self when one's husband's mistress fell ill in one's own home?*

Daphne was smoothing out a scowl with the tips of her fingers when a picture of her mother came into her mind's eye. The ever-present turban crowning her regal figure; her sharp green eyes that saw more than the quizzing glass revealed. Isadora would have handled such a predicament with imperious aplomb. She would never have given Lord Lindley the satisfaction of seeing her turmoil.

Daphne licked her lips. "My lord"—at least her voice sounded steady—"it appears that Mrs. Emmitt has matters well in hand. Let us provide her some privacy and remove ourselves to the parlor. I, for one, could do with some refreshment."

Drawing herself up to her full height, she did not wait for Iain's response, but marched out the door with what she hoped was some degree of stateliness. Once in the corridor, however, she had not any idea of the parlor's whereabouts, and was forced to backtrack along several meandering hallways.

As she passed a portrait gallery she slowed, remembering having passed through there on the way to the east wing. By the look of the silk wall covering, she could tell that many of the portraits had been recently rearranged and that fact struck her as curious. And, although Ashingfords by the score decorated the walls, she could not find a portrait of Iain. She wondered if he had removed it for some reason.

When she finally did arrive at the parlor, she found that Wilkinson had arrived before her and was busy setting out a cold collation.

He quickly completed his task, then excused himself with a remorseful nod of his head, as if he, instead of his master, had been caught in flagrante delicto.

Daphne glanced to the meal and discovered she had no appetite. The day had been a long one and she yearned for nothing more than a hot bath and a soft bed. Her traveling gown was soiled with dust, her shoulders ached with tension, and her stomach felt as if it were a butter churn.

Indeed, she wondered whether she'd have the strength to confront Lindley tonight, then decided that she would do so regardless. In spite of her exhaustion, she knew that she'd be unable to sleep knowing that this conversation loomed before her. Tonight, tomorrow, the next day, made no difference. It was best to get it over with, to take the bull by the horns and wrestle it to the ground.

Or so her mother would have said.

Daphne heard the door open behind her and knew her reprieve had ended. The bull had arrived.

With a deep breath, she turned around to face him, combatting the immediate spark of attraction that flared within her.

Iain Ashingford was every bit as attractive as he'd been

on their wedding day. His black hair was tousled, lending him a boyish air, at odds with his rugged—and currently grimly set—features. He'd loosed his cravat and shirt so that a triangle of dark curls peeped through the gap, as did a hint of the carved muscles beneath.

"I'll repeat my initial question," he said, without preamble. "What are you doing here?"

Daphne leaned back and braced her hands along the top of the sofa. She wished she were wearing some color other than mauve. Mauve was not a color for doing battle; she needed one of her mother's defiant crimson gowns or perhaps a fortifying jonquil.

"Is it not obvious?" she answered with a flippancy she was far from feeling.

He gave no quarter. "No, it is not."

"I am here to determine why *you* are here."

Iain crossed his arms over his chest and leaned indifferently against the doorjamb. "This is my home."

"Home or trysting site?" she tossed back. "Perchance I should be asking why the Comtesse is here, but that would be pointless, wouldn't it?"

A muscle jumped in his jaw. "We will not discuss the Comtesse."

"You know, Iain, you are very good at issuing commands. Unfortunately, I've decided that I am not very good at obeying them."

She cocked her chin. Yes, that sounded good, she thought. A rebuttal worthy of her mother.

His eyes narrowed, although when he spoke his voice was soft. "You've changed."

"Do you think so?" She could not stop the breathless huff of laughter that revealed too much. "If I have, you may thank yourself."

"Should I be thankful?"

Daphne shrugged.

"Why have you come to Ash Park, Daphne?"

"I don't need a reason. This is *my* home, kindly remember."

"You weren't in any rush to claim it. It's been yours over three months now."

She couldn't believe his nerve. "If I'm in a rush to claim it now, 'tis only because you so bluntly informed me I wasn't welcome here!"

Confusion shifted behind his gaze. "So you've come to Ash Park to spite me? I hope you don't think you can drive me away."

"As I did the day of our wedding?"

As soon as the words left her mouth, Daphne wished she could take them back. She didn't want to reveal her hurt to this impossibly aloof man who happened to be her husband.

And yet, she thought, she might be able to dent that shield of reserve. Perhaps even goad *him* into throwing a candle stand.

"I've come for an annulment," she announced.

The corners of his mouth tightened. "Like hell," he softly said. "I won't give you one."

He shoved away from the wall and advanced farther into the room.

Daphne straightened away from the sofa. "You needn't give me one, for I plan to have one with or without your co-operation."

"You haven't grounds."

"I do. Our vows have not been . . ."

"Ahh." His voice lowered a pitch. "So at last we get to the true reason you're here."

"Don't be ridiculous," she sputtered. "I want an annulment. Not—"

"Not what, Daphne?"

"Not . . ." Blast it, she felt her composure not merely

slipping but flailing, floundering. Vexed, she blurted out, "Well, I categorically do not want *you,* Iain Ashingford!"

He stilled, openly assessing her for a long moment. "Are you sure of that, Daphne?"

Oh, how she wanted to cut him off at the knees with a fiery retort . . . but she could only nod. Vigorously.

In a single stride, he was less than an arm's length away from her. "Then why," he asked, skimming her temple with the rough pad of his thumb, "are your eyes nearly black with desire?"

Daphne jerked her head aside, stifling a gasp, dismayed by the effect of his touch.

"And why"—the tip of his finger traced just below the lace ruff of her gown, searing the fine silk—"does your breath come fast and your heart beat even faster?"

Daphne closed her eyes. He was toying with her. To show her that he was in control, not her.

"You realize, Daphne, that you have my name. A title. Wealth, comfort, social position. You've gained a great deal from this marriage.

"If one were to examine the balance sheet"—his voice had dropped to a near whisper—"I'd say you owe me, Daphne."

She snapped her gaze to his. "Wh-what are you talking about? I owe you nothing!"

His unnerving smile widened. "But you do owe me . . . wife."

Realization hit her and she nearly staggered from it. The unprincipled knave! She came seeking an annulment and he twisted everything around to make it seem that she was in his debt! That she owed him—what? Her virginity and an heir?

Angrily she lashed out, shoving against his chest, driving him back a step.

"If I'm indebted to you for anything, Lord Lindley, it's

for the lesson you've taught me, naught else! You've humiliated me beyond endurance and yet I've endured; you've treated me like a child, thereby compelling me to grow up and act like a woman. You've stolen my dreams and my faith because you, unfortunate soul, don't have any!"

Tears began to scald the back of her throat and she knew she had to flee. "I'm sorry," she choked, "but I don't bloody well owe you anything!"

And she dashed around him and ran out the door.

Chapter
Five

Iain glared at the expensively tailored, forest-green, su-
perfine coat and grumbled, "Before I put that on, Dobbs, I
demand you inspect every inch of it for loose pins."

The valet looked down to the jacket he held. "Pins?" he
echoed.

"Yes, Dobbs, pins! Pins! Yesterday the coat you selected
gave me a bloody, nasty *poke* that I have yet to forget."

Dobbs stuck out his lower lip. "A loose pin, you say?"
He gave Iain a patently doubtful look but set to examining
the jacket.

Although many was the time Iain had been tempted to
throttle the man, Dobbs was indispensable to him. He'd
been with Iain for fifteen years and their relationship tran-
scended that of servant and master.

When Iain was young, his father had often been too ill
for company, so Iain had sought out the coolheaded valet

for a sympathetic ear or a word of wisdom. Over the years
the familiarity between the two had grown to where Dobbs
felt free to dispense those words of wisdom, unsolicited or
not. Iain feared he was about to get a healthy dose of unbidden advice this very morning.

"I assure you," Dobbs said, holding the jacket aloft, "that
there are no pins in this coat."

Iain frowned. "Perhaps it was an insect of some sort," he
conceded, slipping his arms into the proffered sleeves.

The valet made a small noise, expressing his skepticism,
then walked around and began to tinker and fuss with the
already perfectly executed cravat. He tugged and pulled
until Iain finally surrendered to the inevitable.

"What is it, Dobbs?" he asked, none too patiently.

"Oh, nothing, my lord. Nothing at all."

Iain bristled. Dobbs rarely "milord"-ed him, and when he
did, the context was usually sarcastic.

"I merely thought to inquire if there was anything I
might do to improve your spirits."

Iain peered down his nose at the valet's shiny, bald pate.
"What makes you think my spirits need improving?" he
snapped.

Dobbs tugged at one corner of the neckcloth. "Pure con-
jecture. A hunch, if you will."

A hunch, Iain scoffed. One didn't need a clairvoyant, or
even a perspicacious valet, to conclude that his mood this
morning had been unusually sour. The debacle with
Daphne had kept him up late, nursing—and ultimately
emptying—two bottles of port; and then, when he'd finally
stumbled to bed, he'd questioned the usefulness of getting
himself pickled since he'd still been up half the night, consumed by the mystery of how his note to Winnifred had
ended up in Daphne's hands.

Last night, after the confrontation in the parlor, he'd returned to the hall to look for the letter. He'd found it on the

floor precisely where Daphne had dropped it. He'd read the note and read it again, outraged that Ash Park's messenger could have made such a hideously fateful error.

And then, before the hapless stable hand could be summoned, he had reluctantly realized that the error could only have been his. It wasn't as if there had been two letters and they'd been accidentally switched; not once had he written to Daphne at her Cotswolds home. Somehow he must have penned her direction, not Winnifred's, on the envelope.

He had lain awake most of the night, loath to accept the only logical explanation to the riddle. He didn't want to believe he had done it. He didn't want to admit that in the darkest corners of his psyche, he might have secretly wished to contact her. That he might have inadvertently sent her the note because he'd been unable to stop thinking of her all these months . . .

But he wasn't even that attracted to the girl! She was pretty enough, he supposed, but he'd had his share of beauties in his day. Why would that dreamy-eyed chit have got under his skin?

She hadn't, he assured himself. There must be another explanation.

"Dobbs, have I seemed at all absentminded to you of late?"

The valet abandoned his fussing over the cravat, and stepped away to fetch Iain's Wellingtons. "No, not that I've noticed."

"I haven't seemed forgetful or distracted?"

Dobbs pursed his lips. "I don't think so. Have you been?"

Iain sat down so that the valet could put on his boots. "I suppose you've heard that Lady Lindley arrived last night."

"Ah, yes, the kitchen staff was discussing her arrival when I went in this morning."

"And did you happen to hear that the Comtesse deCheval made an appearance last night as well?"

"Yes, I do believe mention was made of the fact."

Iain caught his valet's eye. "Deucedly difficult, wouldn't you say?"

Dobbs's lips trembled as if he held back a smile. "I feel confident that you will smooth matters over with your usual finesse."

Iain scratched at his chin. "I was a trifle lacking in that finesse last night, I'm afraid."

"Run into a spot of trouble?"

"You could say so. My wife is not convinced she wishes to continue as such."

"Hmm, I'm surprised to hear it. You've always had good fortune with the ladies." Dobbs put one last polish to the gleaming boots and stood.

"But Daphne is not precisely a 'lady.' She's my wife."

The valet glanced over his spectacles at Iain. "Precisely. You do realize that an annulment would mean—"

"I know perfectly well what an annulment would mean," Iain said.

"Then perhaps you might need to apply yourself more diligently?"

Iain's mouth quirked in annoyance. "I might."

"'Twould be my advice. As you said, a 'lady' is not a wife. One is never quite done wooing a wife, if you take my meaning."

"Court my wife?" Iain leaned back in the chair and laced his fingers behind his head.

Curiously, he did not find Dobbs's recommendation as disagreeable as he would have found it even as recently as yesterday. For, up until yesterday, Iain had been feeling very hostile toward the woman who had taken his name. She was, after all, a Whiting.

Seeing Daphne again, however, had put doubts into his

mind. In fact, part of what had bothered him during the sleepless night was the realization that he might have remembered her unfairly. He had been painting her with the same brush he'd applied to Lady Harkwell, assuming that Daphne had been party to her mother's game of deceit.

Last night had made him wonder. Perhaps she was what he had thought her to be prior to their marriage: nothing more than a sweet, dreamy girl who had been as much a pawn as he had been. That sweet, dreamy girl had shown some backbone yesterday evening, though. She'd surprised him in that.

With a shake of his head, Iain decided it didn't really matter how he remembered her or whether or not she'd been in on the deception. In essence, the point was moot. For if she'd conspired with Isadora or not, he would be a fool to allow any lingering resentment to intrude on what he knew must be done. And Iain Ashingford was no fool.

"I take both your meaning and your advice, Dobbs. I'll confess I hadn't thought it would come to this, but I swear on my father's grave . . . I will *not* lose Ash Park. If woo I must, woo I will."

An hour later Iain strode into his study, his boot heels ringing ominously on the cool, gray marble. He'd been sitting down to his breakfast when Wilkinson appeared like the town crier with his many announcements. First, the butler had informed him that Lady Lindley had already broken her fast in her chamber and would not be joining him. Then, Iain had been provided the latest bulletin on the Comtesse's health, which had been judged by Mrs. Emmitt as "fair to middlin'." And finally, what Iain had deemed the only report of any true significance, Wilkinson had advised him that the steward had at long last returned from his London sojourn.

Over a mouthful of kippers and biscuit, Iain had in-

structed the butler to have the steward await him in his
study. He'd then quite purposefully availed himself of a
leisurely meal and *The Morning Post* while Mr. Thompson
cooled his heels.

As he strode into the study Iain acknowledged that he
was out of sorts and he regarded the steward's lengthy absence as a convenient outlet for his temper. The overseer
might think he could dally in Town and leave Ash Park to
rot, but by damn, he'd set the man straight right now or
send him packing.

His footsteps faltered, however, when he spied Mr.
Thompson standing by the window. Younger than Iain had
expected, the steward looked more like a junior clerk than
the caretaker of a large and prosperous property. Spectacles
clung to the tip of his long nose and it appeared as if a
strong breeze—or a dose of Iain's wrath—could easily pull
him from his feet. Thin and frail, he was whiter than new-
fallen snow, and yet . . .

There was something vaguely familiar about Bertie
Thompson, something in the shape of his jaw and cheek-
bones. Iain did not have time to reflect on it, however, because the steward turned away from the window and saw
him at the other side of the room.

"Oh, my lord," he squeaked, "my most humble apolo-
gies." He began bowing and scraping, scuttling forward
like a crab.

"We hadn't been expecting you, my lord, we'd had no
word of your arrival, or else I would have most assuredly
planned to be here, never would have gone off if I'd known
you were coming—"

Bertie paused for a breath and Iain neatly inserted, "Have
a seat, Mr. Thompson."

The steward instantly dropped into the nearest chair, its
elaborate Rococo style decadently plush against his spare
figure.

Iain studied the man with a measure of annoyance. *What a disappointment,* he thought to himself. He'd been looking forward to giving the man a good tongue-lashing but this will-o'-the-wisp didn't look as if he could stand up to it.

Blast it, he'd have to find some other way to expend his gnawing frustration, perhaps a hard ride later or a round of fisticuffs with the ever-obliging Dobbs.

"Mr. Thompson." Iain fixed him with a gimlet stare that served to drain what color there was from the steward's pallid cheeks. "How long have you been overseer here?"

"Three years, my lord."

"And the Earl of Whiting was satisfied in your discharge of duties?"

Bertie's Adam's apple bobbed like a cork at sea. "I believe so, yes."

"Well, let us make one point very clear: I am *not* the Earl of Whiting."

"Oh, no, my lord."

"And I would not accept the Earl's recommendation under any conditions."

"No, my lord?"

"No." Iain rested his forearm atop the mantelpiece. "I draw my own conclusions. Therefore, during your rather *extended* absence, I've looked over Ash Park, reviewed its accounts, examined the grounds, attempted to familiarize myself with the property.

"And, although limited by the brief time I've been here, I found that, without a master in residence, Ash Park has fared surprisingly well."

"Oh, thank—"

"However, my observations produced a number of perplexing questions that I trust you will be able to answer?"

"I'll do my best—"

"First, I was intrigued to learn that since the Earl's death, aside from you, only three members of the Earl's original staff have remained at Ash Park. Three. Now, in the space of eighteen months, I find that attrition rate to be inordinately high, wouldn't you agree?"

The steward nodded weakly, but Iain did not wait for a response.

"Secondly, Thompson, it appears that many of the servants you hired to replace those who left are only day laborers from Blandford and do not reside here on the estate. This strikes me as both inefficient and inconvenient, especially since I plan to take up permanent residence at Ash Park. Perhaps you'd be so good as to shed light on this arrangement as well?"

Bertie nudged his spectacles with a shaky forefinger.

"And thirdly," Iain finished, his voice hardening. "I am most curious about the many trips you have made since the Earl's passing. From what I could determine, these sojourns have increased tenfold during the last year and a half when compared to your first eighteen months as steward. I would, of course, like an explanation."

With a perfunctory wave, he yielded the floor to the steward.

Bertie gulped visibly and clasped his hands between his bony knees. "There's only one explanation for all your questions, my lord, although I hate like the dickens to have to speak of it."

"Do you really?" Iain dryly asked.

Bertie nodded. "I really do, my lord." He paused with melodramatic effect, looking to his left and then to his right.

Iain frowned.

"Delighted as I am that you're here, Lord Lindley, I feel it my honor-bound duty to caution you. . . ."

The steward leaned forward and Iain unconsciously did the same.

In the lightest of whispers, Bertie announced, "Ash Park is haunted."

Fustian!

Isadora threw her hands into the air, disgusted beyond words. Whatever had prompted jingle-brained Bertie to make such an outrageous pronouncement?

She circled his chair to stare directly into his little, pasty face.

Bertie Thompson, you are the most dreadful nodcock I've ever had the misfortune to meet either in this world or the next. You can't possibly know that I'm here, I'm certain of it—

"What?"

The single word sliced through the room, arresting her mid-harangue. She peered over her shoulder. *I say, Bertie, Lindley looks far from amused.*

By Bertie's harried expression, she guessed he'd assumed as much.

"I know it must come as a shock, my lord, but ever since the Earl's passing, Ash Park's been visited by spooks."

Aha! That proves you haven't the vaguest notion what you're talking about. I've been haunting this establishment a mere three months.

"Honestly, my lord, it's been a frightful experience. Almost all the servants fled. I then convinced the locals to come work, but most insisted on leaving the manor by nightfall. Word of the hauntings spread, and that's when I had to begin traveling so frequently, since many of the tradesmen refused to set foot on the estate." Bertie's final words emerged on a whine.

Shaking her head, Isadora floated over to the other end of the mantel. *Tsk, tsk, you've done it now, Bertie, look at that scowl!* And Lindley was scowling. Fiercely.

"I've kept very well informed about Ash Park and I've heard no rumors of that sort."

"People don't like to talk of it, my lord. Afraid the spirit will take offense and begin haunting them."

"And what about you, Mr. Thompson? Why aren't you afraid of this spirit?"

Bertie lifted his thin shoulders in a small shrug. "Well, I'd always gotten along pretty swimmingly with the old Earl, so I figured he wouldn't be bothering me."

"The Earl?" Lindley's expression hardened even further.

"Yes, they say 'tis the Earl's ghost that haunts Ash Park. He died here, you know. . . ." The steward's voice trailed off feebly. And Isadora saw why. Lindley appeared as if he'd like nothing more than to tear Bertie apart limb by limb.

"Mr. Thompson, let me make myself perfectly clear," Iain ground out from his tightly clenched jaw. "I have no tolerance for fools. And even less tolerance for ghosts."

Pray tell? Isadora laughed.

"While I am in residence here, there will be no more speaking of this nonsense. It is nothing but gibberish for children's tales and superstitious rustics and I won't have another word of it, do you understand me?"

Isadora refastened a loose button on her glove while watching Bertie's head jiggle up and down.

"Yes, my lord," he finally managed in a squeak.

"Good. You are dismissed."

And Bertie vanished as quickly as if he'd borrowed some of Isadora's powers.

Iain, still wearing a thunderous glower, turned to rest both elbows atop the carved mahogany mantel. He dropped his head into his hands, muttering under his breath.

What's wrong, Lindley? Isadora asked with mocking concern. *Is your precious Ash Park harboring ghosts and ghoulies?* She opened her fan, passed it in front of her face, then smiled saucily at Iain over the top.

How can I resist?

With malicious glee, she stepped up behind him and waved the fan at the nape of his neck. The ebony locks fluttered back and forth and Iain yanked his head up from his hands.

He turned to look behind him while one gloved palm patted searchingly at the back of his head. He spun around, frowning first in the direction of the unopened window, then to the closed French doors.

Isadora drifted backward toward the door, waving the fan at him once more. The hair on his forehead wafted with the current.

Breezy, isn't it? she cheerfully called before floating away through the study wall.

One thing that Isadora had learned during her first months as a spectral being was that she was truly bound to Ash Park. She couldn't meander about the fields or explore the wooded areas to the north. Her range, she'd discovered, was limited solely to the physical structures of the estate: the manor, the stables, the steward's cottage, the quaint Grecian temple at the back of the garden.

And it was in the Greek temple that she ultimately found Daphne later that morning. For only the second time since she'd died, Isadora felt thankful for being a ghost. The first occasion had been last night when Daphne had burst through the door of Ash Park.

Not a doting or fussing or clinging mother, Isadora had nonetheless loved Daphne with all the intense pride of her nature. She'd done her best by her daughter, and had wanted only the best for her. Health, happiness. Love. Everything that the girl's sentimental soul had dreamed of.

To leave Daphne as she'd last seen her, sobbing brokenly

over her own dead body, had been the most painful experience of Isadora's life—or death.

Until last night, that is. The sight of Daphne bursting through the door had been like a double-edged sword through Isadora's heart. She'd been delighted, but at the same time the realization that she would no longer be able to share her daughter's life had stunned her. The actuality of her death had hit Isadora like a physical blow.

She would never celebrate another of Daphne's birthdays. She would never hold a grandchild. And then, in a flash, Isadora had felt very grateful that she was a ghost. That she'd been given this additional time on earth meant a little more time with Daphne. Her witty, beautiful, and inexplicably starry-eyed daughter.

Isadora found her in her gray morning gown, pacing and talking to herself as she had done since a young girl when preoccupied or disturbed.

"—hopes to intimidate me, but I refuse to be intimidated. The dour looks and curt commands didn't work, so he tries to frighten me with seduction! He probably thinks I'll run like some poor, terrified virgin, but he's wrong. I won't run. I won't."

Daphne tucked her thumb into a corner of her mouth and began chewing distractedly on her thumbnail.

Where are your gloves, my girl? Isadora looked disapprovingly at the mauve lump lying beneath a bench. *And, my stars, your hat*—Daphne was listlessly swinging the chip bonnet around by one grosgrain ribbon—*you'll freckle, if you're not careful.*

"I am not rich. Neither am I beautiful. I don't have anything he could desire. So why wouldn't he want an annulment?"

Because then he'd lose Ash Park, Isadora tartly observed as she settled herself on the marble bench.

"He can't honestly believe I'll give him an heir! Not after the way he's treated me."

You wouldn't think so, would you, but the man's got more cheek than is seemly.

"And that woman . . ."

Isadora rolled her eyes. *Must you remind me?*

"How can I remain in the same house with his . . . mistress?"

We must be rid of her. Isadora slapped her fan into her palm.

"But if I leave, then I'm conceding victory to him. I'll have to stay at Ash Park until that Comtesse person is well enough to travel, then, once she's gone, I can depart with dignity. In the meantime I will demand that Iain Ashingford tell me why he chose to marry me."

Percy's to blame for your not knowing. I'd wanted to tell you, I did.

"And then I'll go to London and procure the annulment." Daphne paused and stared at her kid walking shoes. "I venture to say it's what I want."

Isadora peered sharply at her daughter. *You're not so certain anymore?*

"I imagine that Roger might offer for me—"

Roger!

"—but I'm not in love with him and he's so dear, he deserves a wife who'll adore him." Daphne sighed deeply and walked over to the bench and sat down next to her mother's spirit. "Although if I tried, I wager I could probably be a good wife to Roger."

I thought you had some notion of marrying for love.

"What is love, anyway?"

With a scandalized look, Isadora whipped her quizzing glass into place. *Is this my Daphne speaking? The hopeless romantic?*

"Not the way my heart aches when he smiles at me. Not

the butterflies that danced in my stomach when he touched me last night."

Isadora's lips puckered with distaste. *Sounds suspiciously like it to me,* she muttered.

"I wonder what Mother would say." Daphne laid her bonnet in her lap, then began weaving the ribbon between her fingers. "She never did wish for me to marry him; she'd most likely be glad to see the marriage annulled."

Yes, well . . .

"She'd want me to be strong."

Yes, but happy . . .

"She taught me to be proud."

But your happiness, Daphne . . .

Daphne tilted her head back and gazed through the open-air ceiling to the robin's-egg blue of the summer sky. "I miss you, Mother," she whispered.

Oh, now, don't go getting all weepy on me, Isadora scolded, fumbling for her handkerchief.

"I realize that you . . . might have done or said something that caused Iain to leave the morning of the wedding—"

Isadora stilled, guilt seeping through her.

"—and I know that I probably will never know the truth of what took place that day. But whatever your feelings had been for the Marquess, I do know that you would have never deliberately hurt me."

I had to know whether he could care for you, blast it. I gambled and the unscrupulous wretch called my bluff.

"And, no matter what might have occurred between you and him, he owed me the decency of a word, the courtesy of a good-bye."

He most certainly did, she huffed.

A soft smile tugged at the corners of Daphne's mouth and she glanced down to where she'd wrapped the bonnet's ribbon around the finger of her left hand, like a ring.

"However, it would seem that Iain Ashingford is as proud and stubborn as you ever were."

That brought Isadora up short.

"Curious, isn't it?" Daphne murmured.

A long shadow slanted across the floor, casting a pale gray form over the white marble. Daphne looked up and her hands went slack in her lap.

"Iain."

Chapter Six

"Am I disturbing you?"

Daphne surged to her feet. "No!"

"No?" Iain questioned with a quizzical smile, advancing one cautious step into the rotunda. "I thought I heard you speaking to someone."

Warmth stole up Daphne's neck. "I . . . I have a habit of talking to myself." She raised her chin defensively. "Peculiar, I know."

"I don't think it so peculiar," he allowed. "You must have a great deal on your mind."

His friendly tone unsettled her. "I do." Then in her agitation, she yanked the ribbon right from her bonnet.

Iain looked to her clumsy handiwork. "A pity. Or had the unfortunate hat been serving as a stand-in for me?"

Daphne eyed him warily from beneath her lashes. Teasing, congenial. Which role was he playing today?

"No," she retorted, "a modest chip bonnet could not do you justice. I'd say you're more of a Yeoman or a Trafalgar."

His gray eyes twinkled. "I believe I've been wounded. As pretentious as the Trafalgar?"

She waved her hand. "If the hat fits . . ."

The banter struck Daphne as a striking contrast to their heated words of last evening, and although she responded to his badinage in kind, she remained guarded, unsure of his purpose.

In her opinion, the man was a chameleon, shifting colors from one moment to the next. She did not know what to expect of him, but she did know she would not be swayed by either his disdain or his charm.

"Did you follow me out here to discuss millinery?" she asked.

"It does seem a safer subject than matrimony," he responded with an arch grin.

She did not return the smile. "One we need to discuss nonetheless."

He turned the subject. "What do you think of Ash Park?" His gaze quickly scanned the massive gardens to the left and the lush countryside rolling out to the right.

"It is beautiful," she had to admit.

"You've not been here before, have you?"

Daphne shook her head, wishing she hadn't ruined her hat. She might have been able to hide her confusion behind its sheltering brim. Why was he suddenly so affable?

"No. Although my mother was raised here, she had not returned since marrying my father."

"Ah. Yes." Iain bowed his head and strolled over to a marble pillar entwined with hundreds of the loveliest, pale pink roses. He picked one perfect blossom from the vine and twirled it absently between his thumb and finger. Without looking at her, he said, "About your mother, Daphne. I owe you an apology."

She stiffened.

"I learned of your loss a few days after the service," Iain said. "I'm terribly sorry. I should have written you."

"Why didn't you?"

"I was angry."

He was angry? Faith, she could teach him a few things about that emotion! She felt the old, familiar outrage threaten to erupt, but before it could take hold, her mind skipped back to the morning of her wedding. *What* had angered him? What had occurred to embitter him so?

"At my mother?" she ventured.

He shrugged, evidently not willing to open up to her. "Merely angry. I should have written you, though, and I can see now it was inexcusable of me not to have done so."

It was inexcusable, she mentally echoed.

He studied the rose for a moment. "I also must apologize for my conduct last night. I behaved badly, Daphne. Shockingly so. I can offer no defense for my boorishness, since, unfortunately, there is none. Your arrival caught me unprepared."

"'Twas evident," she replied, lifting both brows. "Especially since you'd already forbidden me to come. What gave you the right to send me that note, instructing me *not* to visit at Ash Park?"

"Would you believe me if I said that message was misdirected and never intended for you?"

Funnily enough, Daphne almost did believe it. She wasn't sure if she believed it because of its plausibility or because of the dimple winking in Iain's cheek.

"For whom was it meant?" she pressed, refusing to be weakened by that dimple. "Someone of 'many charms'?"

He had the grace to look abashed. "The Comtesse was

under the impression that she'd been invited to visit. I had hoped to dissuade her of the idea."

Daphne clenched her jaw. She wasn't certain if she was more relieved he'd not meant the note for her, or more outraged that he'd invited a woman of loose morals to Ash Park.

"You didn't seem to be dissuading her when I walked in last night," she stiffly pointed out.

"It did look bad, didn't it?"

Daphne tried to hold on to her wrath, she honestly did, but this charming version of Iain was much more difficult to withstand than the cold, harsh man of last night.

As she fought herself Iain slowly closed the distance between them.

"I know I'm asking a great deal of you," he said. "More than you should be asked to give, but . . . can you forgive me?"

She hesitated. The rose's sweet perfume floated up to her on a puff of breeze, its intoxicating fragrance acting on her like a drug. Something inside Daphne began to soften ever so gradually. She could not deny that his apology pleased her. As did his gesture of offering her the rose.

Careful not to brush his fingers with her own, she plucked the rose from his hold, accepting the peace offering. The cool ruffled petals were like velvet against her fingertips.

"Yes," she said in a surprisingly even voice. "I can forgive you for not sending a letter of condolence. I can even forgive you for sending the wrong letter."

He dipped his head, acknowledging her concession.

"But your conduct has been reprehensible and I won't mislead you into believing that *all* is forgiven."

"I thank you for your honesty."

"You value it?"

"I do." His smile warmed. "I believe the last time I used those words, you were carrying flowers then as well."

She started and glanced to the single rose she held, realizing he referred to her bridal bouquet. Something flashed through her, something akin to fear, and she deliberately dropped the rose to the ground.

She was falling under his spell, she could feel it. Even now, as he worked his charm on her, she was ready to forgive him anything. She must be crazed, she told herself. Her mother would never be so easily taken in.

At the very moment she had decided to flee, she felt his finger under her chin, nudging it up.

No, she inwardly cried. *I am furious. I truly am.*

But his mouth claimed hers before she had time to put the thought to word or action.

Daphne had never been kissed, so this was the excuse she allowed herself as his lips slid over hers with gentle persuasion. Not even on their wedding day had he embraced her, so she justified this one kiss by telling herself it was overdue.

What it was . . . was magic.

Heat blossomed in the pit of her abdomen, then spread into her veins, hot and swift. She couldn't believe how powerful it was, the feel of his tongue dancing along the seam of her lips. His teeth pulled softly at her, begging her to open to him, testing and tasting.

As his hand splayed over her lower back, urging her closer, a low moan came out of nowhere.

Her eyes flew open. Not nowhere—that moan had come from her!

Dear God, it was as if her mind and body were divided, one protesting her need that flamed out of control, the other craving it instinctively, desperately . . . madly.

This wasn't supposed to be happening, she told herself as

she focused on cooling her body's ardor. The rational part of her searched for ammunition against the less rational.

Annulment. Abandonment. Adultery.

Those three words proved most effective.

She wedged her arms between them and pushed, relieved when Iain instantly released her.

He was breathing as hard as she was, and looked as shocked as she felt.

Lurching back a step, he shakily combed his fingers through his hair.

"I might owe you another apology," he rasped. "But you won't be getting one for that. I cannot honestly say I'm sorry."

He turned and left her.

"Jane, run down to the kitchen and fetch me some more beef tea. This has grown cold."

With a long-suffering sigh, the Comtesse handed the offensively tepid dish to her maid.

"Yes, madame. Is there anything else you'll be needing?"

Winnifred flung her lawn handkerchief across her forehead and closed her eyes. "These pillows, Jane. How can I rest when these pillows are so deucedly uncomfortable? Can't you do something?"

The maid set down the dish and began plumping the pillows.

"Is that better?"

"Yes, it is. You're a good girl, Jane, now hurry off to the kitchen before I swoon with hunger."

"Yes, madame."

Winnifred heard the door close and immediately after the hinges squeaked open again.

"Jane, I swear it, I shall surely expire—"

"Pipe down, Winnie, it's me."

Winnifred cocked one eye open, then sat straight up in bed. "Dash it all, you shouldn't be waltzing in here in broad daylight. Someone might have seen you come in."

Bertie made a face. "What do you take me for? A complete flat? No one saw me."

"Perhaps not this time, but you must have a care. If anyone learned of our relationship, the entire plan would be suspect. Where in blazes have you been anyway?"

"Ooh, that's a proper sisterly greeting for you. I only just got back this morning and had to speak with the Marquess before I could sneak up here."

She grimaced. "You should have been here when I arrived. I thought I was in the suds when his wife showed."

"So I heard." Bertie sat down at the foot of the bed. "Did she strike you?"

Winnie raised her hand to her bruised cheek. "No. That oaf Lindley stumbled and hit me with his arm. I fell and knocked my head."

"Hmm." Bertie leaned forward to get a closer look. "Lucky for us that you're indisposed or else the Marchioness would send you packing."

"Lucky for *us*? My cheek is three different shades of purple and my head feels as if it might very well fall off and you tell me I ought to feel lucky?"

"You know what I mean," Bertie replied, displaying a lamentable lack of sympathy. "I'm saying that you shouldn't be in any great hurry to recover your health. We might be able to make use of this."

"You're all heart, Bertie," Winnie sulked.

"Ain't I, though?" He simulated a grin. "But back to business. Did you learn anything in London?"

Winnie pushed out her lower lip. "Not a word. I own if I didn't know better, I'd believe Lindley had unnatural inclinations. All I could get out of him was the invitation to join him here and that was given only after he'd downed two bottles of Claude's best champagne."

"Yeah, he's a queer one. Stiff as a poker."

"Are you sure he knows of the treasure? Your letter didn't explain how you'd come to hear of it, much less what makes you suspect Lindley has information."

"Oh, he knows all right."

"How do you know?"

"I just do."

Suspicion narrowed Winnie's eyes. "Give over, Bertie. You're not telling me the whole story."

He frowned and shoved his spectacles farther up his nose.

"I knew it! I can always tell when you're hiding something because you fidget with those ridiculous spectacles."

"Oh, cease your prattle. I'm not hiding anything. I merely didn't wish to raise your hopes until I'd first done some checking on my own. The truth is I *know* that Lindley has information about the treasure because the Earl told me so himself."

"What?"

Bertie cleared his throat. "I was with the Earl of Whiting when he . . . died."

Winnie clapped her hands over her mouth. "Bertie, you didn't!"

"Didn't—oh, no, of course not! Why should I off the old man?" He gave her a testy look before explaining. "We were riding out to the east pasture when Whiting suddenly fell from his horse. I leaped down to see what was the matter and found him clutching his chest and groaning. I was going to ride back for help, but the Earl grabbed hold of me and wouldn't let go. He started babbling about Ash Park and I couldn't make heads nor tails of it till he said, 'Lindley.'

"Now, I'd remembered that the estate had previously belonged to the Ashingfords and for some reason that caught my interest. You know, a dying man calling out another man's name? Odd, I said to myself. So then the Earl says, 'I've hidden it, but young Lindley knows the truth. He'll come after it. He'll come to Ash Park, looking for it.' I could scarce believe my ears, but before I could ask him what he'd hidden or where"—Bertie shrugged—"he died."

"The Earl was right," Winnie breathed. "Lindley did come for it."

Bertie nodded meaningfully.

"But . . . wait. The Earl's been dead nearly a year and a half yet you didn't write to me until just two months ago."

"Yes, well—"

"You weren't even going to tell me about the bloody treasure, were you?" she accused.

"Shh, keep your voice down—"

"Bertie, you always were a devious little toad! You've been looking for the treasure all this time, haven't you? And then when you couldn't find it and Claude died, that's when you hatched the idea of me seducing the information out of Lindley. Isn't that so?"

"You must admit, it's a good idea," he wheedled.

She tossed her handkerchief at him, scowling petulantly. "If it works. How do you know Lindley hasn't already recovered the treasure himself?"

"I've been thinking about it, and I don't believe he realizes that he possesses a clue to the treasure."

"Then why did he marry the chit to get the property?"

Bertie tugged at his earlobe. "That I don't know. But it might prove immaterial, because right before I left for London, I made a discovery that could mean you don't need to play slap-and-tickle with Lindley after all."

"How so?"

"I found that the manor house is riddled with secret passages." Bertie's nose twitched excitedly. "I'll wager the treasure is hidden somewhere in the passageways."

"Ohh . . ." Winnie shrank back against the pillows, shaking her head. "You aren't going to convince me to go crawling about dusty old tunnels and the like. You know I'm terrified of the dark."

"Come now, you know you haven't any choice. If you're going to continue living in the style in which Claude kept you, you're going to have to come up with some blunt. No offense, old girl, but you're not likely to leg-shackle another doddering Frog who doesn't mind if his bride comes from common Somerset stock."

Pouting, Winnie recalled her last discouraging meeting with the Comte deCheval's creditors. "Blast that old Frenchman!" she fumed. "Claude led me to believe his pockets were plumper than Prinny, but what am I left with? A mere pittance, I tell you."

"Enough of your whining. We have to put our heads together. I think it best to alter our strategy—" Bertie abruptly swiveled around. "What's that?"

Rustling could be heard from the corridor, directly outside the bedchamber. "Jane!" Winnie exclaimed in a stage whisper.

"Get rid of her," Bertie hissed, jumping up and pressing himself against the bedpost. He pulled the bed's curtains around him so that his gaunt frame nearly disappeared into the voluminous fabric.

The door swung open and the young abigail stood on the threshold, carrying a tray.

"Jane, set the tray down and leave me. I feel absolutely wretched and cannot bear company at the moment."

"But, madame, don't you want me to bring you your beef tea?" The maid took a step into the room.

"No!" Winnie hastily tempered her tone. "No, leave it there and go. Now."

The puzzled maid placed the tray inside the door and left.

"All right, Bertie, she's gone. Let's hear this scheme of yours—quickly. It's simply too dangerous for you to be visiting my room."

Bertie emerged from the ivory bed hangings. "Listen closely, since I will need your help to carry this off. After the Earl died, I had to be rid of the staff so that I could hunt around for Whiting's secret. So, I concocted a ghost. Whiting's ghost."

"Clever," Winnie grudgingly conceded.

"Yes, I thought so, especially when the plan worked to perfection. Nearly everyone fled and I was able to poke about at will, as well as pinch one or two items that I later pawned in London.

"Don't look sour, I've put aside a little for you." He arched one pale eyebrow. "Provided, that is, you help me find the treasure."

"You're nothing more than a blackmailer, Bertie Thompson."

Bertie smiled smugly. "Now here is my plan. . . ."

Chapter
Seven

Later that evening Iain sat in his bedroom with a razor pressed tightly to his throat. Shaving paste, specially concocted by Dobbs, tickled at his upper lip and filled his nostrils with the tangy scent of clove oil and lemon.

Dobbs was deftly guiding the blade across Iain's jaw when the valet commented, "Are you aware that Ash Park is said to be haunted?"

Iain jerked so swiftly that even the competent Dobbs could not move quickly enough to avoid the nick below Iain's left ear.

"Damn," he muttered, feeling blood trickle down his neck, sticky and hot.

"Jittery tonight?" Dobbs pressed a cloth to the scratch.

Iain didn't answer, thinking the cut was no more than he deserved for overreacting to such nonsense.

"Or is it the idea of a ghost?" the valet asked. "Sorry, I hadn't meant to give you a start."

Iain scowled. "You didn't give me a start. That fool steward Thompson had already told me about the resident spook. Where did you hear of it?"

"Kitchen gossip." Dobbs dabbed an ointment on Iain's neck, the balm's sting sharper than the scratch itself.

"So what do you make of it?" Iain asked.

"Well, in my experience, I've found that the country folk tend to be most credulous of this type of thing. Doesn't altogether surprise me. Easy now." The soft scrape of the blade rasped over Iain's throat.

"It doesn't? Well, it irritates the hell out of me," Iain growled. "After half a century, I finally rid Ash Park of Whiting and now I'm told that I'm still not free of the blighter!"

Dobbs peered over the top of his spectacles. "Was not that 'blighter' the Marchioness's grandfather?"

"You know that he was."

"Hmm-mm."

His lips conspicuously pursed, the valet picked up a linen.

"By Jove, what now?" Iain demanded in exasperation.

"I'd wager you'll not get far with your wife should she hear you refer to her kin in such a manner."

"Oh, for heaven's sake, give me some credit, will you?" Iain jerked upright, wrenching the linen from the valet's grasp. "I'm not so dull-witted as to call her grandfather a rotter to her face. Even if he was a lying, cheating, son-of-a-bitch."

"But is that the point?"

Iain stood and roughly completed toweling off. "What point?"

"The Earl of Whiting might have been a liar and a cheat, but does it necessarily follow that Lady Lindley is?"

Iain felt as if he'd been reprimanded and he had. "Blast it, Dobbs," he mumbled. "I hate it when you're right. I've gone about this all bloody wrong, haven't I? I shouldn't have allowed my feelings for the Whitings to have spilled over into my dealings with Daphne. She's of a sensitive nature and I failed to take that into account. My oversight could prove disastrous."

He didn't need to state aloud: *Should I lose Ash Park.*

"At least I've begun to remedy matters."

"How is that?" Dobbs asked.

"She's dining with me, isn't she? My prettily worded note worked, so I must hope that I'm gaining ground with her. I do believe that I might have made some progress today."

The valet handed him a neckcloth. "Might I inquire as to the nature of your progress?"

"No, you may not inquire," Iain shot back.

Dobbs bowed. "Forgive my presumptuousness."

"Forgive it?" Iain gave him a lopsided smile. "You glory in your presumptuousness, you old dog." He patted the pockets of his Weston-tailored coat. "Now, where did I place that snuffbox?"

"This one?" Dobbs handed him a gold-and-enamel box, decorated with a phoenix resembling Ash Park's fountain. "Lovely piece."

Iain turned the box in his hand. "Yes, it is, isn't it? I found it lying about in the study. I've grown rather attached to it."

Dobbs sidled a sly glance at him. "Ah, that you might someday say the same of your bride."

In spite of himself, Iain barked a short laugh. "You're incorrigible, Dobbs. Utterly incorrigible."

"Yes, my lord. Thank you."

A few minutes later, as Iain headed downstairs for dinner, he reflected on his conversation with the cheeky valet.

In the past he'd had no difficulty in confiding to Dobbs, but this evening he had found himself unable to do so. He couldn't discuss his "progress" with Daphne and he knew perfectly well why not. He'd been too embarrassed. How could he confess that his first attempt to seduce his virgin bride had nearly exploded in his face . . . or more accurately stated, in his breeches?

Iain paused on the staircase, amazed to feel his blood begin to pound again with the memory. Damn, but she'd surprised him. Like a young lad sampling his first taste of a woman, he'd been caught completely off guard by Daphne's passionate response. He'd commenced with only a kiss. An innocuous thing, chaste. Then she'd moaned softly into his mouth and suddenly that kiss had consumed him. He'd been sucked into a whirlpool of need.

Ironic, really. Here he'd been planning to manipulate her with an introduction to desire and he'd been the one forced to stagger away from the temple, aching as though a certain part of his anatomy had been turned to marble.

He could laugh at himself now, but earlier . . . The heaviness in his groin had been almost a painful thing.

His intention had been to smooth over their differences with an apology and a dose of charm. He knew that he had to seduce her. The threat of annulment meant that as long as their marriage remained unconsummated, he was in danger of losing Ash Park. And losing Ash Park was not an option.

He hadn't, however, anticipated the pleasure he might get out of bedding his young wife. The girl wasn't without appeal, nor—apparently—did she lack for . . . fire. He considered himself fortunate in that because he knew he would have to seduce her whether he was attracted to her or not. 'Twould only make it easier for him now.

He recalled Daphne as he'd first seen her, during the week before their wedding. To be truthful, even then he'd found her mildly attractive in an understated way. No, she wasn't a beauty but there was something about her, something indefinable yet appealing.

During that week he had tried not to give her too much thought. She was a means to an end and he had feared if he saw her in any other light, he might have regretted his plan.

She'd been merely a starry-eyed girl with a breathless voice whom he was taking to wife.

But today she'd been more than that. When she'd leaned into him, pressing her soft breasts into his chest, her mouth as sweet and soft as honey . . . He wanted her. Startling enough, he desired this woman, this naive, idealistic girl.

Last night she'd accused him of robbing her of her dreams, her naïveté. He wondered if there was any truth to it. Admittedly he might have wounded her by his actions these past months and she did seem to have matured; but he didn't honestly believe she could have kissed him the way she'd done today if she didn't still harbor fanciful notions of love and romance.

Love and romance.

Iain nearly laughed aloud, but the bitter sound caught in his throat. Good God, he hadn't believed in those inventions since . . . He couldn't even remember when. Once or twice during his younger years, he'd wished there might be something as miraculous as love, something greater than affection or lust. But he'd yet to see it. And Iain never believed in anything he couldn't see with his own two eyes.

He was shaking his head in silent bemusement when the footman pulled open the door to the dining room and his gaze fell on Daphne.

She stood at the mullioned window, her auburn hair shining like molten copper under the waning rays of the sun.

Was it but a moment ago he'd thought her only mildly pretty? She was breathtaking, the golden light bronzing her profile, casting a glow about her—a visible glow. Almost like a halo. Actually, very much like a halo.

Frowning, Iain slitted his eyes and tilted his head to the side.

The halo disappeared.

A trick of the light, he decided. Yet he couldn't blame the lighting for his body's sudden reaction to Daphne. Resolve and desire spread through him in a hot rush and he knew with a certainty he'd do whatever he must to bring her to his bed. And, of course, to keep Ash Park.

Daphne did not turn toward him but he could tell she knew he was there. Beneath the modest neckline of her dress, her breasts rose and fell rapidly, their soft curves a thousand times more enticing than Winnifred's abundant proportions.

"Have we established a truce?" he asked.

At last she turned to glance at him, her gaze wary. Guilt pierced him, but he shook it off.

Slowly she walked over to the linen-clad table, the rustle of her gray-and-white skirts the only sound in the cavernous chamber. She rested her hands between the spindled posts of a chair and, without turning toward him, softly agreed, "Truce . . . for now."

The footman hurried forward and pulled out her chair and Iain joined her at the table. By unspoken mutual consent, they did not mar the fragile peace between them as the servant filled their wineglasses and served from the covered dishes.

From behind the footman's movements, Iain watched her. She was so composed, he thought, his gaze following the flicker of honeyed candlelight across the curve of her cheekbone. Her calm surprised him and he acknowledged that Daphne *had* changed more than he had recognized. She was more self-possessed than she had been three months ago, carrying herself with a graceful confidence reminiscent of . . . her mother.

Iain started, almost spilling his wine. *Now, that's bloody odd. I actually had an agreeable thought about Isadora Whiting Harkwell.*

In truth, the words had entered his thoughts from nowhere, as if they'd been whispered to him by an inner voice. He couldn't imagine where that inner voice had come from or why that voice would favorably recall Isadora the Turbaned Dragon. He mentally shook himself, resolving to get more rest.

The footman had taken his position in a corner of the dining room and Iain signaled him with a brief jerk of his head to leave them. Although he was certain that every staff member had already learned of the drama played out in the foyer last evening, he preferred to conduct this conversation in private.

He sipped at his claret until the servant exited. He then cleared his throat.

"So, have you already sent to Harkwell House for the rest of your trunks?"

Above her plate, Daphne's fork hovered uncertainly. "No."

"Would you like me to see to it, then?" he offered, ever so nonchalant.

She placed the laden fork back onto her plate and confronted him squarely. "No," she repeated, her voice firm. "I have no intention of remaining at Ash Park."

He feigned mild surprise. "Don't you agree it would be for the best?"

"The best for what?"

"The best course for our marriage."

She stiffened in her chair.

"Might I ask, my lord, when *you* became concerned with the wisest course for our so-called marriage? If you'd be good enough to recall, I have already decided on *my* plans for this union and I'll be seeing to them as soon as I leave here."

"You still wish to seek an annulment?" he asked. "Even after . . ."

If not for the sudden blush that stained her complexion, he wouldn't have known that she'd picked up on his reference to their kiss.

Her voice, however, was decidedly cool when she answered. "Naturally."

"But why?"

She speared a turnip with the tines of her fork, her cheeks deepening another shade. "I cannot believe you even ask."

"Because of the matters we discussed this morning?"

Her gaze raised to challenge his. "Too much water has passed under the bridge, Lord Lindley, for all to be forgiven with one mere kiss."

Ah, just the opening he needed.

"But it needn't be but one kiss, Daphne."

She coughed and took a deep draft of wine.

"I am beginning to believe that I gravely erred when I left you at Harkwell House," he went on. "I think we are much more compatible than I had initially reckoned."

"And it was our 'incompatibility' that caused you to abandon me?" she questioned, her sarcasm plain.

"No, my reasons for leaving had little to do with you."
And a great deal to do with your shrew of a mother.

"Please then enlighten me. What were they?"

Iain hesitated. He couldn't reveal the argument he'd had with the Baroness without his motives becoming glaringly evident. And, impossible though it seemed, Daphne did not appear to realize he'd wed her solely for Ash Park.

"Let us simply say I've concluded that my reasons were

very poor, indeed." He lifted a shoulder. "I made a mistake."

"Which mistake are you referring to?" she asked. "Wedding me or deserting me?"

"Marrying you was no lapse of judgment, I assure you." He felt the truth of that statement right to his bones. And beyond.

"Unfortunately, my lord, I disagree. Our union was ill-conceived." She turned her attention back to her plate, her profile unyielding.

Blast. He hadn't anticipated such strong opposition from her. Not after the interlude in the temple. With her new-found confidence, Daphne had evidently acquired a healthy dose of obstinacy as well. And as much as it got in the way of his goal, he found himself liking it in her. The spirited woman she was now was infinitely more intriguing than the girl he'd wed.

He stroked the stem of his wineglass. "You believe it a mistake; I do not. Do you think we might arrive at a meeting of the minds?"

She did not immediately answer and Iain pressed his point. "Would you be willing to allow me the chance to change your opinion?"

From the corner of his eye, he saw her twist into knots the napkin in her lap. The nervous habit was growing familiar to him.

"To what purpose?" she asked suspiciously.

Ah, you are so delightfully naive, my dear. He fought back a self-satisfied smile. "To salvage our association."

She frowned and looked ready to object, but he forestalled her. "Please. At least give me an opportunity to convince you before you do anything rash like secure an annulment. To end the marriage before it has begun would be precipitate at best.

"Moreover, I don't think either of us can deny that there is a certain . . . attraction between us."

At the back of her eyes, a flame glimmered before she masked it behind a sweep of lashes. Iain thought he recognized that flame as desire.

However, her next question doused that spark as effectively as a bucket of cold water. "What of your attraction for the Comtesse?"

Iain stifled a groan. Would he forever be haunted by that rash invitation? Admittedly, when Winnifred had first arrived at Ash Park, he'd been annoyed but had soon decided to avail himself of the charms the Comtesse so lavishly offered. After all, he'd been over six months without the benefit of female companionship and Winnifred had been openly pursuing him since he'd returned to London. Why not make the best of the situation? he'd concluded.

But that was before Daphne's arrival. Now Winnifred was nothing more than a nuisance, a bedridden one at that. A well-endowed obstacle, she stood in the way of his goal: to seduce Daphne and hold on to Ash Park.

"Hell," he whispered beneath his breath.

"I beg your pardon?"

Iain guzzled his wine and set the glass on the table with a thud. He couldn't deny a faint physical attraction to Winnifred and he wouldn't lie.

"As I told you earlier, the Comtesse was . . . mistaken in coming here," he hedged. "As soon as she is well enough to travel, she'll be leaving Ash Park."

"As should I," Daphne replied.

Should, not *shall.* Iain seized on the advantage she'd given him. He reached across and took hold of the hand fidgeting in her lap.

"Will you allow me a week, Daphne? A week to show you that I am not the unfeeling monster I've seemed to be?

Time enough to satisfy you that our marriage is worth saving?"

Beneath his hand, he could detect the trembling of her delicate fingers. And, suddenly, he felt again their touch as they slid over his scalp, clutching at his hair, drawing him close. This morning Daphne hadn't been wearing her gloves. Her fingers had been cool, satiny . . . erotic. Insanely, Iain had to fight back an impulse to caress her hands there and now. Her voice brought him back to sanity.

"I won't even consider your proposal unless you answer a question for me."

"Gladly," he responded, taking hope.

"Why did you decide to marry—"

Boom.

The sound reverberated through the room.

They both looked up in the direction of the din to see the crystal chandelier swinging back and forth, casting multi-colored arcs against the walls.

The door to the hall and the door to the kitchen flew open simultaneously.

"Oh, the Comtesse!" a young woman's voice wailed.

"Oh, 'tis the ghost!" a chorus of voices cried.

Chapter
Eight

By Jove, I've seen it all now, Isadora murmured, staring at the unusually broad backside of the Comtesse deCheval.

In truth, probably more than I ever cared to, she added with an acerbic sniff.

Intending to pop in on the Comtesse, Isadora's powers had unexpectedly dropped her into one of Ash Park's many secret passages, where she had indeed—to her surprise—located Winnifred. She could hardly have missed her.

The widow was crouched on hands and knees on the floor of a dark, dank-smelling tunnel, dressed only in her nightrail. Covered in wispy spiderwebs that trailed from her like mourning bunting, she was gingerly patting the stone floor in an evident search for something.

I wager you're looking for that candlestick over there, Isadora observed, wondering what to make of such a vastly amusing spectacle.

"What the blazes are you doing in there?" The sibilant whisper came from the far end of the passageway.

Isadora recognized the voice. *Is that you, Bertie?* She cocked a brow in surprise. *My, how very intriguing. The bumbling steward and the buxom seductress on intimate terms. What can it mean?*

"I dropped the candle stand," Winnie hissed back. "I can't see a blasted thing."

"Well, you're making enough damn noise to wake the dead!"

"For heaven's sake, Bertie, must you speak of the dead?" Winnie's fingers latched onto the lost candle stand. "It's as dark and as cold as a crypt in here."

Odorous, as well, Isadora added, wrinkling her nose.

"Never mind. You better come on out before someone comes running," Bertie urged. "I hate to think what they've heard below."

"Mayhaps they'll believe it's your ghost," Winnie mocked as she struggled to her feet. The tunnel's low ceiling prevented her from standing fully erect, so she was forced to bend both at the waist and at the knees. With difficulty, she managed to wiggle around in the tight space, then started toward the faint light at the end of the passage.

Isadora followed.

"Step to it now," Bertie called with some urgency. "I think I hear someone coming."

Indeed? Isadora bent an ear in the direction of the corridor. Footsteps were approaching.

Winnie tried to increase her pace, but hunched over as she was like some old crone, she could manage only an awkward waddle.

"I say, Winnie, hurry!"

Rap, rap, rap. Through the thick stone walls, the knocking sounded as if it came from a great distance.

"Madame Comtesse?" The voice belonged to Jane, the young maid. "Madame?"

"Winn-n-nie!" Bertie whined in a whisper.

Isadora smirked. *Now, this could be interesting.*

And it was, for at that moment Winnifred caught her toe on the hem of her nightdress and catapulted forward onto her knees with a thundering crash.

"Aagh!"

Oops.

"Madame!"

A muted rattling followed, suggesting that the maid was attempting to open the locked door. Then her footsteps could be heard racing down the hallway.

"God take it, Winnie, she's gone for help. Hurry up, can't you?"

Winnie labored to rise, muttering curses that burned even Isadora's ears.

La, such language! Isadora tsk-tsked. *And do have a care for your accent, my dear, your breeding is showing.* Winnie's counterfeit upper-crust drawl had conspicuously slipped into Bertie's broad Somerset diction.

"I swear, Albert Thompson, when I get out of here . . ."

Lurching along, Winnifred made her way to the tunnel's end, then stumbled through the hidden entrance at the side of the fireplace.

Isadora snickered while Bertie gasped.

"Dear God, Winnie, you're a sight!"

Isn't she though?

Winnie's pristine white nightrail was streaked gray with dust, a large rip visible at the knee. Her hair had fallen loose from her lace cap, its snarled curls liberally laced with cobwebs. Flushed and perspiring, she glared at Bertie with a look that said she'd like nothing more than to bean him with the candle stand.

"Bertie . . ." Winnie's nostrils quivered with outrage, causing Isadora to burst out cackling.

Oh, dear, Whinny, you truly look like a horse when you do that thing with your nose! Neighhh, she mimicked, chuckling wickedly all the while.

"We haven't got time for that," Bertie snapped. "Find yourself a clean gown before someone arrives to break down the door."

Just then a heavy tread echoed from down the hall.

"Lindley," they said in unison.

With greater agility than Isadora would have expected from either of them, Winnie vaulted neatly over the bed while Bertie dove headfirst into the passageway. Scrambling over to the armoire, Winnie began scattering clothes hither and thither as she searched for a clean nightrail. Bertie, sneezing and coughing from the dust he'd kicked up, tugged at the heavy door to the hideaway as Winnie struggled to pull the tangled gown over her head.

The knock came.

"Winnifred, this is Lindley. Are you unwell?"

"Ah . . . j-just a moment," she gasped, almost inaudibly. She shoved her arms into the gown's sleeves.

A moment of silence followed. "You don't sound well. I'm going to let myself in with the key."

Isadora levitated to perch atop the armoire while Winnie frantically shoved her mussed hair under the lace cap.

"Did you hear me, Winnifred?" Iain called. "I'm coming in."

Huffing and puffing, the Comtesse threw herself toward the bed. "No . . . I . . . I—"

Too late.

The key clicked in the lock and the door swung open as Winnie flung herself back against the pillows.

Iain entered, trailed a few paces by the teary-eyed abigail. Isadora didn't think he looked pleased and she took perverse delight in the knowledge.

With crisp, irritated steps, he crossed the room.

"Dear God." He stilled for a long beat, then grabbed hold of the young maid's arm. "Fetch Mrs. Emmitt at once."

The girl nodded and ran from the room, stifling a sob as she went.

Isadora clucked her tongue.

Lying against the pure white of the pillows, Winnie's beet-red face did appear rather striking, she had to admit. That, coupled with the sweat trickling down her temple and her evident shortness of breath, gave the appearance of a raging, death-heralding fever.

Iain slowly brought his hand to his forehead. "Mrs. Emmitt had reported that you were in fine health this morning," he said, more to himself than to her.

Winnie bit her lips. "Yes, well . . ."

"We'll have to send for a doctor."

"No!" She sat up, wild-eyed. "No doctor!"

"Winnifred," Iain said. "You appear to be seriously ill. Perhaps a brain fever. Frankly, I'm amazed that you're even coherent."

"No, Lindley, really, the fever just came on. I'm certain it will pass soon."

Very soon, I'd say, Isadora dryly put in.

"Your maid said she feared you'd even fallen from your bed," he argued.

"Yes, I did, but I, um, I managed to climb back in."

Iain shook his head.

"Please," Winnie begged, "I loathe leeches. Mrs. Emmitt is the only person I wish to attend me. Do you hear me, Lindley?" Her voice rose to a frantic pitch. "I absolutely refuse to be seen by anyone else!"

Iain's brows met in an uneasy scowl. "Winnifred, please

don't overset yourself. I fear you might be suffering delirium."

"If I could merely be allowed to rest without so many interruptions," she whimpered. "I must be left undisturbed."

Ah, clever. Isadora nodded approvingly. *Undisturbed to venture about in secret passages, eh, Comtesse?*

Already the color was staring to fade from Winnifred's face, the miraculous "fever" disappearing as quickly as it had come. By the time that Mrs. Emmitt arrived with her ever-present basket, the Comtesse had recovered her customary anemic aspect.

Mrs. Emmitt clucked over her patient for a minute then was pulled aside by Lindley, who was looking excessively put out. The two spoke in undertones while Winnie fretted and cast furtive glances to the fireplace.

Ah, poor Bertie. Isadora would have liked to see how the little weasel was faring but she did not wish to miss the exchange between Lindley and the cook. Across the room she floated to hover above the pair.

"—daresay I'll have to keep a close eye, my lord. To all 'ppearances, her ladyship seemed to be coming right 'long, but with a blow to the noggin, you can never be too mindful."

"How long do you estimate until she can travel?"

The cook turned her pudgy hands palm up. "Who can say? Depends whether or not she continues to have bouts of fever like this. I can't say I cared for this one, though." Mrs. Emmitt pointed to the side of her nose. "Did you notice it left a stench to her? Reminded me of death."

Isadora chuckled. *That's strange, Mrs. Emmitt, for it quite reminded me of mildew.*

"Keep me apprised," Iain instructed, shoving his fists into his pockets. "I want reports morning, noon, and night, do you understand?"

The mobcap bobbed. "Aye, my lord."

With one last frustrated look toward the curtained bed, Iain strode from the room, leaving Isadora puzzled yet intrigued.

Daphne sat staring into her plate. Not two minutes had passed since Iain had asked her to remain at Ash Park and where was he now? He had just left the dining room with the Comtesse deCheval's hysterical maid on his arm.

In the midst of pleading with her to give their marriage a chance, her husband had been summoned to his mistress's bedchamber!

And he'd gone!

Daphne shoved to her feet, afraid she might either start weeping into the congealing Bernaise sauce or heave the wine decanter to the other end of the table. Either way, she decided to make a quick exit before she thoroughly disgraced herself before the group of servants, still chattering about the ghost.

With more haste than dignity, she sped from the room and headed upstairs.

Her bedchamber, immediately adjacent to Iain's, occupied a corner of the west wing at the opposite end of the house from the Comtesse's bedroom. Although glad to be so far removed from the winsome Winnifred, Daphne had not been elated to discover the connecting door between her room and her husband's. A lock on the door had afforded her some comfort last night and she habitually checked the latch every time she reentered her bedchamber.

Tonight Daphne failed to do so, as she ran into her room and collapsed face forward onto the bed as limp as a rag doll. Arms outstretched, legs dangling over the side, she lay with the side of her face pressed into the satin counterpane. Against her hot cheek, the satiny coverlet felt silken and cool. Deliciously smooth, like another caress—

Deliberately, she rolled onto her back. Above her, the

bed's canopy of pale blue taffeta, spangled with gold stars, simulated a moon-washed summer sky. The baldachin's celestial carvings repeated the theme, depicting cherubic angels frolicking among the stars and clouds. Behind the bed hung a plate of mirror glass.

Daphne turned to her side, propped herself up on one elbow, and looked at her reflection in the mirror. Unshed tears cast a false brightness to the pink-rimmed eyes looking back at her.

"Dash it, if you aren't a first-rate ninny!" she burst out. Muffled by the thick bed hangings, her anger sounded feeble and sad.

"Your problem is that you're still hoping the frog you married will turn into a prince!"

Not very likely. For if Daphne knew anything, she knew her fairy tales. No matter how comely or charismatic the frog, it could never be transformed into a prince if it wasn't basically a prince by nature. Iain Ashingford just happened to be one extremely attractive frog.

"Ninny," she softly accused before flopping back onto the mattress.

It was true. Despite all that had happened, all the heartache of the past few months, she could not summarily dismiss her feelings for her husband.

At Harkwell House, she'd been able to convince herself that she despised him. How could she not hate him after being left alone three long months to nurture her outrage and humiliation? But, as much as she'd tried to deny it, the minute she'd laid eyes on him last night, her heart had reaffirmed what her intellect had refused to accept. She didn't hate him at all; she was merely very hurt and very angry.

She'd been forced to accept the truth this morning when he'd kissed her. Even if the prince had not lived up to all her fantasies, that first kiss most certainly had. She hadn't known that she was capable of such emotions. When Iain had held her in his arms, she'd felt as if he'd awakened a part of her that had been asleep until now—very much like the tale she'd so loved as a child.

Nevertheless, even after the kiss, she had still been planning to follow through with the annulment. She had her pride, after all. She *was* her mother's daughter. She would not be bound to a man who could toss her away like yesterday's *Post* and whose demeanor changed as frequently as the periodical's lead story. If he did not want her, then she would not want him.

But now he said that he did want her. But whom was she to believe? Which Iain wanted her? Iain the ruthless autocrat? The manipulative seducer? Or, perhaps, the irresistible rogue?

Daphne pulled a pillow to her chest, wrapping her arms tightly around it. She might have feelings for this man, but she was not so naive as to think she knew him.

Good gracious, while she held this internal debate he was, at that very moment, at his paramour's bedside. If she had any sense, she'd pack her bags and be gone by morning.

She sat up and scowled at the girl in the mirror.

"But you have no sense where he's concerned, do you?"

Her reflection's guilt-weak smile answered.

The idea of leaving Ash Park had been easier to accept when his harsh words of the previous night still rang in her ears. But where had that scornful, derisive Iain been today? Was he truly sincere in his wish to mend the breach between them? Or had he some ulterior motive that she had yet to discover?

Peevishly, she tossed the pillow at her image. She should leave, but she wouldn't. It would be too galling to leave her husband and his mistress here at Ash Park while she hied off to London with her tail between her legs, seeking an annulment. No, she'd stick it out and perhaps even give him his seven days.

She shook her finger at the mirror. "But don't forget that no matter what the church register maintains, you are, above all, a Harkwell. For heaven's sake, remember that."

Her expression softened and she added, whispering, "For your mother's sake, remember."

Chapter
Nine

The following morning Iain and Wilkinson stood in the front hall as Iain gave Ash Park's butler a thorough dressing-down.

"You might imagine my displeasure at having my supper interrupted by a band of hysterical servants, wailing at the top of their lungs!"

"Yes, my lord, I might well imagine."

"Good, for I will be holding you responsible, Wilkinson. Any repeat performances of last night's events and *you* shall be called to account. Each member of the staff is to be advised that if I so much as hear the word 'ghost,' I will consider it grounds for an immediate dismissal—without reference. I absolutely will not tolerate any more of this damn business!"

Iain emphasized the statement with a sharp rap of his riding crop against the side of his boot.

"I assure you, my lord, you will hear no more of it," the butler promised. "Not a breath. Not a word. Not a whisper. I, for one, never did countenance such talk," he added haughtily. "Ghost, indeed. As if the Earl of Whiting had naught better to do in his afterlife than—"

Iain narrowed his eyes and Wilkinson instantly silenced.

"My solicitor, Kane, should be by today," Iain said, changing the subject simply because he couldn't take another word of the butler's inane prattle. "If I am out, I want you to send someone for me."

"To the gatekeeper's cottage, my lord?"

"No," Iain answered, his shoulders tensing. "I won't be out that way today. And listen here, Wilkinson, no one else is to know I go out to the cottage, understood? My business there is private and I don't want anyone else out that direction."

"Yes, my lord. Never fear. My lips are sealed, I assure you."

Iain doubted that a pound of nails and a bucket of glue could keep Wilkinson's lips sealed, but refrained from saying so.

He turned toward his study when his eye caught a movement at the top of the landing. Daphne.

Attired in unrelieved black, she should have been difficult to detect among the corridor's deep shadows, but she wasn't. Instead, she looked to be fairly incandescent, surrounded by a golden nimbus of light—

Damn it, she was glowing again!

Iain dug the heel of his palm into both eye sockets. What in blazes was wrong with his vision?

Blinking hard, he looked up as Daphne began to descend the staircase. The luminescence he thought he'd seen had vanished against the bright, morning sunshine flooding in through the front windows.

Perhaps 'twas only her red hair reflecting the light. Although he hadn't truly noticed before, its rich, auburn color was really quite unusual. In fact, the curls framing her face were the exact color of autumn leaves, just as her eyes were the color—

Iain caught himself up with a start. *Faith, Lindley, get a hold of yourself or next you'll be composing odes to her bloody toes!*

It was his extended celibacy that was to blame for such Byronesque dribble, he thought disgustedly. He'd have to remedy that condition and remedy it soon.

Daphne approached him warily—she always seemed to be wary of him since she'd come to Ash Park—her eyes huge and looking as if they hadn't had enough sleep.

"Good morning," he said. "Are you out for a jaunt?"

She glanced to the riding crop he was tapping restlessly against his thigh. "Yes. Have you just returned or are you leaving?"

"I've already been."

Her relief was evident, her emotions so easy to read that, if he hadn't been annoyed by her reaction, he might have laughed. She made him feel like the proverbial spider lying in wait for the fly.

"But what say that tomorrow we ride together?" he suggested. "We'll make a morning of it and have lunch al fresco."

"I—" She was about to balk.

"Splendid. I'll have Wilkinson arrange it. Do enjoy your ride." And he strode away to his study, not once glancing back.

At least, he thought with satisfaction, the riding appointment would keep her one more day—and one more night— at Ash Park. Although he would have preferred for her to agree to his proposal of a seven-day trial marriage, after last night he didn't dare hope for too much.

He slammed shut the door to his study, knowing that the

emergency call to the Comtesse's bedside last evening could not have advanced his cause.

Seducing his wife while the specter of Winnifred hung over them was not going to be an easy task, but Iain did not see that he had any choice. Winnifred's convalescence could not be accelerated merely to suit his plans and he wasn't such a cad that he'd deny responsibility. He couldn't simply throw Winnifred out. His only hope was that Mrs. Emmitt's nursing skills would see the Comtesse up and away from Ash Park as soon as was humanly possible. Maybe sooner.

Seated at his desk, Iain pulled out a prospectus for a business venture he was considering, and set to reviewing the document. The venture involved the renovation of abandoned mills, an idea that Iain had found promising when it had first been presented to him a few months earlier in London.

Eager to review the details, he had not even completed reading the first few paragraphs when his thoughts began to stray. Actually they did not so much as stray as *leap*. He had been thoroughly engrossed in the prospectus when Daphne's name had unexpectedly broken into his thoughts.

He rubbed his eyes with his fingertips and tried again. Two more paragraphs and then—

Daphne.

Damned, if it wasn't the strangest thing. Almost as if an inner voice whispered her name to him.

Focusing intently on the document, he next attempted reading aloud. "Properties located at Shefield—"

Daphne.

"I say," Iain breathed. He sat back in the chair, head bowed, massaging his temples. What was happening to him? First, the acuity of his eyesight, and now his powers of concentration. Were his almost twenty-nine years beginning to take their toll on his faculties?

He managed to read through another page, steadfastly ignoring the haunting echo of "Daphne, Daphne" in his ears. Thankfully, or so he felt, Wilkinson interrupted his laborious attempt to read the document by announcing that Walter Kane had arrived.

Glad for the distraction, and a trifle concerned for his wits, Iain set aside the prospectus.

"Good to see you, Walter," he greeted, rising to shake the man's hand.

"How are you, Lindley? Lovely place, this."

The solicitor, a middle-aged man of nondescript features, average build, and extraordinary intellect, was Iain's idea of the perfect man of affairs. Unobtrusive yet sharp, Walter Kane accomplished what needed to be done without drawing attention to himself or to his client, a quality Iain greatly appreciated.

"Thank you. Ash Park was one of the issues I wished to discuss with you."

"So you indicated in your letter."

The solicitor sat down and Iain held silent for a moment, waiting to hear if Daphne's name would continue to resonate in his head. Mercifully, his thoughts were uninterrupted.

"I appreciate you coming down, Walter, although a post would have sufficed."

"Actually, I was happy to get away from London for a bit. I have an uncle on the other side of Dorchester to whom I owed a visit, so the two trips dovetailed nicely."

"You won't be staying over?" Iain asked.

"Not unless you need me to."

"No, that won't be necessary."

Schooling his expression to one of impassivity, Iain steepled his fingers together.

"Walter, about Ash Park . . . I believe the law is pretty straightforward in this area, but I am curious." He paused, tapping his fingertips together. "Naturally, I can trust your discretion?"

"As you always have, Lindley."

Iain knew the question had been unnecessary, but had felt the need to express it. "Of course. Walter, if perchance my marriage to Daphne Harkwell were to be annulled, would there, in your opinion, be any means by which I could lay claim to the settlement property?"

The solicitor considered. "I believe that would depend on the grounds for annulment. If it were an issue of your bride having contracted a previous alliance . . ." He shrugged. "I cannot say. 'Twould be a weak argument but we might try to claim fraudulent intent."

"And if the reason were other than that?"

"Impotence, familial connection, or failure to consummate are all that remain and I don't believe any of those would serve your purpose." His dark gaze probed Iain's. "However, speaking hypothetically, of course, if the marriage were dissolved and you did lose the property, we might try to purchase Ash Park straight out. Although Lady Harkwell would never have sold to you, her daughter might."

Iain frowned. "How likely is that?"

Walter smiled softly. "I've not met the lady. What do you think?"

Iain shifted in his chair, abruptly recalling the feel of Daphne melting in his arms, her breasts shoved up against him.

"No, she's my wife," he brusquely said. "I don't see why I should have to look for another, especially when she brings me exactly what I desire."

He shifted again, wishing he hadn't used the term "desire."

"So, no annulment?" Walter asked.

"No. There will be no annulment."

The solicitor nodded. "About the other matter you asked me to look into, the Raymond girl."

"What did you find?"

"As you said, she'd been staying at an aunt's this past year, waiting for word from her father. The family had covered it up carefully, no gossip, and from what I could tell, it had been handled well. There didn't seem any reason why she couldn't return home, but it took some 'encouragement' for her father to finally send for her."

"How much?"

"The full amount you'd authorized."

"Greedy bastard," Iain grumbled. "He had bloody well better be treating her properly."

"I knew you'd be concerned, so I lingered in Sussex for a few weeks. There is nothing to worry about; Sarah has been accepted back into the family bosom as if nothing had ever happened. A little bit of money goes a long way in buying Lord Raymond's affections. A lot of money goes even further," he wryly added. "Anyway, it appears that Sarah will even be accompanying the family to London for the Little Season. The younger sister is going to take her chances on the marriage mart."

"Louisa?"

Walter nodded, and Iain could tell that the solicitor had more he wished to say.

"What else?" Iain asked.

Walker looked uncomfortable. "The girl might like a word from you."

Iain brusquely shook his head. "I don't think she needs to be reminded of past heartache. I'll contact her after a decent interval has gone by. What else?"

As expected, Walter followed his lead and dismissed the subject. "Well, Grisham is still waiting for your decision on the mill project. Do you have any thoughts?"

Iain glanced to the documents he'd been trying to read

earlier. He'd had plenty of thoughts, unfortunately, none of them pertaining to the venture.

"I'll let you know," he told him. He stood and Walter did the same.

"My thanks again for responding so quickly to my note."

The solicitor smiled, patting his pocket where he'd placed Iain's bank draft. "Services rendered, services paid."

Although Iain returned the smile, he suddenly thought that his marriage to Daphne was not so very different from his relationship with Walter Kane. He gave Daphne his title, she gave him a piece of property. He agreed to provide for her, and she agreed to provide him an heir.

Services rendered, services paid.

Although it was all perfectly acceptable and logical, for some reason it did not settle well on Iain's conscience. He tried to let go of the comparison as he bid his solicitor good-bye, but the notion clung with him, sordid and unsettling.

Why, he wondered, should his conscience suddenly attack him when it had lain dormant for so long?

Perhaps, he answered himself, because Daphne's name yet echoed through the recesses of his mind.

She had not appreciated Iain's ploy. Short of sprinting across the foyer and shouting after him that she had no intention of riding with him on the morrow, she'd been trapped. Neatly. Deliberately.

Daphne half-entertained the idea of telling Iain that the only reason she remained at Ash Park was because she refused to be driven away by his mistress, but that sounded unsophisticated and childish. *I won't go till she goes.*

Besides, Daphne reminded herself, she wasn't supposed to care. It should not matter to her if Iain kept a dozen mistresses at Ash Park, because she was going to procure an annulment. Wasn't she?

She spurred her mount faster, the wind pulling at her hat and stinging her eyes. She didn't care which direction she took, she only wished to get away, to find a peaceful spot where she could be Daphne Harkwell again, instead of the terribly confused Marchioness Lindley.

After a few miles of hard riding she eased up as she rode into a cool, wooded area canopied green with the leaves of densely branched oak and mulberry. So profound was the quiet in the trees's great shadows that Daphne imagined she'd entered an enchanted forest. The birds and squirrels silently roamed the limbs, casting curious glances at the unfamiliar intruder.

The woods were not deep and she soon entered an open glade in the middle of which stood a cottage. A small single-room dwelling, it did not look as if it were inhabited, although grass worn low around the door gave evidence of recent visitors. Shrugging lightly, Daphne saw no reason she could not be one of those visitors. She was thirsty and might be lucky enough to find water within.

She jumped down from her horse, calling out. "Hello?"

As she'd expected, there was no answer.

The door pushed open easily, the air inside fresh, not stale, and she instantly saw why. Someone had been visiting the cottage, and had been using it as an artist's studio.

Sketches hung along the rough wood-beamed walls and littered a large table at the cabin's center. Aside from the table, a single chair constituted the room's only furniture, the interior surprisingly clean and free of dust.

Fascinated, Daphne walked slowly over to one wall, her heart kicking in her chest when she gazed upon the dozen or so drawings haphazardly pinned into the beams.

The sketches along here were all of one person. A man. A man who bore an indisputable likeness to Iain.

Her eyes widened and she wrapped her arms protectively around her waist. Such pain. She could barely stand to look at the portraits, yet she could not tear her eyes away. Pain shone not only in the man's expression, but also in the way the artist had drawn his subject. Although the beauty of the work could not be denied, both artist and model looked to be in hideous emotional torment.

Daphne caught her lip between her teeth to still its quivering. Who was this man whose haunted eyes so closely resembled her husband's? A brother, father, uncle?

Some of the drawings showed the man at peace, his features less haggard, his eyes focused into the past. Yet even in these portraits, the artist's passion came through loud and clear, angry and bitter, lines slashing and slicing like shards of shattered glass.

Daphne steadied herself on the back of the chair as realization swept into her like the chill of a December wind. The person who had created these testimonies to misery and suffering, the person whose emotions had been poured into these sketches . . . that person was Iain.

Daphne awkwardly lowered herself into the chair, her legs suddenly weak. She felt as if she'd taken a forbidden journey into her husband's soul and the demons she'd seen there had frightened the very breath from her.

In truth, she had seen glimpses of this vulnerability before. He concealed it well, but those brief flashes of pain that lit his gray eyes had not always been hidden from her. Of course, she'd had no inkling as to the cause, but now she thought that she might.

Her gaze slid to the drawings on the table. The sketch on top nearly made her laugh out loud, a welcome relief to the anguished wall portraits.

Iain had drawn his valet Dobbs, peeking over the top of his round spectacles, his eyes sparkling with affectionate reproof. What made the drawing so endearing was that the censure in the valet's gaze was most obviously directed at Iain, yet Iain hadn't shied away from it, re-

vealing his own fondness for the valet in the tender lines
of the drawing.

Beneath the valet lay two renditions of Ash Park, and although well executed, they didn't convey the same emotion
that Iain was capable of capturing in his portraits.

Daphne's fingers stilled as she withdrew a sketch from
beneath the pile. A self-portrait. An Iain she'd never seen
before.

Tears welled in her eyes and she brushed them away before they could fall. If she hadn't known better, she might
have believed Iain had done this sketch with her in mind.
The man looking out from the drawing called out to her
with a naked yearning that pierced her straight to the core.
His eyes were uncertain, only partly revealing their shadowed vulnerability.

The purr of a turtledove abruptly reminded her that the
hour grew late. The last thing she would want would be to
be discovered here, especially by Iain. She had a feeling
that he would not care for her unintentional intrusion into
his private world.

After carefully replacing the sketches as she'd found
them, Daphne closed the door to the cottage with a heart at
once both heavy and light.

Light because she had finally some understanding of the
secret sorrow that afflicted her husband; yet heavy since
she didn't know if Iain would ever freely reveal that side of
himself to her.

As she rode toward home Daphne thought of Iain's proposal to start afresh in their marriage. Seven days he'd
asked for and she'd been too reluctant to give it. Why, she
had wondered, should she open herself up again to hurt, allowing him to breach her defenses?

But the more she learned of Iain, the more difficult it was
to turn her back on him. It appeared that she wasn't the
only one shielding past wounds.

Chapter Ten

"Has everything been taken care of?" Iain asked.

"Yes, my lord, I assure you. I spoke to the entire household and all appreciate your sentiments regarding the ghost. You'll not hear anything more of it, I'm certain."

Iain flicked his impatient gaze over the butler. "Wilkinson, I was speaking of the picnic."

"Oh. Yes, that's been taken care of as well. Cook's prepared all his specialties, the carriage is loaded, and I've instructed Simons as to your wishes. You couldn't have picked a better day for your outing, my lord. It looks to be a lovely day, absolutely lovely."

"Yes, lovely," Iain agreed, but he wasn't speaking of the fine weather. Daphne was approaching from the hall.

Last night at dinner he'd sensed a softening in her, an easing up of her stiff demeanor. She'd been less wary of him, less cautious. He wasn't certain what had wrought the change, but he planned to take advantage of it. Perhaps this very day.

"I hope I haven't kept you waiting," she said, joining them in the vestibule.

"No. Wilkinson and I were just concluding a bit of business, eh, Wilkinson?"

"Oh, yes, my lord, and never fear. You'll hear not a word of that *other* business," he said with a conspiratorial wink.

"What business?" Daphne asked after the butler had scurried off.

"Nothing of import. I've merely instructed Wilkinson to put down this ridiculous ghost talk."

Iain took hold of her elbow and guided her through the front doorway, her scent of honeysuckle floating to him.

"How do you know it's ridiculous?" Daphne asked, adroitly pulling away from his grasp.

Iain glanced down to his empty hand, then frowned at the plumed hat preceding him down the front steps. Perhaps she hadn't softened as much as he'd hoped.

"Of course it is," he answered.

She stopped and turned toward him with a faint smile, the sunshine slanting into her upturned face. "How can you be so sure?"

"I'm sure because . . ." Her smile distracted him for a moment before the neighing of the horses brought him back to her question. ". . . because I'm sure. Never say that you believe in that sort of thing?"

Daphne did not answer him until they'd both mounted their animals, hers a strong-limbed sorrel, his a dappled gray. Then, taking her reins in hand, she raised her gaze to his.

"I would never say that I do *not* believe. To think that one knows all there is to know of life and death is, to my mind, the very height of arrogance." And with that softly voiced reprimand, she flicked her horse into a trot.

Irrationally piqued by the barb, Iain watched her take the lead down the driveway. It wasn't the first time he'd been called arrogant, nor, he reasoned, would it be the last. Nonetheless, he felt much more put out than he should have by the slight. He spurred his horse forward to catch up with her before she disappeared over the rise.

As the butler had predicted, the day was a glorious one, and like a jewel in the proper setting, Ash Park shone brilliantly. They rode through shady woodland and green, open fields, Iain allowing Daphne to set the pace. She proved to be an exceptionally good rider whose stamina impressed him when, two hours later, they'd finally circled back to the spot he'd chosen for their al fresco luncheon.

He smiled approvingly as they broke through the copse of trees and he saw that all had been arranged exactly as he'd requested. A soft blanket stretched over a flat expanse of lawn and a basket full of delicacies waited expectantly next to a bottle of chilled champagne. For musical accompaniment, the River Derwill gurgled melodiously, sparkling in the noonday sun. Secluded, the setting could not have been more romantic. An ideal site for a seduction.

"My, isn't this lovely!"

"It's a pretty spot, isn't it?" he agreed as he slipped from the saddle and looped his reins over a branch. He walked over to Daphne and, reaching up, gripped her about the waist. She slid easily into his arms, his hands lingering boldly even after she'd found her footing. She remained in his embrace with her head lowered, the feather from her hat threatening to make him sneeze.

Iain blew at the impudent plume but it wafted back into his face, brushing his nose with maddening persistence. Short of sneezing all over her bonnet, he had to release her. He did so and she immediately stepped away.

"You're quite a horsewoman," he commented, watching

with interest her nimble fingers unfasten the top two buttons to her jacket.

"It's a credit to my father; he's enormously proud of his stables. He had me on a horse well before I could walk."

Iain shrugged out of his jacket and sank onto the blanket, bracing himself on one elbow. "It's evident by your seat. Few women could have held up to the pace you set today."

He wasn't sure if Daphne had heard him, for she'd gone down to the river's edge to moisten her handkerchief. She dipped the linen into the water, then wiped the damp cloth over her face and throat. Then, to Iain's immense satisfaction, she removed her bonnet and ran the kerchief over the back of her neck. Her movements were so innocent and yet so keenly sensual that he found he could not take his eyes from her. Why was it that she grew prettier to him with each passing day?

"Ah, that feels delicious," she murmured, sliding the cloth into the hollow of her throat.

A surge of desire forced Iain to wrench his gaze away before his expression betrayed him.

"Shall we hope that our provisions prove equally so?" he said, making a show of looking through the basket while from the corner of his eye he continued to watch her.

She leaned over to pick up her hat where she'd dropped it on the pebbled shore, and her slim silhouette was starkly outlined by the sunshine behind her. A simple black figure against the multihued summer background, she didn't look drab or somber, but conversely light and airy, a perfect foil to the colorful landscape. For a moment Iain had the oddest sensation that she belonged to this place, that she belonged to Ash Park.

Unaware of his scrutiny, she picked her way over the rocks, climbing the slight slope. A few feet away she paused and hurriedly glanced up, as if she'd suddenly felt his eyes on her.

Their gazes held. She broke away first, waving her arm over the feast he'd laid out. "I must confess I find all this most impressive. Do you always go to such pains for your wives?"

"Only the most fetching ones," he conceded with a teasing grin, setting to work on opening the champagne.

Daphne advanced a step closer and he sensed the uncertainty in her hesitant stride. He looked up to find her staring at him, her gaze questioning as she twirled her bonnet by its riband.

"And what of your fetching houseguests?" she asked. "Do you treat them as well?"

Iain nearly lost an eye to the cork as it whizzed past his head like a bullet from a pistol.

Winnie. He should have been expecting this. Confound it, it looked as if he'd be leaping this hurdle for some time, at least as long as the Comtesse remained at Ash Park.

He very carefully phrased his response.

"My wife and I aren't currently entertaining any fetching houseguests," he lightly quipped. Winnie might be described any number of ways, but "fetching" she wasn't.

"And, whether you believe it or not, Lady Lindley, if I could arrange matters to my will, I would choose not to have any houseguests at all. Only you and me. Here at Ash Park. What say you to that?"

The bonnet stilled its swinging as she studied him. "I'd say I'm frightfully peckish. What have you brought for our dining pleasure, Lord Lindley?"

She dropped to her knees at the blanket's edge and Iain felt absurdly relieved.

He handed Daphne a glass of champagne and raised his own in salute. "To us."

Skepticism shone plainly in her expression as she returned the salute with a brief nod. "To us."

No doubt parched after their long ride, she drained her

glass quickly and Iain replenished it as quickly. However, he noted that she only sipped at the second glass before placing it on the ground.

"So tell me of this ghost of yours," she said as he began to fill their plates.

He gave her a wry look. "I assure you it's no ghost of mine."

"Whose is it, then?"

Iain shrugged and handed her a plate. "If the tale is to be believed, it's probably more yours."

"Mine, you say?"

"Yes, the spook is rumored to be your grandfather."

Daphne's eyes sparked with evident delight. "Really? Do you think he'll show himself to me?"

"I sincerely doubt it," Iain retorted before sinking his teeth into a cold meat pie.

Daphne looked slightly disappointed by his answer. "You don't much care for this notion of a ghost, do you?"

"I don't much care for any forms of idiocy, if you must know the truth."

"Oh, come now, it's not really idiocy. Isn't it more like imagination?"

"I wouldn't know," he replied, a bit more curtly than he'd meant to.

Daphne tipped her head to the side and stared at him as if he were some exotic, vaguely repellent insect—a regard he found not much to his liking. "What are you saying? That you have no imagination, no powers of invention?"

"None."

"I don't believe it," she declared with an incredulous laugh. "I've seen—" With a guilty look, she cut off what she was about to say, instead remarking, "Surely your parents read you fables; as a child, you must have believed in elves and dragons and the like. Didn't you invent your own stories, your own magical kingdoms?"

Pastry crumbs had fallen on his waistcoat and he flicked them away. "My mother died shortly after my birth."

Daphne's compassionate murmur caused him to glance up and immediately wish that he hadn't revealed so much. He turned away from the pity in her eyes.

"And what of your father?" she persisted, albeit more gently.

"My father?" Iain looked off into the distance, the familiar pain curling around his heart. "He couldn't . . ."

His voice trailed off as his gaze strayed to the quaint cobblestone bridge spanning the river. "That's odd," he mumbled to himself.

Daphne spun around and followed the direction of his gaze. "What?"

It was as if her question had miraculously conjured up a scene from a faraway place, like an illusionist drawing images into a crystal ball. A memory long forgotten from his childhood suddenly surfaced to Iain's mind and he saw himself, six or seven years old, sprawled at the foot of his father's bed, one cold and rainy winter afternoon. He especially remembered the rain beating at the window, for he'd been a little frightened but too proud to say so. He'd been worried that if he admitted to being scared, his father wouldn't finish the tale of the man-eating, wart-covered troll that lived beneath the old cobblestone bridge.

"I . . . I just remembered something I don't believe I've thought about in over twenty years."

"What?" Daphne asked again, but Iain was still caught up in remembering.

Memories of many other afternoons spent at his father's sickbed, enraptured by marvelous stories of Ash Park. Stories of pointy-eared trolls who devoured trespassers and of gossamer-winged pixies who carved secret passageways through the walls of the country house. Precious hours shared with his father that had all been lost to him until this

moment. It was as if merely by asking, Daphne had un-
locked a treasure trove of recollections that Iain had inadvertently buried decades earlier.

"You know, you're right. I had forgotten, but my father
did tell me fairy tales. Wonderful ones."

"You remembered, just now?"

"Yes. Just this minute."

Daphne's smile illuminated her face. "And did you believe in the fairy tales as a child?"

In his mind's eye, Iain could see that little boy, quivering
with fear, but too enthralled not to beg for every gory detail
of the troll's atrocities.

"Yes, I seem to remember that I did."

"So why did you stop believing?"

Her ingenuousness struck him anew. "I grew up, of
course."

"And?" Her tone implied there had to be more.

He frowned and pushed to his feet, then stalked a few
paces toward the river.

"And my father grew ill. Very ill."

"So you weren't told any more fairy tales?"

He peered back at her over his shoulder. She sat with her
legs tucked beneath her, head uncovered, on the red-and-
black plaid blanket. She looked as innocent and trusting as
a child.

"No," he gruffly answered. "Besides, I was growing too
old for them anyway."

Quiet descended on them, the only sound the silvery tin-
kling of the river.

"That must have been a difficult time for you. When
your father became so ill."

Iain's stomach clenched. Difficult couldn't begin to describe it. He'd only been a child, but mature enough to recognize both his father's suffering and his father's courage.
Perhaps he'd forgotten those earlier, happier times simply

because they'd been clouded by the many years of heartache that had followed.

"He'd been an invalid since before I was born. A riding accident." He searched Daphne's expression but she showed no reaction, ignorant of the tragic history that bound their two families. "His back was broken in the fall. He was able to walk through the pain for a number of years, but then his condition worsened. The summer I turned nine, he was confined permanently to his bed."

"Oh, Iain, how awful."

Like a dam once released, Iain found he could not stem the tide of pain and bitterness rushing forth. "Not a day went by that I did not pray to God to end his torture, to show my father a measure of mercy. He suffered so greatly. But the years passed, I went away to school, came home again, and finally . . . quit praying. My father spent twenty years in that bed, never leaving his room, never leaving Sussex." Iain's fingernails curled into the palms of his gloves.

"But the worst of it was that when his time did come, he could not even die in peace, he so regretted—"

Iain jerked his head to the side, checking his words in the nick of time. He'd almost given himself away.

"Regretted what?"

He snapped a dry twig from a nearby tree branch. "He died with regrets, Daphne, that's all."

A tentative hand fluttered on his shirtsleeve a split second after the scent of honeysuckle informed him of her nearness. He half-turned to look down into her solemn, heart-shaped face and all he could see were a pair of liquid green eyes. A curious emotion settled in his chest.

"I'm sorry, Iain."

The weight of that unnamed emotion increased until he felt almost breathless and was forced to look past her to their half-finished luncheon and lukewarm champagne. A blackbird snatched a morsel from his plate and he smiled derisively.

So much for his planned seduction. All the preparations he'd made, and the lengths he'd gone to in order to create the perfect ambience, only to throw a wet blanket over the entire afternoon with his damned melancholy. It seemed he'd have no progress to report to Dobbs this evening.

"Come," he said. "Let us finish our luncheon before the squirrels steal it away."

Daphne did not remove her hand from his sleeve. "Iain, about those seven days you asked for?"

He stilled. He had deliberately not broached the subject since that first dinner. "Yes?"

Her eyes were enormous and so very expressive. She was a little frightened, but trying not to be. "I cannot make any promises, but I'll stay the remainder of the week if you answer me this question: Why did you marry me?"

He inwardly flinched. "Have we not already discussed this?"

She dropped her hand from his arm. "On our wedding day, you claimed that your reasons were probably the same as mine. I sincerely doubt that could be true."

Iain focused on her fingers twitching at her sides while casting about for a truth that would not say too much.

"I'm sure you are aware that I am obligated to carry on the title and family name. I needed to marry."

"But you are still young. You could have waited many years yet."

Shrugging, Iain looked down to his own hands. "Why wait? I was not one to idle about in Town; in fact, I had spent very little time in London over the years."

"Because you were with your father?"

"Yes." He flexed his fingers. "After he died, I elected to get on with my life. I knew I had to wed and I chose a bride."

"But why me?"

Iain hesitated only a fraction of a second. "Your family was known to mine. I didn't have to sort through the Season's latest crop, searching for someone appropriate."

"Oh." Daphne frowned in evident bewilderment. "When you say that our families were acquainted, I had been under the impression that the acquaintance was not amicable."

Iain nearly popped a seam of his gloves. So she did know more than she let on. "The antagonism," he said softly, "was not shared by every member of the Ashingford and Whiting families."

"But—" Daphne caught her lower lip between her teeth and Iain knew she must be thinking of her mother.

Blast it, he didn't want to have to explain about Isadora now. Daphne was just beginning to trust him. If she knew what he and Isadora had argued about, she would finally understand that Ash Park had been his goal all along. Not her.

"Daphne," he said, grabbing hold of her hand. "I've explained my reasons. Will you stay or not?"

She looked up at him and Iain felt as if he'd lost his soul. "Very well," she agreed. "I'll stay."

Chapter Eleven

Winnie tore into the chicken leg with a contented growl, devouring the treat like a woman half-starved. Actually, after four long days of nothing but beef tea and Mrs. Emmitt's special tonic, Winnie *was* a woman half-starved, a fractious one at that.

"I vow, Bertie, if you'd come one minute later, I would have marched down to the kitchen myself and the devil take your mysterious treasure!" She reached for a hunk of cheese while glaring balefully at the provider of her unauthorized meal.

"See here, Win, what with the way Mrs. Emmitt's been hovering outside your door, I had a deuce of a time sneaking in here unnoticed. I daresay the old bird is frightened out of her wits that you're going to take on another fever and Lindley is demanding to know how your recovery is progressing at least three times a day—

"By Jove, we might need to simulate another fever for their benefit."

"Oh, no," Winnie countered, waggling her stripped drumstick at Bertie. "No more fevers and no more inspired ideas from you, Albert Thompson."

Bertie pummeled his small fist into the mattress. "But we must find the treasure. We must."

Winnie gazed up at him, suddenly suspicious. "What have you done?"

He squirmed. "Nothing that you haven't."

"What, Bertie? What is it?"

His face pinched up. "I'm in a bit of a tight spot, Win. When I went to London, I spent more than I should have—you know, a few rolls of the dice went bad—and now I am in dun territory."

"Oh, dear heavens, you fool! I dare not think what type of shady character would loan *you* money."

Bertie looked green around the gills. "Truth be told, a not very understanding character. If I don't come up with some quid soon, I might find myself under the hatches."

Winnie sighed, folding her arms with determination. "Very well then, Bertie, you're going to have to listen to me for a change. I've been thinking this through and have decided that the only way we're going to locate Whiting's cache is to have free run of the manor. Which means being rid of Lindley and his wife."

"How do you propose to manage that?"

"Why, the same way you managed before. We resurrect Whiting's ghost and frighten them off. With both of us working at it, we ought to be able to produce a ghostly trick or two that send the pair hying back to London. Especially if the ghostly shenanigans prove hazardous to their continued well-being."

"Hmm, aren't you the canny one?" Bertie stroked his chin consideringly. "You know, you might just have something there. It should be easy enough to pull off now that the servants are all in a state after the other night. They thought all your bumping about was our dear departed Earl returning for a visit. Besides, at the rate we're going, it could take us forever to search all the corridors."

"And I haven't forever," Winnie pointed out. "If I don't improve soon, Lindley will bring in a leech who'll pronounce me as right as rain. And then I doubt I'll be able to depend on Lady Lindley's hospitality for very much longer."

Bertie cringed. "I fear I haven't forever, either. My lender is growing impatient."

"Then we agree on the ghost?"

"We agree," Bertie concurred. "Of course, you'll have to leave with the Lindleys once they flee, but instead of returning to London, you can claim to visit a cousin in Dorchester, then circle back to Ash Park in a day or so."

Winnie sat up straighter against her pillows. "How shall we start?"

"Stewed eels? Does the Marquess care for eel?" Daphne asked, chewing thoughtfully at her lower lip.

"I assure you, my lady, that the Marquess will adore *my* stewed eel," Ash Park's chef promised, then kissed his fingers with Continental flair.

From her chair behind the escritoire, Daphne shot a doubtful look at Wilkinson, who nodded encouragingly.

"Eel it is, then," she agreed, scanning the rest of the menu. "Yes, the roast quail, pudding, peas, everything looks delicious." She handed the paper back to the chef. "Lovely, monsieur, I will look forward to this evening."

As the servants took their leave Daphne returned the chef's parting smile through gritted teeth, feeling as if she'd just been deftly manipulated by an unseen hand. Not that of the chef or the butler, but by the hand of her husband.

Only yesterday she'd agreed to finish out the seven days at Ash Park, and suddenly the servants were consulting her on menu planning, linens, and the other domestic duties that a lady of the manor would normally attend to.

While Daphne didn't object to such responsibilities, frankly, she'd been surprised when Wilkinson and Gaston had sought her out. In her mind, she had yet to assume the mantle of Ash Park's mistress. Iain's ploy had obviously been designed so that she would begin to think of herself in precisely that manner.

Her jaw relaxed as she considered her husband's motive. Why should she be annoyed when Iain had made it abundantly clear that he wished to keep her at Ash Park?

Her gaze abruptly fell to the blank page in front of her. There lay the reason.

She'd been staring at that same sheet of foolscap for a good half hour and she was bound and determined not to spend another half hour in the same futile pursuit. By all rights, she should have sent this missive a day earlier, but she hadn't found it any easier to compose it yesterday than she did today.

She simply couldn't find the words to tell Roger that she was extending her stay at Ash Park. Intellectually, she knew it should be a simple undertaking, but nothing was ever simple where matters of the heart were involved. And Roger's heart was involved. Daphne couldn't be certain of this since he had never openly declared himself—and she had not encouraged such a declaration—but she had long suspected that Roger cared for her beyond the bonds of friendship.

Forged during childhood, their relationship was as close as that of siblings. Daphne loved Roger and would not have chosen to hurt him for any reason. Hence her desire to word the note as tactfully as possible.

Dearest Roger, I realize that you are expecting me to re-

turn home shortly; however, Lord Lindley and I have decided to put our alliance to a seven-day test. . . .

Daphne pulled fretfully at a loose curl. That would never do.

Dear Rog, my husband has decided he'd like to keep me after all, so don't expect me at Harkwell House for at least a week. . . .

"Oh, dear," she groaned before tossing the pen onto the cherry desktop.

After another ten minutes of fretting, Daphne decided not even to attempt an explanation.

Dearest Roger, I so appreciate you looking after Father in my absence, and I'm sure he finds your company a great comfort. I've been delayed at Ash Park—I'll explain when I return home—so please don't expect me until at least the second. I hope that all is well. I remain your good friend, Daphne.

Roger would no doubt be curious, if not actually concerned, but she saw no other way around it. The situation was too difficult to convey in a letter. It was too difficult to convey outside of a letter. For heaven's sake, she was living it and she still couldn't begin to describe what was happening between her and her husband.

Since that first disastrous evening, Iain had been courting her with a single-mindedness that flattered and perplexed. He hadn't gone so far as to serenade her beneath her window or to leave nosegays outside her door, but he had been solicitous and attentive to a fault. When contrasted to the polite courtesy he'd extended her the week prior to their wedding, his conduct of the last few days could be characterized as no less than charming.

And Daphne continued to ask herself why.

There was no denying that he was making every effort to woo her and she had come to believe that he honestly wished to remain wed to her. Yet why the sudden change of heart? He had been perfectly content to leave her at Hark-well House as a spouse-in-name-only; now he wished nothing more than to convince her to be his wife in truth. What had brought on the about-face?

Daphne fiddled absently at the lace on her gown. It seemed she was always returning to the same question— why Iain had wished to marry her in the first place.

For some reason, Daphne felt there had to be more to the story than he'd revealed to her yesterday.

A man of his position generally married to produce an heir, choosing a properly chaste, well-bred girl whose dowry would augment his financial circumstances. Although chaste and well-bred, Daphne knew that the Marquess had not negotiated a bridal price on her behalf, accepting only what would have come to her anyway—this property inherited from her mother's family. Granted, Ash Park was exceptionally beautiful, but its lands were not unusually extensive or profitable.

More and more, Daphne suspected that Iain wished to preserve their marriage because of his desire for a son. He had insinuated as much that first evening she'd arrived and then, yesterday, at the picnic . . .

Those sketches she'd seen in the cottage had to have been of his invalid father, she now realized. Obviously, Iain had loved his father very much and mourned him still. Did he hope to mend his loss through a son of his own?

Perhaps, too, his father's death shed some light on Iain's decision to relocate to Ash Park. It could have been too disturbing for him to remain in the Sussex home where his father had suffered and then died.

Daphne stood up with a frown, sensing that she still did not possess all the pieces to the puzzle. A vital clue was missing. What, she could not say, but she felt if there were to be any hope for their marriage, she would have to learn what it was.

As usual when troubled, Daphne either talked to herself or took herself off for a walk, sometimes talking to herself while walking, if she was unusually distressed. Outside, the warm summer day beckoned, so she decided to heed its call.

She was planning to take her usual path, around the far end of the manor and down to the river; but as she approached the garden she spied Iain's valet, Dobbs, crouched down among the plants.

He was an amusing fellow, Iain's man, with his owl-like aspect and twinkling eyes. She was going to pass him by when she suddenly thought that the valet might be helpful in helping her find that missing clue. The one that might unlock the continued riddle of her husband.

After all, providence had placed the man in her path for a reason. She should at least share a word with the valet, if only to be friendly.

"Good day to you," she greeted.

He looked up from his stooped stance. "Lady Lindley, how are you this fine day?"

"Well, thank you." She nodded suspiciously at his basket. "Might I ask what you're digging up from Gaston's garden?"

The valet winked at her. "I use some of these herbs in Lord Lindley's shaving paste. It's my special mixture and he likes it just so."

Daphne sat down, choosing a grassy spot at the edge of the garden. "Well, I shan't tell on you," she promised.

The valet must have either read her mind or her expression. "And with what, my lady, must I reward your silence?" he asked amiably.

His shrewdness caught her unaware. She shrugged, though she doubted it came off as nonchalant. "I thought— just an idea, mind you—that perhaps you could help me, Dobbs. Help me to understand Lord Lindley."

He sat back on his heels, sending an appraising look toward the manor. "That sounds reasonable enough to me."

"Oh." Daphne brightened. "But I wouldn't want you to disclose anything that Iain would prefer kept confidential. I shouldn't care to spy on him nor to get you into trouble."

Dobbs smiled roguishly. "Don't you worry about me. I can take care of myself where his nibs is concerned."

The valet's familiar manner struck her as peculiar, but he was so pleasant about it. . . .

Daphne folded her hands in her lap, unsure where she should start, when Dobbs dove right in.

"You should first understand that Lord Lindley's mother died of childbed fever before she and the Marquess had been wed a full year."

"How sad!"

"It might have been if the Marquess had cared for the girl, but—" He stopped, eyeing her judiciously. "But James had married Susan Hern in the wake of a jilt, so his heart was not involved."

"Oh."

"Iain never knew his mother, not even through stories his father told of her. In many ways, for him, she never existed."

"Not even to have the memories . . ."

"Quite right." Dobbs shook his head mournfully. "Thus, as a young child, all of Iain's love was directed to his father, since James was the only family the boy had ever known. And while the Marquess was a good man who cared deeply for his son, he was embittered. Fiercely so."

"Because of his infirmity?"

Again, Dobbs bestowed on her that assessing regard. "That was a large part of it," he agreed.

"Oh dear, poor Iain."

Dobbs folded his arms across his chest. "You don't know the half of it, my lady. The lad never had a childhood. He

couldn't run about and shout for fear of disturbing his father. There was no one to teach him to ride or to hunt or to
fish. His was a sad home. Dark and sad."

Daphne's fingers were twisted like knots in her lap. The
picture Dobbs painted was touching and she wanted to
know more.

"What else, Dobbs? I'd like to know as much as you're
willing to tell me."

And Daphne sat in the herb garden for a good part of the
afternoon, unraveling the mystery of Iain Ashingford.

Moonlight and roses.

Iain felt as if he could teach a course on creating romantic settings, although, in good conscience, he could not take
credit for the moonbeams or the perfumed breeze of late
evening. He did take credit, however, for having the good
sense to bring Daphne out here. The stars sparkled like
dewdrops against the blue-black velvet of a summer sky
and the inviting shadows hinted of an intimacy that begged
to be explored. Perfect.

Daphne stood at the balustrade, her face turned to the
stars. Her lips were moving slightly.

"What are you doing?" he asked. "Praying?"

She kept her gaze fixed skyward. "I'm wishing on a
star."

"Hmm. I ought to have guessed."

"You really shouldn't make fun, you know." She turned
to him with a confident smile. "My wishes almost always
come true."

"Do they?" he asked with an indulgent smile of his own.
"Then you'll have to tell me your secret, since I'm sadly
overdue to have any of mine realized."

"Have you ever thought that you've been wishing the
wrong wishes?" she asked, cocking her chin in an appraising manner. "Why don't you try again? Tonight."

Iain shook his head. "Very well. My wish is for the sun to rise in the morning."

"That's not much of a wish!"

Iain laughed. "I like to play it safe, hedge my bets."

"Oh, pooh. My mother was always quoting me *ad astra*. Aim for the stars, she said."

"I wouldn't have pegged the Baroness for a dreamer."

The teasing light faded from Daphne's eyes. "She wasn't. Not really."

Iain could have kicked himself. Why, in God's name, had he brought up Isadora? More than anything, he wished he might do something to bring the radiance back to Daphne's smile. "May I fetch you a shawl?" he asked instead.

"No, thank you."

"It's really quite pleasant tonight, isn't it?"

"Yes, it is."

In truth, Iain was more than pleasantly warm, for each time his gaze fell to Daphne's décolletage, he felt in danger of overheating. By London standards, the gown was far from risqué, but it was the most revealing that he'd seen her in to date. It would take only a flick of his finger to slip the sleeve from her shoulder and—

He cleared his throat. "We're fortunate to have the breeze from the river. Come autumn, we should still be very comfortable."

Daphne sidled a step away from him and he could almost read her thoughts.

"Yes," she said, "you should enjoy autumn here."

"*I* should?"

She was standing in profile, so that he saw her throat working as she swallowed. "Surely, you understand that although this was my mother's home, and I am ostensibly mistress here, I cannot remain at Ash Park. How could I possibly stay unless . . ."

"Unless?"

"Unless we were able to reach some manner of agreement."

Iain lowered his eyes to hide a satisfied gleam. She was coming around. "Do you think, Daphne, that we might be able to reach such an agreement?"

"I cannot say. I think it unlikely unless we can begin to speak frankly with each other."

"Then by all means, let us do so."

He saw her take a halting breath that shuddered through her chest in the most titillating fashion.

"What was it you wished to discuss?" he asked.

Her hand trembled as she brushed her hair back from her forehead. "I want to know what happened, Iain. I want to know why you left the morning of our wedding."

His jaw locked with tension. Blast it, it seemed that she would not be satisfied until he gave her the truth, and that he would never do. He wouldn't lie to her, but neither would he risk absolute honesty.

When he did not immediately answer her, Daphne grabbed hold of his arm, demanding, "Tell me, did someone anger you? Was it my mother?"

Iain's conscience denounced him, although he answered truthfully. "Yes, Daphne. I left because of a conversation I had with your mother."

"It was the quarrel between our families, wasn't it? She threw that up at you."

He nodded. "Yes, she spoke of the feud and made clear her resentment toward both me and my family."

Grief washed over Daphne's expression and she spun away from him.

His conscience flared again. This time more loudly. *Cad. Deceiver.*

He followed her to the other side of the veranda and gripped her bent shoulders from behind. Dipping his head to hers, he said, "Daphne, whatever she said, she didn't intend to hurt you. To spite me, perhaps, but never you. In hindsight, I might even say she said what she did to protect you from me."

Daphne stilled, then slowly turned in his arms. Tears quivered at the tips of her lashes and he wanted to curse.

In a quiet voice, she said, "That's kind of you to say so."

"No, it's not kind," he roughly replied, squeezing her shoulders beneath his palms. "I'm not trying to be kind! I only want—"

Her eyes widened, dislodging a tear.

"I only want to kiss you," he said with a sudden sense of defeat, and lowered his lips to the single teardrop clinging to her cheek.

It tasted salty and warm and he savored it on his tongue.

She sighed. He trailed small, pecking kisses to the corner of her mouth and rested there, waiting. She turned her head ever so slightly, inviting him to take more. He did.

And exactly as it had in the temple, need stormed through him like thunder and lightning. Blinding and deafening, it overtook him. He crushed her to him, wrapping his arms around her back, ravishing her mouth. She ravished him back. Her passion fed into his until they were both breathing hard, their hands holding to each other with feverish desire.

"Daphne, I want you so very much," Iain whispered, tracing his tongue along the curve of her ear.

"Iain, I . . ."

He stole her words with a kiss as he pressed his knee between her legs. Pinned against the balustrade, her hips cradled him as he gently rocked against her, wrenching moans from her between each kiss.

"Oh, God, Iain," she cried.

Later Iain would wonder what had caused him to look skyward when he'd been so thoroughly occupied with plotting a course to the nearest bedchamber. But, for whatever reason, he glanced up.

The full moon shone brightly on the statue teetering on the edge of the parapet. There was no time to think, only to react. He grabbed hold of Daphne and lunged sideways at the same instant that the statuette smashed to the balcony floor in a spray of splintering stone. When Iain looked up again, he saw nothing but sky and stars.

Chapter Twelve

Up until now, Isadora had found the Thompson siblings' antics mildly amusing. She was no longer amused. If not for Lindley, Daphne might have been seriously injured. And if not for her intervention, Lindley wouldn't have been able to prevent it.

Isadora herself would have failed to see the statue falling if she hadn't been alerted by her supernatural senses. Once matters on the balcony had begun to grow amorous, she'd quickly transported herself to Iain's study; she hardly wished to spy on that sort of thing, after all. However, no sooner had she emptied the fireplace ashes into Lindley's pipe than her ghostly intuition had called her back to the balcony. And just in the nick of time. She'd whispered a warning in Iain's ear at the same moment the statue tumbled from the ledge.

Flying up to the roof to take a look, who should she discover fleeing the scene but that miserable pair, Winnie and Bertie. The two were racing off as fast as their legs could carry them, and Isadora couldn't determine whether the bumbling duo had accidently jarred the statue or if they'd pushed it with malicious intent.

Over the last few days she had been occasionally following the two, trying to decipher their scheme. She knew they searched for something, but she knew not what, nor could she ascertain what role Lindley might be playing in the affair. The only thing Isadora was sure of at this point was that Bertie and Winnie had just gotten her dander up.

If any harm comes to Daphne, you two will live to regret it, she vowed, shaking her fan at their retreating figures. She scowled down to the balcony, realizing that Winnie would be safely ensconced in her sickbed, and Bertie long gone from the manor, before Lindley would be able to reach the roof to investigate.

She rapped the fan into her palm. If only she could take action to delay the pair. She looked questioningly into the heavens, then shook her head in frustration. As much as she would have enjoyed playing a trick or two on the steward and his sister, she was strictly prohibited from exercising her powers on anyone but her chosen subject.

Only Lindley was fair game, and right about now, her son-in-law wasn't exactly in her good graces either.

Isadora glanced skyward once more. *He isn't making this at all easy, you realize. It's beastly difficult to play Cupid when I can scarcely tolerate the scoundrel!*

No sympathy came from above.

Allowing Daphne to believe that I was responsible for his wedding-day disappearance! she huffed. *He's afraid to tell her the truth because he knows how she'll react. Just as I did thirty years ago. Daphne will be gone like that—* Isadora snapped her fingers—*and Lindley will have lost the only thing he cares about, the only thing any Ashingford ever cared about: this blasted property!*

Isadora flung her boa over her shoulder and scornfully gazed out onto Ash Park. Gilded by moonbeams and mist, the rolling hills and steepled treetops could have been heaven itself, their beauty was so breathtaking. And yet, beauty deceived. Isadora knew this land for what it was—a stealer of souls. Throughout the years too many hearts had been broken by this cursed plot of dirt; she could but pray that Daphne's would not be the next in line.

Movement below lured her back to the balcony, where she found Daphne pressing a handkerchief to the back of Iain's hand as a breathless Wilkinson arrived on the scene.

"It's only a scratch," Iain was saying.

"Don't be silly. That shard sliced through your glove like a knife. Just look at it."

Daphne indicated a blood-soaked glove lying on the balcony floor.

Oh, I say, Isadora murmured, hastily closing her eyes. For all that she considered herself of stalwart character, she never had been able to abide the sight of blood.

"Wh-what has happened?" Wilkinson gasped. Debris littered the terrace from one end to the next. It looked as if a meteor had crashed to earth.

"Our sphinx dove from the roof," Iain answered.

Wilkinson looked up to the parapet. "I . . . I don't understand."

"Neither do I, Wilkinson." Iain gave the butler a significant look. "Why don't you take a footman with you and see what you can find. I wouldn't want the 'wind' to send any more statues hurtling down upon us."

The butler's right eyebrow lifted with comprehension. "Oh, yes, my lord."

Iain jerked his head toward the balcony's French doors. "Go on. I'll join you in a moment."

"Not before I put a few stitches in this," Daphne interjected. "Let's go inside where I can clean your hand and have a better look."

"It will be fine," Iain insisted.

"Only as long as I keep this linen pressed to it," Daphne argued. "Otherwise, you're likely to bleed to death."

Do you think so? Isadora uncharitably asked.

Although mildly grateful to Iain for saving Daphne's life, Isadora was not at all happy with her son-in-law. Even before he'd deceived Daphne about his role in the wedding-day disaster, the conversation he'd had with his solicitor had confirmed in Isadora's mind that Iain Ashingford was an unscrupulous wretch. From the sounds of it, he'd despoiled some poor girl, then bought her father off to keep the scandal hushed up.

Of course, what should she have anticipated from an Ashingford?

"Very well," Iain said, conceding to the stitches. "Let's get it done quickly, then."

Isadora trailed after them as they made their way to the kitchen. *Such a fuss over a little scratch. That scrape is no less than he deserves, you know.*

The kitchen was empty as they entered, but for the lingering scent of rosemary and smoke. Their steps echoed loudly from the spotless limestone floor to the top of the vaulted ceiling. Copper pots and utensils hung from every windowless wall, so that the only light came from the fire blazing in the hearth.

Daphne lit a candelabra and set it on the trestle table in the center of the room.

"The water is still hot," she said as she dipped her finger into the kettle suspended high above the fire. "I'll wash you up and then we can see how many stitches you're going to need."

Iain sat down on the bench. "Don't you think we should call Mrs. Emmitt?"

"Why?" Daphne began rummaging through the shelves for supplies. "It's late and she's probably abed. My needle-work is more than adequate."

Iain placed his hand with its bloodied makeshift bandage atop the table. Isadora averted her gaze.

"Here it is." Daphne set Mrs. Emmitt's healing basket on the bench next to Iain. "Do you want anything to dull the pain?"

"No, let's get on with it." He gave Daphne an assessing look. "I must say you're admirably composed for a woman who nearly got flattened tonight by an oversized paper-weight."

"Composed? Not any more than you are, I'd say. What did you expect?"

Iain shrugged. "Oh, I don't know. A mild case of hyster-ics?"

Isadora sniffed. *You don't know my daughter, sirrah.*

"Sorry to disappoint," Daphne replied, "but I'm not gen-erally prone to fits of hysteria."

"I'm not disappointed," Iain rebutted. "Merely sur-prised."

Daphne paused in the process of threading a needle. "I cannot imagine why you'd be surprised. Do you think you know me so well?"

Not as well as he'd like, Isadora put in.

"Well enough to marry you," Iain answered.

Daphne returned her attention to the needle and said softly, "I'm not certain I knew *you* well enough to marry."

"You seemed content at the time."

Daphne didn't answer, but removed the folded kerchief from Iain's hand. Isadora swiveled around to stare into the fire.

"At any rate, that's all the more reason for you to allow

us this week together," Iain said. "Once we strengthen our
acquaintance, we'll be much more comfortable starting our
married life."

"We shall see," Daphne said. "And remember, we agreed
to a week in total, four days of which have already passed."

Isadora expected Iain to cleverly counter that point, but
all she heard from him was a low, hissing sound. She
turned about, her gaze automatically dropping to the table.
Daphne was pulling the needle through the torn flesh of
Iain's hand as blood oozed from the cut—

Gulping, Isadora clapped her hand over her eyes, but it
was too late. Her ears grew hot, her stomach pitched, and
she fell to the floor in a heap.

"What was that?"

"What?" Daphne asked, carefully drawing another stitch.

"That noise. Didn't you hear it? That thump."

"I didn't hear any thump."

"Come now. It came from directly behind you."

Concerned, Daphne looked up from her gruesome
needlework. "Iain, you didn't knock your head or anything,
did you?"

His brows came together in a single black line. "No." He
peered over Daphne's shoulder. "You honestly didn't hear
that?"

"I honestly didn't. Are you sure you're all right? Maybe
we should awaken Mrs. Emmitt."

"No, I'm fine."

Daphne peeked up at him from half-veiled eyes. "There
wasn't any wind tonight, you know."

A muscle tensed in Iain's jaw. "Most likely a loose stone
gave way."

Daphne nodded, thinking it the most plausible of expla-
nations. Even if she were to believe that her grandfather's

spirit was lurking about, she didn't think he'd be guilty of such pernicious pranks.

She neatly tied off the thread and wrapped Iain's hand in a clean bandage. "Tomorrow I'll ask Mrs. Emmitt to put some salve on the cut. We wouldn't want it to become infected."

"We wouldn't?"

Daphne hid a small smile as she stowed the implements back into Mrs. Emmitt's basket. They'd played this word game earlier in the evening. "Yes, in this case: we. I wouldn't like to see your hand become gangrenous any more than you would."

She made to rise when Iain abruptly gripped her wrist with his injured hand. Startled, her gaze rose to his and her heart fluttered at what she saw there. His eyes held promises, intimate ones.

"I'm glad to hear that, Daphne, for I think you'll be pleasantly surprised by the good use I plan to make of this hand."

Her face flamed. Only a half hour earlier that hand had freely roamed her body, touching and caressing, igniting a fire in her still not doused.

"Iain, this . . ." She sank back onto the bench. "This is impossible."

He released her wrist. "Of course it's possible. We're husband and wife."

"In only the strictest interpretation. In reality . . . I think it would be wrong of us to rush this aspect of our relationship."

"Why in God's name? This 'aspect,' as you call it, is flourishing nicely."

"Ye-e-s." She couldn't dispute the point. "However, it's the only thing . . . It's all we share."

Iain grimaced. "What difference does that make? Three

months ago you'd have come willingly to my bed, knowing me less well than you do today."

"That was different," Daphne argued. "Three months ago our relationship was a clean slate. It isn't today. There are issues that must be resolved—"

"Such as?" he testily broke in.

"Such as that woman sleeping upstairs. And I do not refer to my abigail."

Iain rolled his eyes. "Oh God, Winnie again! Don't you think I'd be rid of her if I could? I didn't want her to come to Ash Park in the first place."

"Then what led her to believe she was invited?"

Thankfully, Iain didn't have to answer, for Daphne charged ahead with her accusations.

"I've heard of your reputation, you know."

"From whom? Your mother?" Iain huffed. "My reputation is the work of many fertile imaginations, Daphne, and not half as inglorious as you seem to think. I told you yesterday that I spent very little time in London, and when I was in Town I didn't go about a lot. The gossips assumed I was occupied with other prurient activities, I suppose. I won't claim to being a saint, mind you, but I've nothing to be ashamed of, either."

He could tell that he'd shaken her assumptions. He took hold of her hand, his voice gentling. "Daphne, let's not look to the past when we've got our future before us. Can't you forget that Winnifred is upstairs and let us work from that clean slate you spoke of?"

Daphne stilled, wondering what held her back. Three months earlier such a plea would have sent her flying into Iain's arms, but she'd learned too much about herself since then. Although the romantic in her wished to succumb, her instincts told her that something was amiss, that one barrier yet stood between them.

"Are you frightened, Daphne? Of what happens between a man and wife?"

She turned away, blushing. Yes, she was frightened, but not of *that*. Gracious, every inch of her cried out to learn where those luscious feelings might end.

No, what she feared was the hurt. The hurt of being rejected. For just as she couldn't deny her attraction for him, neither could she deny the heartbreak she'd been living with these past months. She needed to proceed cautiously, to protect herself.

"No, that doesn't frighten me," she explained quietly. "'Tis only that I'd feel more comfortable if we . . . slowed down that aspect of our relationship."

Iain wriggled slightly. "As long as we don't have to close the door on that 'aspect.'"

Daphne thought back to the moonlit balcony and the strange, hot, strangled feeling she'd experienced in her abdomen. Faith, that door wasn't closed, it was off its hinges! But she didn't want to tell Iain that.

Realistically, she didn't quite know what she was waiting for. What might convince her to stay at Ash Park, to pick up where their marriage should have begun? Even as she asked herself the question, in her heart of hearts, she knew the answer.

On the day of her wedding, Daphne had realized that Iain did not love her. How could he have? But in her dreamy, fairy-tale way, she'd believed that eventually, sooner or later, he would have to fall in love with her. Simply because she had always believed in happy endings.

But that was before her faith in happy endings had been shaken and before she'd been hit with a severe dose of Iain's brand of reality. Now she wasn't so certain that her husband would come to love her. And she wanted him to. Very much.

She stood up swiftly, not daring to look at him while she

returned Mrs. Emmitt's basket to the cupboard. "We'll just have to see what the next three days bring."

From the safety of the other side of the room, she turned around. Iain was staring at her, his gray eyes kindling with desire.

Those three days seemed very long indeed.

Chapter Thirteen

Iain jerked awake.

Something, some noise, had awakened him. He remained perfectly still, waiting for it again. There. Dammit, what was that clanking? It sounded almost like the rattling of . . . chains.

He shot straight up in bed. Despite the trouble he'd been having with his hearing, there was no mistaking that *clink-clink*.

He rolled out of bed as quickly as possible, the floor uncomfortably cold against his bare feet. The moon had risen higher in the sky, casting less light than it had earlier in the evening, but enough for Iain to see by.

His first thought was for Daphne. Padding to the connecting door, he laid his ear against the wood, but could hear no stirring from within. He hoped that she still slept. Whatever this was about, he didn't want her frightened in the dead of night by someone's idea of a prank. Thankfully, her suite at the corner of the house could not be reached without first passing by his apartment. He had a vision of himself in the role of a teeth-baring watchdog and was surprised by his sense of protectiveness.

The faint jangling sounded again from the opposite end of the bedchamber. As noiselessly as the wraith he pursued, Iain raced into the corridor.

Adjacent to his bedroom was a *cabinet de bain,* a rather large chamber equipped with an oversized copper tub. Iain pushed open the door and entered cautiously. Light and shadows crisscrossed the floor in a haphazard pattern while cloaking the room's perimeter in darkness. Iain began a meticulous search of the chamber. He checked both the garderobe and the closet that housed the closestool, all the while straining to hear any further chain rattling. Although he would have sworn that the noises originated from inside that room, his search produced neither clues nor clanking.

He returned to the hall and waited. And waited. No more sounds disturbed the night.

A cool draft swept through the corridor, bringing goose bumps to his arms and legs. Abruptly he realized that he was standing in the hallway as naked as the day he was born.

"Good God," he muttered to himself. He'd been a bit of a loose screw ever since he'd come to Ash Park, but this was the outside of enough. Seeing and hearing things was one matter, but dashing about the house unclothed . . .

Briefly he considered checking Daphne's door to ensure that it was locked, but he feared her reaction should she awaken and find him outside her room in this condition. Instead, he went back to his bed and left the door wide open for a clear view of the corridor.

Folding his hands behind his head, he sat back against the quilted headboard and stared into the hallway. Not for one minute did he believe that a ghost was responsible for the clattering he'd heard. It simply wasn't in him. There had to be a logical explanation for an illogical occurrence; there always was.

By the time the sky began to shift from charcoal to gray to rose, Iain had convinced himself that the noises he'd heard must have come from the bathroom pipes. He'd thought through all the other possibilities and had decided that human involvement was unlikely since he'd inspected the source of the clanking within seconds of hearing the noise. No one could have slipped away so quickly. Add the fact that Daphne had bathed earlier in the evening, and Iain concluded that what he'd heard was water draining from the pipes.

Perhaps the incident with the statue had caused him to be unusually skittish, he thought. After Daphne had retired for the evening, he'd gone up to the roof to investigate and had discovered no evidence of foul play. He had, however, found at least two sites where the masonry was loose, loose enough to result in an accident like the one they'd narrowly avoided. To reassure himself that the episode had been purely random, he'd tested the weight of a companion statue, deducing that only an uncommonly powerful man would have had the strength to topple the figure.

Nonetheless, Iain was still thinking of the fallen statue when he heard Daphne moving about next door. The past three days he'd arisen at dawn and spent the morning hours in estate business, not meeting up with her until midday. This morning she was up early, and he wondered if she'd slept as poorly as he had done. Actually, he hadn't slept at all after the clinking had roused him. He'd been imagining what might have happened had Daphne discovered him un-clad at her bedroom door.

The soft sounds next door were driving him mad. What did she look like first thing in the morning? Was her hair down? Tousled? Did she still smell of honeysuckle? After hours of fantasizing, he couldn't resist.

Pulling on his robe, he walked over to the connecting door and knocked. The muffled activity stopped. The door opened slowly and Daphne's head appeared around the corner. Her hair was down, curling around her shoulders, and definitely tousled.

"Good morning," he said, feeling suddenly foolish.

"Good morning."

He tugged at the robe's sash as his body reacted to her appealing, bed-rumpled image. "I heard you moving about and thought that since you'd awakened early, we might take breakfast together."

"That would be nice."

She eased a little away from the door so that he could make out the white cotton sleeve of her nightrail. He'd rarely seen anything so provocative.

"Did you sleep well?" he asked.

Color surged to her cheeks—a guilty admission of her own fantasies at work? Then Iain did something he never did. He blurted out the first thing that came into his mind.

"You know, for a Whiting, you wouldn't make much of a cardplayer," he joked. "Those blushes of yours would give you dead away."

As soon as he'd said it, Iain could have bitten his tongue. Daphne's eyes widened so that her eyelashes fairly skimmed her brows.

"'For a Whiting'?"

"I, er . . ."

"How very odd that you would know of mother's secret vice," Daphne said wonderingly. "Or did she hoodwink you into a game as well? Whist was her passion, you know. She loved nothing better than to fleece unsuspecting house-guests in a hand or two."

"Yes, who doesn't enjoy a good hand of whist? Shall I meet you downstairs in a quarter hour?"

Daphne's frown reflected the abrupt change of subject. "Very well," she said.

Iain waited until the door clicked shut before slamming his sore fist into his forehead.

"Fool. Why don't you just confess everything?"

Daphne wasn't aware that he knew her family tree backward and forward, probably better than she knew it herself. The Whitings' weakness for gambling, the red hair that went back six generations, the bigamist great-uncle in Staffordshire. She might have expected him to know something of the family he'd married into, but for him to possess such intimate knowledge of her relations would definitely strike her as peculiar. He'd damn well better watch his tongue, especially where her grandfather was concerned. A blunder at this stage might prove very costly indeed.

"Cods-head!" he admonished himself again.

"I beg your pardon."

Iain twisted about to find Dobbs on the threshold, looking a trifle put out.

"Not you," Iain said. "Come in and shut the door."

Dobbs complied. "I do hope, Lord Cods-head, that you've agreeable news to report."

Iain glared at him. "Cheeky bastard."

The valet-cum-tormentor merely grinned in response.

Despite himself, Iain returned the cocky smile. "Yes, for all my blundering, I believe that last night proved to be the turning point, Dobbs. The safe money says that the Marchioness will be residing permanently at Ash Park at the end of this week."

"That is good news, my lord. I have become rather fond of your lady."

Iain splashed water onto his face, then accepted a clean

linen. "Have you? I hadn't realized that you'd become acquainted."

"Oh, yes."

Iain squinted at the valet, who waggled his eyebrows mysteriously. "I'll have to warn my wife to keep better company."

"I daresay you'd be surprised by many of your lady's activities," Dobbs airily put in.

Iain chuckled. "Am I to take that bait?"

"Oh, no, my lord. There's no need. You'll understand soon enough."

It was a big step and Daphne knew it. But after the discussion with Iain last evening, she'd decided to take a risk and make a leap of faith. Daphne Harkwell would have made that leap without a second thought, but Daphne Ashingford was a wiser woman, a more prudent one. Daphne Ashingford had been burned.

In fact, those very words had passed through her thoughts today when she was returning from her morning constitutional. After breakfast with her husband she'd walked down to the river, questioning herself aloud—as she always did—about her marital circumstances. Approaching the front of the manor, she'd stopped to admire the fountain when she'd been struck by the story of the phoenix. Burned, yet risen again. Her decision was made.

True, she'd been wounded, but she couldn't allow that disappointment to darken the rest of her days. She couldn't be forever doubting, living her life in ashes; she had to believe.

Besides, she reasoned, it wasn't as if there'd be *no* turning back. She could still go forward with the annulment, awkward though it would be, after she'd publicly announced herself as the Marchioness Lindley. When she thought back to her chat with Dobbs, however, Daphne knew that she'd never be able to forgive herself if she didn't do this for Iain, at least once.

"To think that he never had a birthday party."

Her abigail, Rose, accustomed to her mumbling, didn't even look up from arranging Daphne's hair.

Thanks in part to Dobbs, Daphne was slowly beginning to understand what Iain's childhood must have been like. No mother's lap to cuddle in; an invalid father who couldn't teach his son to fish or to ride. None of the simple pleasures a child should have experienced had been Iain's. She could not stand to picture him alone on his birthday with only his valet and bedridden father as celebrants.

"No, he's going to have a party this year. Maybe not the largest nor the grandest, but a wonderful surprise party."

She still couldn't quite believe the chance concurrence that Iain's birthday would fall on the seventh day of their agreement. At first, she'd thought Dobbs was pulling her leg, but the loyal servant had convinced her. The first day of August would mark the Marquess Lindley's twenty-ninth birthday.

Dobbs had told her that Iain hadn't observed the anniversary for almost a decade, so he probably wasn't aware of the remarkable coincidence of dates. Daphne never had believed in coincidence anyway. This had to be fate. She was destined to throw this party for Iain on the final day of their experimental marriage and perhaps, just perhaps, this party was going to be a special one. . . .

She was doing it again. Allowing herself to get her hopes up too high. Iain wasn't going to suddenly decide that he loved her simply because of a small birthday party.

"No, Rose, I cannot pin my decision on that."

"No'm."

"The real question is: Can I be happy and help him find a measure of his own happiness?"

"Yes'm."

And that question was an especially troubling one because Daphne doubted that Iain had ever been truly happy. Somewhere deep inside, an anger ate into him like a cankerous sore. She suspected that it was tied to his father, to the fact that he'd been raised in a home where suffering was the norm and where the moments of joy had been few and far between.

She could make his home a happy one. If she were willing to make another leap of faith.

Earlier this afternoon Daphne had given Wilkinson eight invitations to be delivered to Ash Park's closest neighbors. She'd realized that Iain might not yet know those on the guest list, but had thought that he'd want to meet with them sooner or later, so why not at his birthday celebration?

"My lady, er, the Viscount and Viscountess Royce don't go about much," Wilkinson had said, staring uneasily at the invitation on the top of the pile.

"All the more reason for us to issue them an invitation, wouldn't you say?" Daphne had cheerily replied.

The butler had then glanced to the second letter and his nose had begun twitching. "Pardon me, but the Dowager Countess of Angshire?"

"Yes, Wilkinson?"

He'd answered her in an oddly strangled voice. "There is a reason, my lady, that the family has secluded her at the dower house."

"Yes, the poor old thing is probably dying to get out for some fun. I do hope she'll be able to come on such short notice."

Wilkinson hadn't appeared nearly as hopeful but had dutifully gone off to see the invitations delivered.

Once Daphne completed her toilette, she snuck down to the kitchen to meet with Gaston before dinner. With only two days to work with, plans for the festivities needed to be put into place as soon as was possible.

The kitchen was bustling with activity as she entered and the first person she ran into was a flour-drenched Mrs. Emmitt.

"Oh, Lady Lindley, you shouldn't be comin' in here. The smoke'll get into your pretty gown."

"I'm not going to stay long, Mrs. Emmitt. I just need a word with Monsieur Gaston."

"Monsieur Gaston, eh?" The sous-chef rolled her eyes. "Well, His Royal Eminence has gone out to the herb garden. He'll be back in a pig's whisker. Why don't you wait in the dinin' room and I'll send him in?"

"Oh, no. I don't want the Marquess to see me. I'm planning a surprise."

Mrs. Emmitt smiled coquettishly. "Oh, aren't you two the regular turtledoves? Though it's a pity you can't enjoy your honeymoon to yourselves." She bobbed her head toward the ceiling. "That one upstairs . . . tsk-tsk."

Curious, Daphne attempted to appear sympathetic as she asked, "How is our guest faring?"

"Pshaw. That woman's hale as an ox, I'd say. She gave me a scare at first, but for all her grousin' and bellyachin', I can't find nothin' wrong with her."

"Perhaps she's recovering her strength," Daphne suggested while privately wondering why the Comtesse would feign an illness.

"Could be," the cook conceded. "But to my way of thinkin', that woman should be up and gone by now." Mrs. Emmitt gave her a wink. "To your way of thinkin', too, I'd imagine."

"You'd imagine correctly. I'll allow her another day or so, and then the Comtesse and I might need to have a chat."

Mrs. Emmitt nodded approvingly. "That's the way, my girl. You need to set the course right from the start. I like the new master just fine, but he's a man and a man needs a guidin' hand. But you'll take care of it, I can see that. You got grit."

"Why, thank you, Mrs. Emmitt. What a lovely thing to say."

At that moment Gaston reappeared, and Daphne and he passed a half-hour laying out plans for the birthday dinner party.

Afterward Daphne circled around to the garden and entered the dining salon through the French doors. Iain was waiting for her, looking breathtakingly handsome in his dark evening clothes. As he smiled at her Daphne felt something inside her twist with longing, a need to wrap her arms about him and press his head to her breasts.

"Out for another stroll?" he asked.

She flushed at her thoughts. "Yes, I came through the garden. It's a beautiful evening."

"Ah, beauty but recognizes its own," he replied as he bent over to brush his lips across her fingers.

Although she knew the flattery to be untrue, Daphne was willing to deceive herself. Iain had never before told her she was either pretty or attractive, so tonight she would let herself believe that he thought her beautiful.

She slid her fingers from his. His were bare except for the bandage.

"How is your hand?"

"For the sixth time today, my fretful little wife"—he smiled slowly—"it's fine."

My wife. Like Cupid's arrow, those words flew straight to Daphne's heart, exposing a truth she had failed to see. She hadn't consciously perceived it, but today when she had decided to surprise Iain with the birthday party, she had also decided to remain at Ash Park. She was going to give their marriage a second chance.

The realization startled her, but not nearly as much as the flash of understanding that followed it. Why, she asked herself, had she been willing to make such an enormous leap of faith? The answer weakened her knees.

Because she was in love with Iain.

Her heart hammered and she knew that she was more than startled by its revelation; she was a little frightened as well. In five short days she had gone from wanting their marriage to be dissolved to wishing on stars that it might be saved. No wonder she'd wished so desperately for Iain to be able to love her; she had already fallen hopelessly in love with him.

Turning away to hide her turmoil, she pretended interest in a nearby floral arrangement.

She had no idea how long she'd been staring into the peonies when Iain spoke from behind her. "It's an attractive arrangement, but I must be missing something. Do you see something in there that I have failed to?"

Daphne felt herself caught between tears and laughter. Iain's question had hit on the crux of it: she had always seen what he had not. Hope, trust, faith. The very qualities that made life both bearable and beautiful . . . he was blind to. She bit her lip, daunted by the task she was taking on. Somehow she must teach Iain to open his eyes—and his heart.

The remainder of the evening was a test of Daphne's self-control. They dined *à deux,* then adjourned to the parlor for a game of piquet. Daphne had found it nearly impossible to eat, and no matter how hard she tried, she simply could not keep her attention on her cards.

Iain would be discussing repairs to the manor and then ask her opinion and Daphne would find herself unable to answer. When she ought to have been listening, she'd instead been staring at his mouth, mentally sketching its contours.

And evidently, she was not alone in sensing the mounting tension between them. Their fingers brushed while exchanging cards, and Iain's breath caught loudly enough for her to hear.

Without an outlet, such keen awareness was wearying. Especially tonight when Daphne was still grappling with the knowledge of her newfound love.

"I think I'll retire," she breathlessly announced after she'd lost five consecutive rounds. "I'm feeling inordinately tired this evening."

Iain laid his cards down with a gusty sigh. "I believe that I'll do the same. I didn't sleep well last night."

Their gazes clashed, both aware of what disturbed their rest.

Daphne surged to her feet and Iain followed suit, then they silently wound their way upstairs.

Outside her bedroom door, he raised his hand to knock.

"Oh, I never ask Rose to stay up for me. I've always managed on my own."

As soon as she'd spoken, Daphne blushed. Merely revealing that her maid was not waiting for her wasn't a request for him to join her, was it?

Her doubts multiplied when Iain pushed open the door and preceded her into the room. She hesitated on the threshold, uncertain as to what she might say. She wasn't ready for this, not yet at least. She didn't know if—

Suddenly Iain froze, his attention riveted to the bed.

Oh, dear.

"Iain, I don't think that—"

"Have you seen this?" he demanded in a voice that chilled her to the bone.

Daphne hurried forward, confused. "Seen what?"

Iain pointed to a sheaf of foolscap laying atop the satin counterpane, and resting beside it was a Whiting banner.

Daphne had to lean forward to read what was written on the note. *Leave now before it's too late.*

Chapter
Fourteen

"That leaves us with Allen, Mallory, or that chambermaid. What was her name again?"

"Blanton. Chrissie Blanton, my lord." Thompson answered.

Iain clenched his hands behind his back and paced to the other end of the study.

He was in a foul humor—the blackest, foulest humor he could remember being in for many a year. He'd spent the better part of the last two days questioning the staff, submitting each servant to three rounds of interviews with himself, Wilkinson, and Thompson. And yet, despite all the time invested in this asinine affair, he still could not find the culprit responsible for leaving that message in Daphne's room.

"Goddammit, who could it be?" Iain demanded.

"W-e-ell . . ."

Iain shot the steward a dangerous look. Thompson cringed where he sat, his head sinking into his shoulders like a frightened tortoise.

"Don't you dare," Iain threatened.

"No, my lord." The steward shook his pale head. "I shan't."

Iain turned away in disgust. The man was a buffoon. Thompson hadn't said so straight out, but Iain knew that not only did the overseer believe in Ash Park's ghost, but that the man also believed Whiting's spirit to be the guilty party in this business.

Even more vexing, Iain realized that Thompson was not alone in his conviction. Although no one had presumed to say so aloud, it had been clear in Iain's discussions with the servants that they all believed him to be on a wild-goose chase. *The ghost did it, who else?* their wide-eyed, almost pitying expressions had proclaimed.

Iain rather thought it a testament to his character that he hadn't throttled one of them in his frustration.

Only Wilkinson seemed to have a modicum of sense where any of this was concerned and the butler believed it to be nothing more than a prank. Iain was reluctantly beginning to come around to his way of thinking.

"What of those three?" Iain asked.

The steward poked his spectacles farther up the bridge of his nose while referring to some notes. "After hunting around, I found Mallory at the pub in Blandford yesterday. Three sheets to the wind he was. Went on and on about how he couldn't work in a house with a gho—" Thompson swallowed as if he'd got something stuck in his throat.

"Yes, yes, get on with it. A ghost," Iain tersely supplied.

"Yes, my lord. That *was* what he said."

"Well, did you believe him?"

"Yes. I don't think Mallory would have engaged in such a trick. He's afraid of his own shadow, that one."

Pot calling the kettle black, Iain thought, but held his tongue. "All right. What of Allen and the girl?"

"No news of Allen. His brother says he hasn't seen him. I did go to Widow Blanton's place and she told me that her daughter had come running home two days ago and had fallen into bed, terrified out of her wits. Seems the girl's taken it into her head that she'll be the next to be visited by the uh . . . er . . ."

"Ghost!" Iain shouted. "For heaven's sake, man, you can use the bloody word!"

"Oh, yes. Thank you, my lord."

Iain had the most irrational urge to slap some color into the overseer's pallid cheeks.

"What do you know of Allen? Might he have thought this some clever lark?"

Thompson shrugged indifferently. "I cannot say. He seemed a decent enough sort. I think it more likely he felt as Mallory and the maid did. Wanted to get as far away as he could from . . ."

Pale lips quivering, the steward timidly peered up at Iain.

Iain just stopped himself from lunging at him.

"From the ghost," Thompson finally whispered.

Iain feared he might explode. He couldn't take another minute of this insanity. "Go," he said, pointing to the door. "And let me know if you discover anything more about Allen's whereabouts."

With a bob of his head, the steward scurried out the door and Iain watched him go with annoyance. Why was the man always scuttling about like some many-legged spider?

He sighed, tugging impatiently at his cravat. Allen had to be their man. He was the only suspect left and the fact that he had disappeared before he could be questioned reinforced the likelihood of his culpability.

However, two points about Allen's supposed guilt continued to trouble Iain. What had been the man's motive? And second, where had a kitchen hand learned to write?

He was pondering those questions when a footman rapped at the door.

"Excuse me, my lord, but your man, Dobbs, asks that you join him in your chamber."

"You may tell him I'll be up shortly," Iain answered, thinking it a pretty sad state of affairs when his valet summoned him to dress as if he were still in leading strings.

A few minutes later Iain was walking down the hall to his chamber with the suspicion that Dobbs had more on his mind than which waistcoat Iain would be wearing this evening. Tonight was the last night of Daphne's seven-day agreement.

Wearily he pushed open the door to his room only to find the insufferable Dobbs smiling from ear to ear.

"You do know, you old tyrant, 'that the master summons the valet, not the other way around?" he asked.

Dobbs waved him off with a superior grin. "You're here, aren't you?"

Iain grumbled, shutting the door behind him. "Isn't it a bit early yet to dress?"

"Any other night, yes. But not tonight."

The lilting emphasis on "tonight" caused Iain to scowl.

" 'Tonight,' " he mimicked in a high-pitched voice. "Must you be so blasted cheerful? I cannot imagine what you're so pleased about unless you're gloating, but why you should gloat I cannot guess. I thought you were playing happy matchmaker in all this. Well, I swear to you, for all I know Daphne could be packing her bags this very moment."

"Is she?" the valet prodded.

"Hell's bells, I don't know." Iain collapsed into a chair, his legs sprawled wide, his chin sinking into his chest.

His inability to uncover the perpetrator of the ghostly

hoax was galling enough; but what truly rankled—and what he'd been avoiding thinking of the entire day—was the realization that his seven days were up and he had yet to seduce his wife.

He slammed one boot heel into the floor.

"You have been occupied," Dobbs pointed out.

"Yes, but I've spent every spare moment riding, reading, dining, playing cards. Even fishing. I've done everything with Daphne but—"

"My lord," the valet cautioned.

"Don't worry, I'm not as indiscreet as all that. I only wish I knew if she were planning to remain at Ash Park."

"You could ask her."

Iain frowned and stared at the toe of his boot. "I didn't want to have to ask."

Dobbs actually chuckled. "Well, on the bright side, if Lady Lindley does leave Ash Park, at least you won't be left without companionship."

Iain flung back his head. "You're a monster, do you know that, Dobbs? God, what *am* I going to do with Winnifred? I ought to be grateful she's remained in her bed these past days. I doubt if Daphne even remembers she's here."

"Oh, I don't know about that."

Tilting slightly forward, Iain peeped at his valet through one eye. "I suppose she does remember, eh?"

"Her ladyship's memory strikes me as a keen, albeit forgiving one."

Iain heard the reprimand hidden in that statement, but chose to ignore it. "Well, whatever Daphne decides, I'll have to tell Winnifred she must leave. If Daphne stays, obviously the Comtesse must go, and if Daphne returns to Harkwell House, I'll simply have to go after her."

"That's the spirit," Dobbs said. "Persevere."

"Of course, I'm going to persevere," Iain replied. "I

made a vow to my father and I'll see it done. I will not lose Ash Park."

Dobbs shook his head in patent disappointment. "You're a stubborn one, Iain Ashingford."

"I never claimed to be anything but," Iain retorted, sitting up as the valet wrapped a linen around his neck.

After the shave, Dobbs ushered Iain into the *cabinet de bain,* where a bath had been drawn. As Iain soaked and scrubbed he thought of the night ahead.

This would be his last opportunity to get Daphne into his bed.

Last night he might have succeeded had he been more persistent and less of a gentleman. The kiss he'd requested when bidding her goodnight had quickly stormed out of control—both his and hers. However, when Daphne had pulled away, disheveled and pink-cheeked, he hadn't pushed his advantage. He'd abided by her wishes, leaving her at her door with only that kiss lingering between them.

But when would she not pull away? When would she succumb to the desire that he knew burned as hot in her as it did in him?

The bathwater had begun to cool when Dobbs at last appeared again.

"What kept you? I've been soaking in here forever."

"Busy, busy," was the valet's mumbled reply.

Back in his bedchamber, Iain's thoughts returned to the importance of this single night; this night would have to unfold as a flawless evening of seduction. He could not hold back any longer. His time had run out.

"Damn Isadora," he muttered.

Dobbs paused in dressing his hair.

"If she hadn't interfered, Daphne would already be my wife in every way that matters. The meddlesome woman was far too full of herself, didn't know when to keep her nose in her own busin—*ouch!*"

Iain grabbed at his scalp. "What was that for?"

Dobbs held aloft the comb. "What was what for?"

Scowling, he rubbed at his smarting pate. "*That.* You nearly ripped half the hair from my head!"

Dobbs glanced at the comb. "I didn't—"

"For heaven's sake, man, leave some, will you? I've no desire to resemble you anytime soon."

The valet smoothed a palm across his barren crown. "I'll have you know that Mrs. Emmitt finds my smooth top most appealing."

"Mrs. Emmitt? Well, take a care she doesn't smother you in that bosom of hers, old boy."

Dobbs smirked. "Beg pardon, but I don't seem to be the one requiring advice in those matters."

Iain could hardly dispute that claim.

Still smirking, Dobbs then proceeded to bring out Iain's finest evening wear. "You may as well look your best tonight since I understand her ladyship is to be in fine twig."

"Where did you hear that?"

"Er, I believe Rose might have mentioned it."

Iain slipped into his black coat, feeling somewhat heartened. If Daphne were taking extra pains with her appearance . . .

Dobbs had only just set the diamond pin into Iain's cravat when a knock sounded at the door.

"Ah, your escort awaits," Dobbs pronounced.

"My escort?"

The valet opened the door and there stood Daphne in a shimmering gold evening gown, looking as if she had been dipped in a moonbeam. Although she was smiling, she appeared unsure of her welcome, teetering at the threshold's edge.

Iain felt Dobbs nudge him in the back and he stumbled forward, shaking himself out of his surprise.

"You look lovely, Daphne. How nice to see you out of mourning."

She ran her hand lightly over her skirt. "I know it's early, but Mother wouldn't have wanted me to wear black for her."

"No, I'm sure that she wouldn't have." He offered her his arm. "Shall we go down?"

Laying her hand on his arm, she leaned across him. "Thank you, Dobbs."

The valet winked in response.

Bemused by that interplay, Iain didn't notice the delicate strains of a Mozart's Haydn arrangement until they were halfway down the staircase.

"You ordered in a quartet?" he asked, further encouraged.

Daphne nodded, her smile both shy and secretive.

They arrived at the salon to find the doors closed, without a footman in sight. Iain reached forward to pull open the door when Daphne put her hand on his.

"No, allow me," she said. With a flourish and another mysterious smile, she flung both doors wide. "Surprise!"

Iain stared dumbfounded into the crowded room.

"Wh-what's this?" he croaked.

"It's a party. For you." Daphne took his hand in both of hers. "Happy birthday, Iain."

Iain gazed down into her smiling face, so confused he could scarcely remember his name, much less the date of his birth. But he did remember.

"It's . . . it's not my birthday."

Daphne squeezed his fingers. "Dobbs said you'd probably forgotten," she said with a laugh. "But I didn't. I've invited all your neighbors and we're going to have a lovely celebration just for you."

"But, Daphne, it's really not—"

And then he looked into her eyes, deep into those olive-green eyes, and he saw something there he'd never seen before. Not in her eyes, not in anyone's. He had no idea what it could be, but he knew that it was utterly beyond him to crush it.

"I . . ." He floundered, struggling for words. "I thank you," he simply said.

By the way Daphne's face lit up, one would have thought that Iain had just given her a priceless gift. Before he could add to that meager thank you, Daphne pulled him into the room and he was suddenly surrounded by a sea of unfamiliar faces.

Without a doubt, Iain's twenty-ninth birthday celebration (observed nearly six weeks early) was the strangest affair he'd ever attended.

The first of his neighbors Daphne introduced him to was none other than the infamous Dowager Countess of Angshire. By happenstance, Iain's London acquaintances included her son, the Earl of Angshire, who—in Iain's opinion—bore the cross of his mother's lunacy like a long-suffering martyr.

"This is an unexpected pleasure," Iain said after Daphne had made the introductions.

A tiny woman who couldn't have weighed even four stone, the dowager smiled up at him from a face unexpectedly youthful. Silver-white hair, arranged like a young woman's, draped over her shoulder in coquettish curls and her gown, a pink frothy thing, would have been more suitable for a girl of sixteen instead of a woman of seventy.

When she spoke, her voice was soft, not roughened with age, and outrageously flirtatious. "You may kiss my hand," she told him, fluttering her white lashes.

Iain obliged and the dowager tittered playfully behind her fan. "Oh, you're a bold one," she teased.

Iain glanced to Daphne, who appeared to find the dowager completely enchanting.

"Lady Angshire insists she be called Gilda," Daphne informed him.

"But you," the dowager said, poking Iain in the chest with her fan. "You may call me Gildie."

"Why, thank you, Gildie. I'm honored."

The dowager tittered again and Iain asked her to save him a dance before he was pulled along to meet the rest of his guests.

The Viscount and Viscountess Royce were a fascinating pair, each hoisting a miniature terrier in their arms, one of which was busily chewing the sleeve off Lady Royce's gown. Apparently brought together by a love of dogs, the Royces' idea of social conversation was a detailed history of each of their beloved twenty-three pets.

"Now Juno, you understand, can't tolerate the cold and we have to keep the fires going all winter in case the poor darling catches a chill," the Viscountess solemnly informed him.

"But Rory," the Viscount interjected, "has a skin condition that's exacerbated by the heat, so he, little fellow, must be kept in the east wing with Floppy and Topper."

"Unfortunately, Topper here"—the Viscountess indicated the terrier with a mouthful of her dress between his jaws—"doesn't get along with Mercury and we must be ever vigilant that they don't quarrel."

"Yes, you wouldn't wish them to quarrel," Iain politely answered while privately wondering how Daphne had been able to find so many candidates for Bedlam in this quiet corner of Dorset.

Iain met Colonel Thoroughgood, who'd lost an arm at Elba and regaled one and all with the particulars of the incident. Sir Mortimer and his wife seemed a likely enough couple, though Iain could not look upon them without wanting to recite the Jack Sprat nursery rhyme. And then there were the Devereux, the McDonalds, the Koenigs and the Reddingtons. Pleasant enough people who seemed, to all initial appearances, to be blessed with the full complement of their God-given faculties.

All in all, the dinner passed without major incident, except for Topper falling into the soup tureen and ruining the lobster bisque. Even that trifling disaster couldn't wipe the smile from Daphne's face and Iain felt rather proud of her. She was a perfect hostess, dignified without being cool, composed yet vivacious. She had a gift for making those around her feel comfortable, a skill Iain had never truly appreciated until now.

In fact, Iain had not appreciated much about any social event before this evening. He'd not been much for tonnish festivities, never caring for false flattery or the backbiting gossip that passed for small talk in certain circles. But tonight was different—he was honestly enjoying himself amid this oddball assortment of guests—and it didn't take him long to figure out why.

Daphne.

She laughed. She sparkled. She was iridescent. Many times he caught her glancing at him as if to assure herself that he was having fun. Her concern charmed him and he was touched by her efforts. She had obviously gone to some trouble to arrange this little fete. When was the last time anyone had gone out of their way to please him, with no thought to their own gain? When was the last time he'd been in a position to thank someone for even the smallest kindness?

The evening had grown late before Iain finally found a moment alone with his wife. Nothing had yet been said about this being the last day of their trial week together, and although he was feeling more confident, he needed to hear Daphne say she would be staying on at Ash Park.

She was speaking with Wilkinson when he approached.

"Let her have as much champagne as she wishes," Daphne was saying. "The dear doesn't get out often and she deserves her fun."

"Are you speaking of Gildie?" Iain asked as Wilkinson left to bring in more libations.

Daphne spun around, her smile warm and intimate. "Yes, do you think she's had too much?"

Iain lightly massaged his ribs. "Although I'm going to be black-and-blue from her flirtatious pinches, I'd say let her have another bottle if she chooses. At seventy-seven, one should be allowed one's excesses."

"You've been very kind to her. Thank you."

Iain answered her with a saucy grin. "You needn't thank me. Gildie has earned the right to kick up her heels."

Daphne's gaze moved to the floor, where the dowager was whirling about like a pink dervish. "I think she must be lonely all by herself in that house."

Iain's gaze joined hers. "I'll have to speak with Angshire," he said.

The Earl, that self-absorbed fool, didn't realize how fortunate he was to have a mother alive and well. Granted, Gildie was a bit dotty, but not so bad off that she needed to be sequestered as her son had done.

"She is enjoying herself," Daphne said.

"Everyone is, Daphne. You've put together a lovely party and I want to thank you."

He took hold of her hand, and as he did so he felt a ridge beneath her glove. Specifically, beneath the fourth finger of her hand. Her left hand.

His gaze shot to hers.

She nodded, color rushing into her cheeks.

She was wearing her wedding band. "You're . . . you're going to stay?"

"Yes."

Emotion jolted through Iain with the force of a blow. Desire. Relief. Something else he didn't recognize.

He wanted nothing more in that instant than to pick her up and carry her out of the salon, straight to his bedchamber. He wanted to take her in his arms and show her how he felt, how much he wanted her.

His fingers began to shake as soon as he'd realized what he'd admitted. He wanted Daphne. He didn't want her because she was Ash Park, he wanted *her*.

More than the physical attraction, he needed her smile, her idealism, her light. He needed what only Daphne could give him.

Gently he tugged at her hand, drawing her closer. "Do you think," he asked, leaning close to her ear, "that this party is almost at an end?"

Daphne's eyes widened. "We're . . . we're to have the cake at midnight."

Twenty minutes. They were perhaps the longest of Iain's life. Only the sixty minutes that followed the twenty proved even more unendurable, as the guests ate their cake, then slowly began to make their good-byes.

The dowager's coach was the last to pull up and Iain suffered one final pinch before Gildie took her leave.

At last, Iain and Daphne were alone. The domed foyer seemed cavernous, the walls throwing back at them each breath, each anxious scuff of a shoe.

Iain laced his fingers through Daphne's, inordinately pleased to feel the wedding band marking her as his.

No words were necessary. Together they climbed the staircase, pausing only a moment outside Iain's door. He couldn't be certain who had hesitated first, but for some reason, he wanted Daphne to take the lead. It no longer felt right for him to be the pursuer and she his quarry.

He brought their joined hands to his lips, lightly kissing

the inside of her wrist. He could feel her pulse beating rapidly under his mouth.

"I'd like to be with you tonight, Daphne," he said, his voice barely a whisper.

Her eyes were luminous in the shadowed hallway. "I'd like that, too," she answered.

Chapter
Fifteen

Iain closed the door, his hand slightly shaky as he turned the key in the lock. He tried to steady himself with a deep breath, but the intoxicating aroma of honeysuckle filled his lungs. Daphne's scent.

He swung around to find her standing in the middle of the room, only the light of a single candle illuminating her. He saw her tongue flick across her lips.

"I have a gift for you," she said.

His gaze followed hers to a small package resting on her dressing table, but he didn't go to it. Instead, he walked over to her and rested his hands at her waist. "I could want no greater gift than this," he said.

He felt her shudder beneath his palms. He would have liked to believe she quivered with impatience, as did he, but he reminded himself that his wife of three and a half months was still a virgin. This night—her first night—she deserved more than the feverish tumble his body cried out for.

But God, how he wanted her. He could not explain it, he knew only that she fired his blood like no other woman had ever done.

Gently he kneaded the firm flesh at her waist. She felt pliant and warm. He feathered a kiss at her brow and her eyelids fluttered shut like a butterfly's wings.

As her eyes closed he decided to take the most difficult aspect of this process out of her hands. He scooped her up and walked toward the bed. Her soft cry of surprise was muffled in his chest.

He set her down on the satin counterpane, the shadows deeper behind the bed hangings. Pressing a kiss to her neck, he slid his tongue from the hollow of her throat up to beneath her jaw. He couldn't be certain if it was the lingering taste of champagne, but she tasted buttery and sweet. And hot. Very, very hot.

He kissed the point of her chin, and the small indentation beneath her lower lip. As his tongue traced the curve of her jaw she moved slightly, her mouth seeking. Seeking his.

He smiled and caught her lower lip between his teeth. She moaned and his manhood swelled in response.

He worried her lip, alternately nipping, then licking, until her mouth had opened to him, vulnerable and inviting. He did not hesitate, but claimed it. Faith, she was sweet, sweeter than he'd even remembered.

He felt her hands settle tentatively on his shoulders as he reached down and pulled her shoes from her. He tried to go slowly but he was eager. He'd already sketched her as he had pictured she might look, and as he slowly peeled her gown and petticoat from her, he realized that his pen had not done her justice.

She was smooth strokes and softly curving lines. She wasn't perfectly proportioned or symmetrical but she was the most beautiful woman he had ever seen. Her breasts were small and round, peaked with tiny pink nubs, and her legs were long and willowy like those of a young colt. Her skin was a lustrous shade somewhere between gold, ivory, and white that reminded him of clotted cream.

"Do you . . . like me?"

Her hushed query made him realize that he'd been staring while she lay bare beneath his scrutiny.

"I like you very much," he answered, his voice raspy with need.

Quickly he discarded his jacket and tie, not once taking his eyes from her. That he might paint her like this, he thought. At the very least, he could put her form to memory.

Kneeling at her feet, he ran both palms up and over the backs of her calves, his hands lingering at the sensitive flesh behind her knees.

The texture of her skin was like no other's. He molded and shaped her calves and thighs, then traveled higher to firmly cup her buttocks.

He leaned forward to trace the ridge of her hipbone with his tongue and teeth. She was trembling, her skin like fire under his questing mouth. He circled her navel with kisses while delicately massaging her buttocks, then buried his face in her stomach. She gasped and her fingers clenched in his hair.

He felt as if he could enter her this way, simply lose himself in the honeysuckle sweetness of her flesh. He felt his control beginning to slip, and pulled away from her to shed the rest of his clothes. As his gaze devoured her he knew a moment's gratitude that Daphne was not shy about her body. And yet, even in her innocence, he somehow had not expected her to be.

"Take the pins from your hair," he asked, joining her

again on the bed. She did as he requested, her gaze ranging curiously over his chest and arms.

He drew his hands through her hair, spreading the thick, auburn curls over the pillow while dropping kisses across her shoulders and throat.

"Do you know what this is about?" he asked.

She nodded. "I think so."

"I'll make it as pleasurable for you as I can."

She nodded again and her trust amazed him.

He brought his mouth back to hers, that same powerful need he'd experienced before surging through him. His hands memorized every turn of her elbow, every curve of her breast.

"Touch me," he invited.

She did, her fingers lightly skimming his chest. As she grew bolder, venturing across his stomach and lower, Iain knew he'd made a mistake. Her touch was sending him over the edge.

He grabbed her hand and linked both of his through hers, then drew her arms up above her head. He then took the tip of her breast into his mouth, rolling the tight bud over his tongue and teeth, suckling.

"Oh, Iain. Oh." She tossed her head fitfully back and forth, her small cries whittling at his self-control.

His heart was pounding a rhythm that matched the pulsing in his groin. He wouldn't be able to hold out much longer.

He suckled deeper at her breast, pulling at her, feeling as if he could draw her light from her as a babe draws nourishment from its mother.

Her lower body was twisting beneath him, yearning for a pleasure it knew only through instinct. Her hands were still gripped in his, stretched high above her head.

Pressing his knee between her legs, he nudged them apart. She opened to him. He tested her, his fingers nimbly stroking up and over her. She bucked when his fingers flicked over the most sensitive part of her. She was more than ready for him, her honeysuckle-sweetness dampening his fingers.

He rose above her, then took her in one sure stroke, her slight resistance giving away easily to his invasion.

Claiming her mouth again, he waited to be certain she was all right. She moved beneath him. Eagerly.

He established a tempo, slow at first, which Daphne accelerated of her own accord. She urged him on, meeting his every thrust, giving of herself freely and naturally. Iain had never felt more aroused by a woman, so sensitive to a caress, so uncontrolled in his passion.

Daphne's cries grew more frantic, her movements more urgent.

"Yes," he said. "Yes, Daphne. Come to me."

With one final, ragged cry, she shuddered beneath him. Her climax sent Iain exploding in a flash of light. Brilliant, white light that wrapped around his body and squeezed his muscles taut.

He called out, the power of his own release wrenching her name from his throat. "Daphne!"

Then he collapsed, his arms giving way beneath him. He rolled sideways, careful not to crush her with his weight, his chest heaving as he labored for breath. Beside him he could hear Daphne's own breathing, irregular and shallow.

After a minute he heard something else. Whispering.

He curled over onto his side to look at her. She was staring up at the blue-and-gold-spangled canopy.

"What are you doing?" he softly asked.

"Wishing on a star."

"And what are you wishing?"

She smiled. "If I tell, it might not come true."

"Tell me anyway," he teased.

She turned her head toward him, her beautiful eyes shimmering in the dim light. "I was wishing that it might always be like this."

A pang leaped through him and he gathered her into his arms as he, too, made a wish. He wished that he had the power to make her wishes come true.

Wake up. Wake up, Lindley.

The sun had not yet crested the horizon, and the room was still shrouded in a blanket of dusky gray. Iain groaned, throwing his arm across his eyes and pulling the sheet from his bare chest.

Oh, for heaven's sake, Isadora murmured, averting her gaze. 'Twas a bitter enough pill to swallow to find Lindley in Daphne's bed without having to gaze upon his blatant nakedness.

I hope you're proud of yourself, she muttered, turning her back on him with an angry toss of her boa. *You've got what you wanted. Sacrificing Daphne's happiness to this worthless piece of land—*

Isadora stopped herself before she could build up a good head of steam. Although she would have loved nothing better than to give the unprincipled pup a severe tongue-lashing, there simply wasn't time for that. Bertie and Winnie were at this very moment prowling about the hidden passageways, intent on some form of deviltry.

Come on, Lindley. They're going to sneak off again before you can apprehend them!

She gave his shoulder a convincing shove and his eyes snapped open. A frown creased his forehead and he glanced over at Daphne, who was sleeping peacefully.

Look lively, boy! Isadora snapped. *Over by the fireplace.*

Iain's gaze immediately traveled to the hearth, and she realized with some satisfaction that her powers were growing more effective every day. She had only to concentrate and he could hear her, heeding her suggestions as if they'd come from his own thoughts.

Keep looking, she encouraged him.

Propped on one elbow, Iain was studying the fireplace, searching . . . searching. Suddenly he sat up.

He'd seen it. Her plan was going to work.

As he started to climb out of bed Isadora turned away and tartly instructed, *Clothe yourself, won't you?*

To her relief, when she finally deigned to look at him again, he'd slipped into his trousers—no shirt, alas—and was fingering the torn piece of cloth she'd wedged into the secret entrance.

Good. Now see if you can't locate the triggering device.

As directed, Iain set about exploring the numerous crevices and notches of the intricately carved wood mantel.

Isadora would have liked to have sped things along but she hadn't seen the Thompsons release the hidden door, so she didn't know how to activate it either. She floated upward to perch atop the bed's canopy, anxiously waiting while he searched.

Against her knee, she tapped her fan in an agitated rhythm. She wasn't feeling herself this morning. By all rights, she should have been pleased to discover that Iain and Daphne had mended their differences. Was that not her ghostly mission?

But then again, how could she expect to be content with the current circumstances? Nothing had changed. Lindley didn't love Daphne, he was only using her as a means to get his greedy hands on Ash Park. He might still very well break Daphne's heart now that he'd achieved what he'd set out to do.

Equally disconcerting, Isadora wondered if their reconciliation meant that her time as a ghost was over. This concerned her, for she had been worried about Daphne's welfare ever since Bertie and Winnie had left that threatening note in her daughter's room. She didn't honestly believe that the bumbling pair were capable of harming Daphne—the note had probably only been intended to frighten her—but she wasn't about to take any chances with her daughter's well-being. The Thompsons had to be exposed, and the sooner the better.

Hence her decision to rouse Iain from his bed this morning. Once she'd seen that Bertie and Winnie were planning to enter the tunnels, she'd decided she could not pass up this opportunity to be rid of the two. Even if she had to use Lindley to do it.

It did gall her that she was forced to rely on Iain to keep Daphne safe. She was still furious that he'd allowed Daphne to believe that *she* had been the guilty party in the wedding-day debacle. He'd never told Daphne the true reason he'd stormed out that day—that once he'd learned he couldn't have Ash Park, he had decided he didn't want her, either.

And then there was the matter of all that she'd overheard these past weeks. Lindley calling her a "dragon," "meddlesome," a "foul-tempered Tartar." She'd never been the sort to forgive and forget, and by Jove, she'd have her revenge before she was called away. See if she didn't.

A sharp click cut through the quiet and the fabric scrap tumbled to the floor as a panel in the fireplace swung open. Lindley fell back a step, obviously nonplussed by his discovery.

Splendid. Isadora floated down to where Iain was peering into the tunnel.

Frowning, he lit a candle and stepped into the passage. She saw him hesitate and cast an uneasy glance back at Daphne. Then he plunged forward into the tunnel.

Isadora followed him slowly, also uneasy about Daphne. She didn't want her daughter to awaken and find the panel open. The last thing Daphne needed to do was go crawling about these dusty, spider-infested corridors. That was Lindley's responsibility.

Isadora waited until Iain was a few yards into the tunnel before she pulled the panel shut. The loss of light and the door clicking shut alerted him and he spun around so swiftly that he knocked his head on the low ceiling and nearly extinguished the candle.

"Damn."

Isadora chuckled spitefully. If she were going to do Lindley a favor and lead him directly to the culprits, she saw no reason why she couldn't have some fun while doing so. After all, she did owe him.

A quick check on Winnie and Bertie in another branch of the tunnel confirmed that she had a few minutes to toy with Lindley. The Thompsons, with the aid of her father's portrait, were evidently trying to fabricate their own version of a ghost, complete with the requisite chains and white sheet. In any other situation, Isadora might have found their pathetic efforts entertaining.

As if a ghost remotely resembles a bed linen, she scoffed.

On her return to Lindley, she found him hobbling down the tunnel, his large frame hunched over.

Where shall we start? she asked, poking him in the ribs. He jerked.

She laughed, loudly enough for him to hear.

He whirled about awkwardly, striking his head again.

She snuffed out his candle. The tunnel grew darker than the blackest night.

A dragon, am I? she taunted. *Meddlesome? A Tartar?*

Down the dustiest forks of the labyrinth she led him, baiting him forward with whispered calls and taps against the wall.

This way.

Tap-tap.

Over here.

He stumbled through the icy darkness but pushed on, his face set in grim, determined lines.

Initially Isadora was enjoying her cat-and-mouse game, but as Lindley refused to exhibit any fear, to cower or to cringe, the sport began to lose its appeal. He was too full of nerve, this Ashingford, made of stouter stuff than she'd believed.

Not like his father had been.

Intent on her game, Isadora had lost track of Winnie and Bertie's whereabouts until she recollected her purpose. She flitted away to search for the pair, when suddenly she realized that they had heard Lindley approaching and were preparing to flee.

Fustian.

Hurriedly she attempted to lead Iain in their direction before they could escape the tunnel.

They mustn't get away, she told herself. *There might not be another opportunity to catch them red-handed.*

Weaving along the narrow confines, she rounded a bend and cried out in frustration. *Blast it!*

Light spilled into the empty corridor from a half-open panel. Bertie and Winnie had already fled the passage.

Hurry now, she urged, *we might still be able to trap them with their counterfeit props.*

She heard Iain shuffling behind her toward the light. He pushed at the small door that stood partly ajar and stumbled through the opening into the room.

He stood up, blinking, apparently trying to adjust his vision to the bright light. Morning had broken and was streaming through the windows, sparkling and white.

Isadora was about to pull Iain along to pursue the Thompsons when she recognized the chamber.

Winnie's bedroom. Of course, she should have known.

"Lindley!" an astonished voice cried.

As one, both Iain and Isadora turned to the voice that had come from the curtained bed.

Isadora wanted to scream or pull out her hair. There lay Winnie in her nightrail and cap, tucked into her bed, as calm as you please.

"Goodness, Lindley, how frightfully clever of you," Winnie said, flashing him a coy smile. "No one will ever know you're visiting me through there!"

But someone did know. And she stood in the corridor outside the open door to Winnie's bedroom.

Daphne's small sound of distress carried into every corner of the room, low and keening like the cry of a wounded animal.

No-o-o! Isadora groaned.

"Daphne," Iain said, clearly disoriented.

Isadora saw him glance around the room, finally taking in exactly where he was. His gaze then tore back to the doorway.

"Daphne!" This time a note of despair threaded his voice. He took three halting steps toward her before she stopped him.

"No!" she cried, extending her palm straight out, warding him off.

"But it's not—"

Daphne clasped her hands over her ears and closed her eyes, folding into herself.

Iain made a move toward her and her eyes snapped open.

"Don't," she brokenly pleaded. "Don't."

Then before Isadora fully realized what she had done, Daphne turned and ran.

Chapter
Sixteen

A rapping at the door disturbed her dreams.

"Daphne."

She smiled sleepily into her pillow. *Iain.*

Fighting to hang on to the dreamy, warm contentment, she burrowed deeper into the blankets.

"Daphne," the voice called again, familiar, yet not her husband's.

Slowly she opened her eyes.

Shadows stretched eerily across the strange room and she struggled to get her bearings. Then memory rushed over her in a suffocating rush. She wasn't asleep in her gilded bed at Ash Park; she was huddled beneath a threadbare blanket at some squalid inn in the middle of Wiltshire.

She sat up, her muscles pulling with fatigue. She'd walked for hours and hours today before Mr. Leslie's cart had come upon her and her feet were blistered and sore.

The rapping grew more demanding.

"Daphne?"

"Roger?"

Her legs cramped when she stood, but she limped to the door and fumbled in the darkness at the lock. As soon as she'd slid the bolt, the door swung open, forcing her to stumble back out of the way.

Roger charged into the room, his greatcoat swinging about him, his blond hair in chaotic disarray.

"Dear God," he gasped, and came to a standstill.

Daphne followed his gaze and looked down at herself, abruptly recalling the condition of her gown and the fact that she hadn't bathed since her long, dusty trip down the Dorset highways. Before she could offer an explanation, however, she felt herself swept up in Roger's embrace.

"My dear girl," he murmured, patting her back consolingly.

Over his shoulder, Daphne could see into the corridor where a sleepy-looking maid stood holding a lantern aloft.

Gently she pulled herself from his arms. "I . . . I cannot believe you're here," she stuttered, still half-asleep and a little dazed. "You traveled through the night?"

"Of course." Roger gripped her by the shoulders while his anxious gaze passed over her. "Your message scared the very wits from me. Are you sure you're all right?"

She nodded. "Yes. I'm sorry, I didn't mean for the note to frighten you. I was just very tired and ready to come home."

He looked past her into the dark, sparsely furnished chamber. "Well, I'm sure you won't wish to remain here one more minute than necessary." His pale brows drew together. "Where are your trunks?"

"They're, um . . . they're at Ash Park. I'll send for them later."

Roger looked poised to say something but must have thought better of it. He put his arm around her and guided her out the door, the maid lighting the way down the treacherous staircase.

As they passed through the inn's front room the smell of ale and onions caused Daphne's stomach to clench and she swallowed hard against a sudden wave of nausea. She'd eaten nothing more than a chunk of bread and a few bites of cheese since this accursed day had begun.

Outside beneath the moonlight, a fresh team was being hitched to the carriage. Daphne shivered and Roger pulled her closer to his side. Once the horses were ready, he helped her into the coach and she immediately tucked herself into a corner of the leather banquette.

Roger draped his coat over her, but she closed her eyes, remaining silent. She was too tired to face his questions tonight, wanting only to escape into the painless oblivion of sleep.

When next she awoke, the sky was still dark, although the sounds of early morning could be heard over the rumble of the coach wheels. The birds had begun their daybreak song and the cows lowed mournfully in the distance.

Daphne stretched her cramped legs, yawning behind her hand, then met Roger's watchful gaze.

"Good morning," he said.

She smiled self-consciously. "I . . . I must have been even more tired than I'd believed."

He dipped his chin in acknowledgement, but she could see by his expression that he had been waiting while she slept. Waiting for an explanation.

She chewed gently on her lower lip. "I can never thank you enough, Roger, for coming to fetch me. I hadn't expected a coach until morning and I certainly hadn't expected you to come yourself."

He looked at her askance. "Did you honestly believe I'd send John Coachman to get you after receiving a message like that?"

"Oh." Daphne flushed, embarrassed.

"Would you like now to tell me what you doing in an establishment like the Bronze Whistle?" he asked.

"Yes. Of course." She glanced down to her once-white gloves, now gray with dust. "First, let me say that I acted very foolishly. I can see that now."

Roger frowned. "I couldn't agree more. You should never have gone to see Lindley alone."

"Well, I . . . Perhaps you're right, but I wasn't speaking of that. I meant that I shouldn't have run away from Ash Park the way I did, dashing off as if I hadn't a bit of sense. I'm ashamed of myself. Mother would have been ashamed of me as well."

Roger straightened, his boyish features growing hard. "And what exactly did Lindley do to cause you to flee in such a manner?"

Daphne looked to her gloves again. Roger's possessive tone disturbed her, for although she greatly appreciated him traveling half the night to come to get her, she couldn't mislead him either. It wouldn't be fair.

"Iain is my husband," she said quietly. "What happened between us was between man and wife."

Roger bristled. "You needn't protect him, for God's sake. We'll contact your solicitors straightaway and take care of the annulment before any—"

"Roger . . ." She shook her head.

First puzzlement, then understanding clouded his blue eyes. Turning away, he brushed the curtain aside to stare out the coach window. "Did he—if he forced you . . ."

"No . . . it wasn't like that."

A tendon in Roger's jaw spasmed. "I see."

For the first time since yesterday morning Daphne felt tears burn at the backs of her eyes. She felt horrible, despicable. How could she have given her heart to someone like Iain Ashingford when a dear, sweet man like Roger would have had her for his own?

Roger continued to stare out the window and Daphne wished she could say something to ease his disappointment, but neither could she give him false hope. She was married to Iain and nothing could change that now.

"Your father has been asking for you."

Daphne stiffened with alarm. "He's barely acknowledged me these past months. Has he grown worse?"

Roger turned back to her, although his gaze didn't quite meet hers. "Actually, I believe he's faring better. He's still closeted in the library, but I've spoken with him nearly every day and he's beginning to break out of it, I think."

"Does he know I'm returning home?"

"I didn't inform him of your note, but I believe he was expecting you back soon."

Daphne frowned, losing herself in her concern for her father. The final minutes of the trip were passed in silence. When next she looked out onto the advancing dawn, Harkwell House loomed ahead.

"Are you not coming in?" she asked after Roger had helped her down from the carriage but had made no move to follow her into the house.

"No, I don't think I will, but I'll come by later this afternoon to see how you're getting on."

He took a step, then hesitated, his hat in hand. "You know, Daphne, I'm going to be returning to London next week to join my mother and sister. You might think about coming down as well. It would be good for you to get away and see the Town and I know that Deborah would love to have you stay with us."

"London?" she echoed.

"Yes. It's fairly quiet this time of year, but there are still plenty of diversions. I think you'd enjoy yourself."

Daphne gazed unseeing into the distance. When she'd fled Ash Park, she hadn't been thinking any further than returning home to safety and security. To a familiar haven.

Yet now, when she looked into the future, she saw the life that awaited her at Harkwell House as too safe and too secure—with too much time for reminiscences and regrets.

London had always been a dream of hers. Why shouldn't she seize it? Of course, her father's welfare was a consideration, but if he were well enough to travel . . .

"Yes, I'll consider it. I truly will."

Roger appeared surprised, yet pleased. "Fine, then. I'll see you this afternoon." With a perfunctory salute, he turned to leave but Daphne stalled him with a light touch at his arm.

"Thank you again, Roger. I owe you so very much."

His crooked, slightly melancholy smile nearly broke her heart. "'Tis no more than I'd do for any other friend," he answered.

Shoving his favored beaver onto his head, he left her standing on the porch, lamenting the unpredictable turns of the heart.

An hour later, after breakfast, a bath, and an interview with Jansen, Daphne stood uncertainly outside the door to her father's study. Although eager to see him after her week away, she was also frightened of what she might find.

Her father's health had suffered during these long months of mourning. Where once he'd been stout with the pleasures of life, the period of self-imposed isolation had left him thin and frail, aged beyond his years.

Not once since the day they'd buried her mother had he left Harkwell House and only rarely had he left his study. Too frequently, Daphne had found him in the cold, unlit room, slumped in a chair, silently weeping.

The severity of her father's grief unnerved her. Although she, too, had mourned her mother, she couldn't understand the depths of his torment. She had waited, allowing him to grieve, while hoping that someday he might be able to talk to her about his loss. Perhaps, she thought, that day had come.

She pushed open the door, calling into the gloom. "Papa?"

A shadow moved across the emptiness. "Daphne?"

Light from the hallway slanted a single beam into the study, revealing her father standing before the fireplace. His eyes were red-rimmed, his cheeks hollow.

She dug her fingernails into her palms.

"Here, let me open the curtains for you, Papa. You should see what a beautiful morning we have today." She walked across the room, and as she began pulling at the heavy curtains, dust billowed out from the fabric.

She coughed behind her hand. "You really must allow Jansen in to clean. It can't be good for you—"

"I'm glad you're here, Daphne."

His weary voice cut through her like a knife. She let go of the curtains and hurried to him, taking his hand in hers. His fingers were as cold as death.

"Roger said you'd asked after me. I . . . I had to go away for a few days—"

"Did you see Lindley?" her father interrupted.

She swallowed. "Let's go into the drawing room to talk. There's a lovely fire that will warm you right up."

He disregarded her plea. "I need to talk with you, Daphne. I should have done so before but . . . How could I have known?"

"I don't know how any of us could have," she answered, unsure if they were speaking of the same thing.

Her father's eyes abruptly focused on her as if seeing her from a great distance. "Is Lindley at Ash Park?"

She nodded, bewildered. She had thought he would wish to discuss his wife, not her estranged husband.

"How is the boy?"

"I—I'd rather not speak of Lord Lindley right now, Papa. Wouldn't you prefer to discuss . . . Mother?"

He wagged his head. "It's one and the same, Daphne. One and the same."

She tried to hide her disappointment. Roger had claimed Papa was improving, but in her opinion, he appeared even less coherent than before she'd left for Ash Park.

"Mayhaps you should rest," she suggested, leading him to a chair.

He obediently sank into it and Daphne folded onto her knees at his feet. She waited, expectant, hoping that by listening she might ease some of her father's heartache.

"You cannot know how difficult it is," he said slowly, painfully. "To forgive is no easy matter, especially when you must begin by forgiving yourself."

She looked up at him, confused.

"Do you know, Daphne, that not a night goes by where I don't fall to my knees and pray that your mother might come back to me? For only a moment. Just long enough to say that I am sorry."

"Whatever could you be sorry for?"

"I should have listened to her, Daphne, she felt so strongly about it all. If only I had listened, she might be alive today."

"That's madness." She clutched at his hand. "You cannot hold yourself responsible."

"But if I had relented and done as she asked. If I hadn't forced the marriage—"

"Papa! Is this what torments you?" she asked in horror. "I wanted to marry Iain, you know that I did. You cannot possibly blame yourself for that.

"We both know that it wasn't the marriage that killed Mother. She simply . . . died. Yes, it's easier to find fault, to cast blame, but it still doesn't hide the truth. And the truth is: Her time had come."

"But it was too soon," her father cried. "If only I'd had time to tell her that I loved her."

"She knew that you loved her."

"But I never told her."

Daphne caught her breath.

During thirty years of marriage her father had never told her mother that he loved her? But why? Their union had been a happy one, if stormy at times. Granted, her mother's domineering personality had overshadowed her father's, but the two had shared many interests: a love of music, literature, horses. They *had* been content, Daphne knew it.

"Oh, Daphne. I often accused your mother of being proud, but I was as guilty of that sin as she ever was. She wouldn't declare her feelings, so I never spoke of mine."

"I—I don't understand."

Her father slouched back in the chair and stared vacantly at the empty hearth as memories seemed to carry him back decades earlier.

"I knew she didn't love me when we married—she told me so straight out—but I had decided that I didn't care. I wanted her. She was magnificent with her flaming red hair and a spirit to match. I was determined to have her on any terms . . . even if it meant marrying her when she was in love with another man."

"Mother?" she echoed in a near whisper.

"Yes." His voice cracked. "She'd been in love with the young Earl of Yorkton."

Yorkton. The name was familiar. . . .

"James Ashingford, the Marquess Lindley's son."

Daphne felt as if her world were tilting out of control. Her mother in love with Iain's father?

"But you said that she despised the Ashingford family," Daphne weakly protested.

"She did. Fervently. But only after she ended her romance with Yorkton. Her father, the Earl of Whiting, had convinced her that Yorkton was only interested in her marriage settlement. That he wanted Ash Park, not her."

Ash Park. The words rang through Daphne's mind like the toll of a bell.

"Although Isadora followed Whiting's counsel, she never forgave him for forcing her to see the ugly truth of the matter. She broke it off with Yorkton, but she also left Ash Park, furious with her father. She went to London, where she and I were wed within the fortnight."

"So she jilted Iain's father—the Earl of Yorkton?"

"Yes, she believed he'd proposed only to bring the Ashingford estate back to his family."

"What do you mean 'bring it back'?"

"Ash Park belonged to the Ashingfords until your grandfather won it in a card game almost fifty years ago. The Ashingfords claim that Whiting cheated them of the property."

"Did he?"

Her father shrugged. "The truth will probably never be known."

"So Mother was right about Yorkton's intentions?"

"Not entirely. You see, I know for a certainty that Yorkton honestly and truly loved her."

Daphne went cold, premonition bringing goose bumps to her arms. "Why do you say that?"

Her father closed his eyes, his expression pained. "Yorkton was gravely injured in a riding accident. It was a rainy night and he had been riding recklessly, jug-bitten. He had just received word of our engagement, you see, and he was on his way to stop the wedding."

"Oh—" Daphne clasped her hands over her mouth, holding back her gasp.

"When we learned of the accident, your mother refused to believe he'd been coming for her. Her pride wouldn't allow her to admit that she could have been wrong.

"I, on the other hand, never completely forgave myself.

Although I loved Isadora dearly, I suppose I always felt as if I had her at Yorkton's expense."

"Oh, dear God. Did Iain know all this?"

"Yes, he knew."

Daphne was glad she wasn't standing. She could scarcely believe that their two families had been so hopelessly entangled dating as far back as . . .

Her shock began to recede as she slowly pieced the rest of the clues together. "So, even though Iain's father eventually fell in love with Mother, he had initially sought her out because of Ash Park?"

"Yes."

Understanding swamped Daphne in a sickening wave. "But James Ashingford didn't succeed, did he?" she asked. "He didn't secure the estate. Therefore his son, Iain, took up where James had faltered." Dear heavens, why hadn't she known before? "He married me for Ash Park, didn't he?"

Her father's eyes were sad. "Many fine marriages are built on less."

A mirthless laugh caught in her throat. "And this was why Mother opposed Iain's suit, wasn't it? She feared history was repeating itself."

"But you cannot forget, Daphne, that Yorkton *did* love Isadora," her father argued. "Who's to say Lindley might not feel the same for you?"

"I say," she retorted.

"But you haven't yet given it a chance. For the love of God, don't make the same error your mother did. Don't let pride blind you to the truth."

Daphne was going to blurt out the truth of finding her husband in his mistress's bedchamber, when suddenly she realized that her father was more animated than she'd seen him in months. His face was alive, his voice vibrating with emotion.

Anger slowly seeped out of her.

"And what of you, Papa? You cannot believe that Mother continued to love another man all these years?"

"No." His mouth turned up in a half smile. "When we wed, she told me she would never love me and I answered her that it didn't matter. But you know your mother—she couldn't allow, even decades later, that she'd made a mistake. She did come to care for me, I know. She simply couldn't bend her pride enough to say so."

"La, she was stubborn."

"Yes," her father fondly agreed. "Very much like your Lindley."

Daphne frowned. *Her* Lindley.

The numbness she'd wrapped around herself was beginning to wear thin. It hurt to hear his name; it hurt to even think of him. She needed an escape.

"Papa," she said hesitantly. "I was contemplating perhaps taking a trip to London. What would you say to that?"

Her father eyed her shrewdly, like the father of her past. "I'd first say forgive and forget, daughter. Then I would say enjoy yourself."

Daphne ignored the former statement. "Are you not going to come with me?"

He glanced around the study as if seeing it for the first time. "No, not yet. I'm not quite ready."

"But you will be soon?" she asked encouragingly.

He smiled, softening his drawn features. "Don't worry about me, my dear. Think of yourself and where you want to be."

"I told you, Papa. I'm going to London."

He nodded. "Yes, Daphne. Where you want to be."

Chapter
Seventeen

"I thought I might find you here."

Iain looked up from his sketch pad with a frown. He'd been so absorbed in his work, he'd failed to note the cottage door opening.

Dobbs stood on the threshold, a newspaper tucked under his arm, smiling like the proverbial canary-eating cat.

"I'm going to have to get a lock for that door," Iain commented, nonchalantly placing his sketch pad facedown on the rustic farm table.

Dobbs stepped into the cottage. "Not that it would do you any good, you know. You can't be rid of me so easily."

"If it were easy," Iain retorted, "I'd have been rid of you years ago."

The grinning valet strolled into the one-room cottage, gazing around. "So this is where you've been hiding, licking your wounds."

Iain shot him a forbidding glance. "I haven't been hiding. I've been busy."

Dobbs cocked a graying brow. "Right. Busy."

He approached the table and picked up one of the pastels lying beside the pad. "A thoughtful offering," he remarked in a manner far too offhand to be casual. "How do you suppose she knew?"

Iain glanced to the set of chalks. After Daphne had fled, he'd been reluctant to open her "birthday" gift, but Dobbs's persistence and his own curiosity had eventually broken him down. When finally he'd torn open the beribboned package, he'd experienced a strange combination of surprise, outrage, and . . . despair. He'd put the set away, unable to bring himself to use them until today.

"I presumed you'd told her."

Dobbs shook his head with an exaggerated frown. "Not I. Your doodling, as you insist on calling it, is your affair."

"Hmm-mm," Iain murmured disbelievingly, plucking the pastel from his valet's fingers. "What was it you wanted, Dobbs?"

The valet withdrew the paper from beneath his arm. "There was a fascinating little bit in the *Herald* that I thought I might share with you."

"What? You came all the way out here to—"

Dobbs thrust the periodical under his nose and Iain had no choice but to focus on the illustration at the top of the page.

"Quite a good likeness, wouldn't you say?" Dobbs's voice seemed to come to him from miles away.

The drawing depicted Daphne at a gaming table, surrounded by a pack of besotted young bucks. The cartoonist had actually drawn the young men as bucks, complete with antlers, their adoring expressions comical in the extreme.

Only Iain wasn't laughing.

Underneath the cartoon, the caption read "The charming Marchioness Lindley gambling with Hearts."

Iain thought that he might very well explode. Most literally. Blood pulsed through him so hot and furious that he didn't believe his skin could possibly hold it in.

"Damn it to hell!"

He shot out of his chair like a cannon blast, the paper falling to the table.

"What the bloody hell is she doing in London?" he demanded. "Kane had said she'd gone to Harkwell House!"

Dobbs smiled slyly. "You sent someone after her?"

"Well, I had to make certain she returned home safely, didn't I?" Iain thrust both hands into his hair, more to keep his head on than for any other reason.

"Hmm-mm."

Iain rounded on his valet. "Did you know she was going to London? Did you?"

Dobbs smiled sweetly and shrugged. "I had no inkling, my lord. None at all."

Iain slammed his fist onto the table. "Gambling of all things! The Whiting curse! She'll lose every farthing she's got."

"And how much that might be?" Dobbs put in.

Iain turned to him, comprehension curdling his stomach. "My God. She'll lose every farthing *I've* got. A man is legally responsible for his wife's debts, after all. She could . . . she could even wager away Ash Park!"

The valet leaned over his arm to take another gander at the drawing. "And that's why you're so upset, eh? Worried about losing Ash Park?" Dobbs gave him a dubious look.

"Of course I'm worried about it!" Iain retorted. "The silly girl couldn't bluff herself out of a sack the way she allows every blasted emotion to show on her face."

"And you, my lord, are such a stoic," Dobbs murmured dryly. "You do realize, I hope, that if you'd heeded my advice you'd have known Lady Lindley's whereabouts these past two weeks."

Iain glared at him. "I have what I wanted from this marriage. I see no reason to chase a runaway bride half across England."

"No. No reason at all," his valet concurred, casting another pointed glance at the cartoon.

Narrowing his eyes, Iain wondered where Dobbs must hide his pitchfork and horns. "You are a demon, you know that?"

The bald, round-faced valet smiled at him like a cherub. "I merely serve my master."

"Hmm-mm. I imagine you've already begun packing?"

"We should be ready to depart by noon. I sent a message an hour ago to alert the townhouse staff of our arrival."

"Splendid," Iain said, openly sarcastic. "Did it never occur to you that I might not choose to go to London?"

"No, my lord. Never occurred to me."

Iain scratched resignedly at his chin. "Perhaps it's for the best. While I'm in Town, I can have Stephens come by."

"The physician?"

"'Tis nothing, I'm certain," Iain said. But to himself he privately thought, Only my vision, my hearing, and my memory. "Probably naught more than fatigue."

Dobbs grinned. "I doubt Mr. Stephens can help you with your particular ailment. There hasn't been a man yet who's found a cure."

After imparting final instructions to the steward, Iain sat down at his desk and set to gathering up his business papers.

He'd been uncharacteristically lax in attending to his affairs during the past fortnight and certain documents required his attention sooner rather than later. He'd informed Thompson that he'd only be away a few weeks, but he wasn't truly certain how long he might have to remain in Town.

Restraining an errant wife might prove to be a time-consuming endeavor.

For all of Dobbs's needling, Iain acknowledged that more than a fear for Ash Park was sending him haring off to London. The rapt expressions on those antlered faces had struck a chord of jealousy that Iain could not dismiss. It galled him to think that Society's first introduction to his wife was under such circumstances. The gay, young newlywed kicking up her heels. Who knew what type of scandal she could be visiting upon his name? Could he be the joke of the *ton,* the absent cuckold?

Daphne was unquestionably a passionate woman, who might very well have revenge on her mind. He knew what she thought. He knew that he could have gone after her and dissuaded her of the misconception. But he hadn't.

And he didn't know why he hadn't.

A small part of him felt that if he had pursued her, it would have been tantamount to an admission.

But an admission of what?

He raked his fingers through his hair with a heartfelt sigh. It had been a damned difficult two weeks at Ash Park. Silent, unearthly so. Where once he had found the estate's quiet peaceful, he now found himself straining for the sound of Daphne's laughter. He didn't like admitting it, but he missed her light-filled smile, her perpetual cheerfulness. He couldn't gaze at a night sky anymore without counting the stars. He couldn't sit beside the creek without searching for a four-leaf clover.

And while he'd been occupied with these frivolous distractions, Daphne had been in London, taking the *ton* by storm. Toying with young blades' hearts. Gambling.

The Whitings's predilection for wagering was of genuine concern to him. Many of Daphne's forebears had met financial ruin in games of chance, her grandfather having resorted to chicanery to ensure his winnings. Iain didn't like to think of Daphne, unsupervised at a gaming table, with the blood of the Whitings singing through her veins.

Frankly, he didn't like to think of Daphne at all.

He knew that when he finally confronted her, she would be furious with him and reasonably so.

Their wondrous night of passion had left even him feeling raw and exposed; how must she have felt to have found him in Winnifred's room?

He could have raced after her and explained, but he had been shocked and disoriented. The nightmarish journey through the coal-black tunnels, the strange noises and bumps, had had his imagination running wild. Then, suddenly, he had ended up in Winnifred's bedchamber with Daphne standing in the doorway.

To be honest, her immediate condemnation had disappointed him. The situation had been damning, true—but she hadn't afforded him one fraction of the trust she seemed to give so freely to others. She hadn't given him the chance to explain and he had been too bloody proud to beg for it.

Once he'd learned that she'd fled the estate, he'd rationalized his decision not to follow her. He'd achieved his goal. Ash Park was firmly in his grasp. Yet that knowledge had yielded scarce comfort during the past fortnight.

Unable to sleep, he had roamed the halls at night while his eyes and ears had played tricks with his sanity. Noises without source, images that faded in the flash of an eye. He suspected that lack of rest accounted for the weakening of his senses, yet to his surprise, his sketches had emerged sharper and clearer than ever before.

Hours he had passed in the gatekeeper's cottage, each day producing a fresh portrait of Daphne. He had tried to draw anything else—the countryside, his father, even another self-portrait—but his muse had only one face. Heart-shaped with moss-green eyes and a wide, generous mouth.

Iain snapped his head to the side, wresting the ever-present vision from his mind's eye.

Forcing himself back to his paperwork, his gaze fell on the phoenix-embossed snuffbox resting on the corner of his desk. Impulsively he reached out and tucked the box into his waistcoat pocket. It was a sentimental gesture, since he dipped snuff only on occasion, but Iain felt as if he'd like to take a piece of Ash Park with him to London. A good-luck charm, his wife would have dubbed it.

As directed by the efficient Dobbs, the small entourage left Ash Park by midday. They passed the night at a posting inn, then spent the following day entirely in travel. Loath to spend another night in an unfamiliar bed, Iain instructed his driver to push on, so that it was nearing midnight when the carriage pulled up outside the Ashingford town house on Grosvenor Square.

Light shone from the front windows in evidence of his anticipated arrival. As Iain stepped from the coach the stagnant aroma of London assailed him, and he unconsciously reached for the fragrant relief of his snuffbox while climbing the few steps to the entrance.

Dobbs and the footman had preceded him, so that the door stood open as Iain walked in. He was momentarily blocked by the valet and two other servants, all loitering on the threshold.

"What's going on here?" Iain grumbled, having to push his way into his own home. "Step aside."

They did and Iain saw what had held them in place.

Daphne and a strange man were frozen in an intimate tableau at the center of the foyer. The man, tall and blond, hovered behind Daphne, arrested in the act of placing a gold satin cape about her shoulders. Daphne, her shoulders bared by the daring cut of her evening gown, stood with her chin high, her eyes wide, her manner dignified.

She didn't look the least ruffled. She looked . . . beautiful.

Iain could not take his eyes from her as emotions ricocheted chaotically through him. He had never expected to find her here. At his house. His home. Naturally, he hadn't known where she was staying in London but he hadn't thought she'd have the nerve to take over his residence. Strangely enough, he secretly liked that she had.

He hadn't quite gathered his wits before Daphne coolly introduced him, her eyes shuttered behind half-lowered lashes.

"Iain, what a pleasant surprise. Allow me to introduce Sir Roger Cunningham. Roger, my husband, the Marquess Lindley."

Iain automatically nodded and the other man curtly returned the salute.

Daphne hooked the clasp to her cape. "You must be tired from your trip," she said, running a disinterested glance over his dusty figure. "Roger and I were just on our way out for the evening."

She stepped toward the door and her movement released Iain from his momentary paralysis.

"Wait!" he instructed.

Daphne and her shadowlike companion paused halfway across the front hall. Iain glanced about as if seeking assistance and noted that the servants had all slipped away. Only he, his wife, and her escort remained.

"Yes?" Her polite query held the slightest tinge of impatience.

Iain breathed in, hoping to steady himself, and the scent of honeysuckle wrapped around him like a noose. Impotent fury held him speechless as his fingers tightened spasmodically around the snuffbox in his pocket.

Daphne smiled, like no smile he'd ever seen from her. "Until later, then."

And before Iain could free himself from his immobilizing rage, she and the stranger were gone.

He stood there for a long moment, battling for self-control. He lost.

With a vile oath, he flung the box he was clutching across the foyer, where it hit the wall with a satisfying smack.

"Ouch!"

Iain looked to the wall, his gaze swiftly encircling the room.

"Dash it all, Lindley, you can't kill me twice!"

His gaze jerked back to the far side of the hall. "Who is that?" he demanded. "Who's speaking to me?"

"It's me, you imbecile! Don't you recognize my voice?"

His heart commenced an agitated tattoo. That throaty voice was familiar, but . . .

Slowly Iain crossed the room, looking left, then right, then left again. Every creak of the floor, each hiss of the lantern was magnified in the interminable seconds it took to traverse the small foyer.

He stopped and stood directly over the snuffbox lying sideways on the parquet floor. The lid was ajar and a faint glow seemed to be coming from inside the box.

He didn't move. He didn't breathe.

"Oh, for God's sake, Lindley," the voice petulantly proclaimed. *"It's me. Isadora."*

Chapter Eighteen

She had to give him credit. The rascal kept his feet, although his sun-browned face paled two shades. He staggered back a step and almost overturned an urn behind him.

"This is a joke. Some type of prank." His gray eyes madly swept the foyer. "Dobbs is behind this, isn't he?"

"No, although I must confess, I like your Dobbs. He's an entertaining sort."

Like a man facing the executioner's ax, Iain stared down at the snuffbox where she resided.

"Come now," she chided. *"You shouldn't be so excessively put out. Hadn't you suspected I was here?"*

"Who here?" he demanded, his palms pressed to his temples, his eyes looking a bit buggy.

"Me. Your mother-in-law."

Iain weaved his way backward to the staircase, where he sat down clumsily, his head in his hands, elbows on knees.

"Dementia. My God, I'm too young. Can't be the pox and there's no history of insanity in the family—no, Aunt Eugenia! Damned if the old girl wasn't short a sheet!"

"You're not mad, Lindley, though I wager everyone will believe you so if they discover you out here, talking to yourself. We really should adjourn to another room for this conversation."

His dark head tilted up. "What?"

"Someone's bound to come along and I'm not permitted to reveal myself to anyone but you."

"You aren't, are you?" His voice sounded half-strangled.

"Don't you have a library in such showy lodgings?"

He looked as if he'd just been tossed a lifeline. "Yes, the library. A brandy is what I need."

Seizing a candelabra, he lurched to his feet in the direction of a closed door.

"What about me?" she called. *"You cannot simply leave me here in the foyer for anyone to find."*

He stopped, looking furtively about. "What am I supposed to do with you?" he hissed.

"Pick me up and take me with you. I'm hampered under these circumstances, you know."

By his expression, she could see that he didn't know at all, but he approached her cautiously.

"I won't bite," she goaded.

His face screwed up in patent repugnance, he picked the enameled box up from the floor, gingerly dangling it between a thumb and forefinger.

"I *must* be mad," he muttered. "Taking orders from a snuffbox."

He fairly ran to the library, slamming the door shut behind him. Her, he disrespectfully pitched onto the bar next to a decanter of port.

She watched him throw back two snifters of brandy before commenting, *"Quite the Lord Thirstington, aren't you, Lindley?"*

He set the snifter down, his gray eyes hardening. "I see only two feasible possibilities here. Either I am all about in the head or this is one exquisitely elaborate hoax."

Isadora smirked. *"Had your share of hoaxes lately, haven't you, Lindley?"*

He gazed down at her temporary quarters. "How do you know that?"

Isadora bit her lip. Oh, now she'd done it. By mentioning the pranks, she implicated only herself—when the Thompsons were as much to blame as she was. Already she'd been reprimanded for her involvement in trying to unmask Bertie and Winnie. The spectral authorities had made clear that she wasn't to involve herself in anything but the reuniting of her daughter and Lindley or else forfeit her chance to ascend to heaven.

She squirmed, ill at ease. *"I've been with you for some time, months now."*

Iain refilled his glass and dropped into a wingback chair, his brandy sloshing over onto his hand and shirt cuff. He seemed not to notice. "I've never heard of it being like this," he whispered.

"Like what?"

"Insanity. I believe I'm lucid, but look at me. I'm holding a conversation with a chunk of wood."

Isadora sniffed. *"Mind your tongue, boy. I'm no chunk of wood, I'm merely inhabiting one."*

He cocked a belligerent brow at her. "What's that supposed to mean?"

"I'm not a snuffbox, for heaven's sake. I'm a ghost!"

Iain closed his eyes and laughed. "Of course. How obtuse of me. How could I confuse a talking snuffbox with a ghost?"

His ridicule set Isadora's teeth on edge. *"Listen to me,*

you fool. I am a ghost, bound to Ash Park. I didn't believe I could leave the estate, but I'd been experimenting and discovered that I could inhabit an object native to the property. The snuffbox, for one."

"Ah, what tremendous luck that I didn't leave you at home," he mocked.

Luck had little do with it, but Isadora saw no need to tell him so. Her whispered suggestions were an advantage she'd just as soon keep to herself.

Iain tossed down another shot of brandy, then replenished the snifter once more. This time when he fell into the chair, the liquor splashed his trousers and boots.

"I'll tell you what, little ghost, why don't you go back to Ash Park and do your haunting there?"

"I cannot."

"And why not?" Iain asked.

"My mission isn't to haunt Ash Park. You, Lindley, are my designated project."

"What?" He let out a surprised bark of laughter. "You didn't get a big enough piece of me when you were alive?"

"Hmmph. You're bosky."

"I'll say one thing, you've certainly mastered the Harkwell sniff." He tipped his glass in her general direction. "But I still maintain that you are nothing more than a fancily concocted, very convincing prank. How can you assure me that you're really the dragon-lady's spirit?"

She gritted her teeth. *"You're a bold one when I'm trapped in this box,"* she muttered.

"Let's have it," he insisted. "Either I have proof of your identity or I'll toss you into the street with the horse offal."

"Ah!" Isadora gasped.

"Don't test me," he warned. "I'm not in the most benevolent of moods. My wife is, at this moment, gadding about Town with some blond bloke I've never laid eyes on, probably gambling away half my fortune. So I'm not of a mind to be merciful."

"As if you ever were," she snapped. *"Very well, Lindley, if you must have proof. Do you remember when you floored your charming friend Whinny?"*

"That's Winnie," he corrected.

"Whatever. Do you recall the poke in your ribs that had you spinning around like a top? That was me, you goose, not a bedbug."

He sat up in the chair. "Never say!"

"Yes, that was me. And how do you suppose Daphne received the note you had drafted for the Comtesse, hmm? Did you never figure that one out?"

Iain was straining forward now. "*You* were responsible?"

"I was."

"What of the other incidents? The breeze without wind, the midnight noises, the glowing objects?"

Isadora waffled. *"Now, I cannot take credit for all those occurrences, but many, yes."*

Iain sank back into the chair with a *whoof* of relief. "So I'm not going deaf or blind or bird-witted. That is . . . if you are to be believed." His expression grew suddenly grave. "What about the threatening note to Daphne?"

"Really!" she exclaimed. *"As if I'd do such a thing to my own daughter! Ghosts have principles like everyone else, you know."*

"Principles, hmm?" He tapped his fingertips thoughtfully against the snifter cradled between his hands. "And I would imagine that you have certain . . . powers?"

"I do, although I assure you they didn't come easily. As I said before, I've had to work at it. When I first arrived at Ash Park, why, I could barely even levitate."

"Do it now, then," he commanded, waving a hand into the air. "Levitate for me."

"Aren't you listening, Lindley? I cannot leave the snuff-

box while I'm away from Ash Park. I cannot levitate or float about or anything else."

He still looked skeptical. "Why, then, haven't you spoken to me before tonight? Or does the snuffbox liberate your powers of speech?"

Isadora rolled her eyes. Her son-in-law was a truculent drunk. *"I've had to work up to it. These skills come slowly and only with practice."*

He rose unsteadily to his feet. The brandy decanter was empty, so he switched to port. "I fail to understand why you must haunt *me,* Isadora. I would think that during your natural lifetime you would have wreaked enough havoc on the Ashingford men."

Isadora tensed. *"This has naught to do with your fath—"*

"He loved you, you know."

The slurred words caught her like a blow. *"Lindley, don't,"* she directed in her most compelling voice.

"Didn't want to believe it, did you?" he persisted. "But he did. And he suffered for it."

Isadora drew herself up as best as she could in the confines of the snuffbox. *"I was no more liable for your father's accident than you were for my death,"* she haughtily pointed out.

That observation seemed to penetrate his drunken haze. She could see him mulling over the comparison.

"If anyone is to be held accountable for the way they've mistreated someone, I suggest you take a good look at yourself, Iain Ashingford. And the manner in which you've exploited my daughter."

He had the good grace to look momentarily abashed. "Just how much do you know?"

"Enough."

"So you've been sent by the Ghost King to reprimand me?"

"Flippancy doesn't suit you, Lindley."

"Then why the hell are you here, Isadora?" he growled, growing more combative with each gulp of his drink.

"I'm not allowed to tell you the purpose of my mission."

Iain let loose a foul expletive.

"Watch your language, you insolent creature! There is a lady present."

He chuckled wickedly. "I think you'll be hearing worse where you're headed, Baroness."

Isadora clutched at her throat. Oh dear, she had to get to heaven. . . .

"Look here, Lindley, although I can't disclose my assignment, if you will only cooperate with me—"

"Ha! This is a far cry from our last interview, wouldn't you say, Lady Harkwell? Last time we spoke, you were issuing ultimatums."

"Must you be so stubborn?"

"I must."

"La, if you weren't so deucedly pigheaded, you wouldn't have walked out on Daphne in the first place!"

Iain screwed up his mouth in a bitter smile. "Now Daphne has walked out on me."

"It's no more than you deserve, you bounder. Why, if I'd had—"

Isadora literally bit her tongue. She could not forget what she had been appointed to do, no matter how desperately she longed to throttle the tipsy fool.

"Ah, interesting point you bring up about getting what you deserve, ghostly lady. What of your role in this nasty affair? Who were you thinking of that day, yourself or your daughter? Wasn't it really a case of your decades-old bitterness barring the way to Daphne's happiness?"

"It most certainly was not!"

Iain shook his head, his dark hair flopping ungracefully across his forehead. "Alas, Isadora, I have higher fences to jump than settling the score with one dead mother-in-law."

He grabbed up the snuffbox.

"What are you doing, Lindley?"

"I do apologize, but I have just realized that I cannot allow you to interfere again."

The distant click of a key in a lock hushed them both.

"Is that Daphne returning?" Isadora asked.

The squeak of a hinge, followed by a soft tread, supported that deduction.

Iain stumbled hurriedly to the desk, then opened the uppermost drawer, tossing the snuffbox inside.

"We'll have to finish this conversation later, Isadora. I must speak to Daphne."

"No, wait, Lindley, listen to me—"

The drawer slammed shut on her plea, thrusting Isadora into darkness.

As soon as she let herself into the town house, Daphne spied the light beneath the door of the library, that also served as Iain's study and sitting room.

She wasn't altogether surprised that he had waited up for her, yet felt slightly irritated that he had done so. She'd been enjoying her time in London—the freedom, the attention, the frivolity—all new and exhilarating intoxicants when compared to her staid country upbringing.

She picked up a candle stand from the foyer table and deliberately turned her back to the library door.

"Home early, I see?"

The sardonic voice checked her steps.

"Yes," she answered, without turning around. "Good night."

"Good night?"

She lifted her skirts to climb the stairs, but his heavy stride sounded behind her. The next thing she knew Iain was standing in front of her, barring her path.

Her gaze skimmed him with what she hoped passed for disdain. In reality, his appearance had given her a start.

Iain was usually so meticulous in his dress, but he hadn't yet changed and his traveling clothes were rumpled and soiled. The cuffs of his shirt were stained a pale amber, his limp cravat hung loosely about his neck.

But what disturbed her most were the new lines around his mouth and the bleakness at the back of his eyes. He looked as if he hadn't slept in weeks. The bones of his cheeks jutted out sharply, emphasizing the dark circles beneath his eyes.

"You look frightful," she said.

"Frightful or frightening?" He leered at her, his breath hot with the tangy bite of liquor.

"And you're foxed."

"Guilty as charged."

She didn't find his glibness amusing.

"Excuse me. I'm going to bed," she announced, attempting to slip past him.

"Not alone, I hope?" He moved to block her. "Or have you already been to bed this evening?"

Daphne drew in her breath. "You are offensive."

A corner of his mouth twisted down. "I'm many things, dear wife, none of them nice."

His self-pity should have left her unmoved, but it didn't. Her memories recalled many nice things about Iain Ashingford, many wonderful, beautiful things.

Instead she remarked, "Pray don't expect me to argue with you."

"I don't."

She held her ground, wondering how long this standoff might last. The candle stand in her hand wavered, scattering serpentine images across the Chinese wallpaper.

"Where were you this evening?"

Daphne was tempted not to answer. "Lady Campton held a small soiree."

"Was there gaming?"

Her lips thinned with annoyance. "Yes, Iain, it was like any other party. Cards, music, people."

"How much did you lose?"

"I beg your pardon?"

"Did you play the games of chance? You and Roger?" he added contemptuously.

Daphne's temper rose. "Oh, this is absurd. I needn't tolerate this."

She tried to push by him but he grabbed at the hand holding up her skirts.

"Answer me, dammit. Did you gamble?"

"No!" she fired back. "Why do you care?"

Their gazes locked.

Suddenly he loosened his grip on her, twisting his hand so that his bare fingers were stroking the inside of her wrist. "Don't you know that I care about everything concerning you, Daphne?"

His voice had softened to a rumbling tenderness that left her breathless and bewildered.

How could he do this? How could he play her as deftly as a musician played a violin? One minute he had her strung tight and high-pitched, the next he had her vibrating to his merest touch.

"Why are you here?" she asked, unable to mask her confusion. "Why did you come to London?"

"I need to talk to you."

"What if I don't wish to speak with you?"

"I would beg your indulgence."

She arched an incredulous brow. Iain Ashingford begging?

"Cannot it at least wait till morning?"

He gave her one of those diabolically appealing smiles. "I'm feeling rather brave at the moment."

Unfortunately she wasn't—only lemonade bolstered her courage—but she nodded her head in acquiescence. She was headed for the library when he stopped her.

"No!"

She swung back to him. His color had risen.

"I'd prefer to go upstairs," he explained.

Her expression must have revealed her ambivalence, for he clarified, "The drawing room."

She nodded, preceding him up the stairs by the light of the single candle. In the drawing room, she lit another stand and placed it on the mantel. The room was still very dark, the windows shuttered against the night.

When she turned, she found Iain staring at her.

"You look beautiful, Daphne."

She glanced to the dress of French gauze over a gold silk slip that had cost, to her mind, a small fortune. It was a daring gown, but she had been feeling extremely reckless the day she had ordered it.

"I'm glad you like it. You paid dearly for it."

He smiled. "I admire my taste, although I wasn't speaking of your gown. You are beautiful, don't you know? I hadn't thought so when we first met, but you truly are."

Daphne frowned as he drew closer to the mantel.

"It's not a conventional beauty, but whenever I think of you, I see you as full of light. Luminous."

She felt a blush steal into her cheeks. "Just how much have you imbibed this evening?"

"Too much," he confessed. He took another step toward her and Daphne darted around him, swiftly seating herself in a stiff, spindle-back chair.

Iain sighed and leaned awkwardly against the mantelpiece, looking as if he might tip over at any moment.

"You know, I told myself I was coming to London to make certain that you weren't gambling away my riches—"

Daphne nearly choked. "Y-you what?"

He hefted a shoulder. "With your family history being what it is, I was concerned that you were afflicted as so many of the Whitings have been—"

"You're daft, do you know that?"

She was halfway out of her chair, poised to march out of the room, when Iain tossed a scrap of paper at her. The cartoon from the *Herald*.

She pressed her lips together and sank back into the chair.

"'Twas nothing more than a sorry jest," she said. "One evening at a card party and then this." She waved her hand disparagingly over the illustration.

"What of the drawing's other implication?"

She glanced up and met his gaze, intense and smoky gray in the shadows. Could he be jealous? she wondered. Iain Ashingford?

Coolly suffering his regard, she put the question to the test. "What's sauce for the goose . . ."

He erupted. "No, damn it, I won't be a laughingstock, a cuckold, a joke for your friends! Do you understand me, Daphne? I will not abide infidelity in a wife, I will not have it!"

She rose slowly to her feet.

His flare of temper didn't disturb her as much as the realization that it wasn't jealousy motivating him, but a fear of public humiliation.

"I do not see where you have a choice."

"That's where you're wrong," he snarled, then snatched her into his arms.

She did not fight him, allowing him to crush her lips against his, to ravish her mouth with his brandy-laced tongue. Quiescent, she remained motionless, trying to hold herself back from him. She might have succeeded if he hadn't gentled his kiss, eased his embrace.

Instead of conquering, he was courting; instead of subduing, he was seducing.

Daphne succumbed. She'd never been able to resist him; his touch had always possessed the power to sap her of her will. She dug her fingers into his shoulders, holding him close.

"Oh, Daphne, Daphne," he murmured against her neck. "This is why I came to London. This is the reason."

Her heart thrilled to hear those words even as she questioned her surrender. She wasn't truly yielding to him, she knew. She wanted Iain, she wanted his passion. Why shouldn't she take it?

Arching into him, she sought the heaven she had known but one night of her life. She ceased to think. She wanted only to feel, to forget, and . . . to forgive.

Chapter
Nineteen

Iain awoke feeling warm and fuzzy. Warm because a body was draped over him and fuzzy because he couldn't immediately recall where he was or how he'd gotten there.

The soft form atop him stirred, sending a strand of auburn hair floating over his eye.

"Daphne," he whispered in relief. At least he'd done one thing right in the wake of last night's binge.

He remembered making love to her—slow, exquisite lovemaking that had sent him spiraling into the stars, wondering if he'd ever experienced such agonizing pleasure.

He also remembered the discussion that had prefaced the tumble into bed, and his muscles grew taut. He prayed she had only been retaliating, seeking her own form of vengeance in empty words. He *needed* to believe they'd been meaningless, because he couldn't stomach the thought that it could be true.

Daphne with another man.

Last night she had thrown the taunt in his face and he had believed it, but now he wasn't so certain. During their lovemaking she had tasted as virginal and sweet as he had remembered her from their first time nearly three weeks ago. She had been passionate, generous, radiant. . . .

Dear Lord, he couldn't allow himself to believe that she might have been with someone else. It made him feel murderous.

The idea of murder, oddly enough, flashed another image into his memory. Isadora Harkwell.

Iain's brows snapped together. By Jove, how much brandy and port had he put away last evening? He couldn't recall ever hallucinating under the influence of a stiff drink or two. Or even eight or nine.

"Whew," he breathed. A pot of coffee and a hot bath were just what he required to dispel the lingering effects of last night's excesses.

Carefully he extricated himself from beneath Daphne, admiring the soft curve of her breast, the creamy color of her gold-kissed skin. Nearly tempted to awaken her, he thought better of it, deciding that she probably needed her rest. They'd both been insatiable last night in their hunger for each other.

Tiptoeing out of her chamber, a rarely used guest room, he went in search of Dobbs. He didn't have far to look, for the omniscient valet had a bath already drawn and waiting for him in his room.

While soaking in the tub and sipping at Dobbs's famous "hair-of-the-dog" concoction, Iain began to ponder his brandy-fed delusions of the previous evening. They seemed so clear, so solid. He could almost hear Isadora's distinctive, resonant voice; its exact pitch, her derisive sniffs. He could hear her calling him a scoundrel, he labeling her a dragon—

He couldn't stand it any longer. He had to know. He clambered out of the bath and set to toweling himself vigorously, all the while telling himself that he wasn't a candidate for Bedlam.

They simply didn't exist, he assured himself. No ghosts, spirits, specters, or phantoms. No such thing as a heaven or a hell or an afterlife or a soul. He didn't believe in any of it and hadn't for years.

Miracles, angels, pixie dust, and magic were but crutches for those who needed more than the real world had to offer, who needed the emotional support of fantasy. People like Daphne, who put faith in the power of good-luck charms, wishing stars . . . and eternal love.

Iain flinched as he scrubbed the towel a bit too roughly over his back, where Daphne's nails had raked passionately into his skin.

The irony of it was that he wanted Daphne to think she loved him. He might not believe in love, but he wanted her to. He liked that she believed in happily-ever-after. He wanted to be her prince gallant.

Perhaps it wasn't logical and he couldn't explain it, but sometime during the last few weeks he'd lost his scorn for life's illusions. Not that he would ever be the romantic optimist Daphne was, but he'd learned from watching his wife that not all dreamers were ignorant and that believing didn't necessarily make one a fool.

He dressed himself and hurried down the two flights of stairs to the library. He felt like a thief stealing into the room, noiselessly, not wishing to be seen.

Sun spilled in from the east-facing windows, pale and airy as only the early-morning sunshine can be. It reflected off the gilt lettering on the leather-bound books, showering the floor in a pattern of white flecks. The room was redolent of tobacco and leather.

Iain scoffed at his foolishness. In the light of day, his hallucinations seemed no more substantial than the dust floating through the sunbeams.

He walked purposefully across the room to the ivory-in-laid desk and pulled open the drawer. The snuffbox lay atop a pile of calling cards. An innocuous piece of wood adorned with the Ashingford phoenix. A snuffbox, nothing more. A simple—

"Well, it's about time!"

Iain lunged back from the desk.

"Don't tell me," the voice mocked. *"You'd convinced yourself I was a bad dream concocted over a decanter of brandy, hadn't you?"*

Dear God. It hadn't been a delusion or a dream.

"Isadora?" he questioned weakly.

"Yes, Lindley. And let me say here and now that I didn't appreciate your conduct last night. You cannot stuff me away, hopeful that I might disappear, you know. It doesn't work like that."

"Evidently not," he whispered beneath his breath, blindly feeling his way to the chair behind the desk. He sat down, still staring into the drawer.

"This snuffbox isn't exactly the height of comfort," she complained. *"I've been thinking that I might try—"*

"Try what?" he asked in alarm.

"Raise the lid and I will show you."

Iain debated a moment, then decided, why not? The situation could not possibly become more bizarre than it was.

His fingers tingled when they came into contact with the box and he recalled that last evening he had noted the snuffbox glowing in the same manner it was doing now.

He sat back, his breath lodged in his throat.

The glow expanded, reaching up toward the ceiling. It shifted and swirled, like fog on the Thames, until a figure slowly began to emerge from the whiteness.

Before his astonished eyes, he saw it take shape, a form . . . Isadora.

"Bloody—"

"Oh, bother, look at the wrinkles in this gown," she muttered.

He was looking and he still couldn't believe it.

Transparent—he could see straight through her—she floated up from the snuffbox in perfect detail. The feathered turban, the boa, the Roman nose, the hawklike eyes. She was a colorless, substanceless replica of the Isadora Harkwell he'd last seen alive over four months ago.

"I—I thought you couldn't leave the snuffbox," he inanely remarked.

"I cannot." She pointed to where her shoes should have been. *"You see that I am still anchored to it."*

Iain's gaze darted from the snuffbox to the door. "What if someone comes in?"

She sniffed. *"No one else can see me but you, Lindley. And you only if I choose to allow it."*

Inexorably he came to his feet, compelled to get a closer look, yet equally repelled. He sketched a wide circle around her, knowing that his mouth must be hanging open.

"By God," he whispered. "I'm living every man's worst nightmare. I'm being haunted by my mother-in-law!"

Her lips pursed.

"How will I be rid of you?" he asked.

She floated down, perching herself primly on the edge of the desk. *"I must complete my assignment."*

"To drive me mad?"

She gave him a sour smile. *"Appealing as that might be, no. I have been charged with a different task. If you wish to help, Lindley, you must keep me with you."*

"You mean carry you about in my pocket? No offense, old girl, but I didn't much care for you alive. The idea of lugging you around dead simply doesn't hold much attraction for me."

"Pooh! As if I enjoy—"

Tap-tap.

"Iain?" Daphne's voice came from the other side of the library door.

Iain spun around. The door pushed open and Daphne stepped inside.

"I'm sure that you are busy," she said.

His heart pounded. Couldn't she see her mother's ghost?

"But I feel it imperative that we talk. About last night," she added, lifting her chin determinedly.

He glanced back to Isadora. He could see her as clear as day, but, most obviously, Daphne could not. The hairs on his arms stood up like porcupine quills.

Then he realized that Daphne awaited an answer.

"Yes, of course. Can you give me a moment?" He turned his back to her and walked stiffly to the desk, coming to stand at Isadora's side.

"Begone," he gritted between his teeth.

"Why should I? I have as much right to—"

"Isadora . . ."

"Iain, is everything all right?" Daphne asked.

He twisted to look at her over his shoulder. "Indeed. I'll be just one minute." He then turned his back to her again.

"I promise you, Isadora, if you don't get back in that box . . ." he threatened in the barest of whispers.

"You'll what?"

Iain clenched his fists.

"Tsk-tsk, you needn't fly into a temper," she huffed.

Then, *poof,* just like that, she was gone, with only the muted glow of the snuffbox evidencing her presence.

Iain picked up the box and clasped shut the lid. He stalked over to the wall safe hidden behind the portrait of his mother.

"Lindley, don't you dare!" Isadora cried. *"You'll regret this, I promise you."*

He ignored her. "Let me put this away, Daphne, and I'll

be right with you. Please sit down," he invited as the safe swung open.

"*Lindley, you are making a grievous error,*" Isadora said shrilly. "*I am your only hope!*"

"Hope be damned," he muttered beneath his breath, and firmly closed the safe on her.

Daphne selected a low-backed chair that would not dwarf or overpower her, and calmly smoothed out her skirts. She knew that the bottle-green morning dress showed her at her best, providing her the extra edge of confidence she needed this morning.

When she had awakened in her bed, all tangled among the sheets, it had taken but a stretch of her arm to remind her that she had not spent the night alone. Sore in every muscle of her body, she'd flushed scarlet recalling the abandoned manner in which she'd given herself to Iain. And the shocking way she'd taken him.

It had been a night of feverish lovemaking, of claiming and demanding, as if in their frenzy they could banish the questions yet unanswered between them. Last night Daphne hadn't wanted to ask those questions, but this morning she knew that she must.

Not that she regretted what had passed between them. She had wanted it. Desperately. But she wouldn't deceive herself into believing that it had meant anything more than it had.

The door to the safe clicked shut and she glanced up.

Iain was seating himself across from her in a companion chair. He looked overwarm, the color high in his cheeks. She didn't wait for him to speak first.

"I don't want there to be any misconceptions between us," she began decisively. "What happened last night was . . . unusual."

"I don't know if I should be glad you recognize that," he said with a cryptic half smile.

"That is," she clarified, sitting up straighter, "it will not be happening again."

"I wouldn't bet on it," he murmured.

"I would," she firmly shot back. "I meant what I said, Iain. I will not tolerate two sets of rules. You cannot demand faithfulness of me when you . . . consort with other women."

His brows met in a scowl. "Who says I'm consorting with other women?"

Daphne inhaled angrily. "Pray, let us not play games! I saw you at Ash Park."

He leaped to his feet and paced around to the back of his chair. "And what did you see, Daphne?"

Her eyes widened. Would he force her to relive it for him?

"Iain, I found you unclothed in her room! I heard her applaud your ingenuity for finding a way to sneak into her bed, for heaven's sake! Must we do this?"

"Damn it, Daphne, you saw nothing!" He slammed his palms atop the back of the chair. "Implausible as it sounds, I had discovered a hidden passageway through the manor. I was exploring it when I inadvertently ended up in Winnifred's room. I never touched the woman!"

"You expect me to believe that?" she countered, incredulous. "I was already suspicious of the Comtesse's supposed illness. I simply hadn't yet deduced that you were using it as a ploy to keep her ready and available to you!"

"For the love of God, why won't you believe me? Why would I lie to you?"

She swallowed an ache in her throat and said quietly, "You've lied to me all along, Iain."

His stance grew rigid. "What are you talking about?"

"You know what I'm talking about. You married me for Ash Park."

He remained motionless while something flickered at the back of his eyes. "Is that such a crime?"

"It might not be a crime, but sacrificing my virginity to a piece of property is nothing short of immoral."

He flinched as if she'd struck him. "It wasn't like that, Daphne." His voice rasped softly. "I wanted you. I want you now."

Her abdomen clenched.

"Tell me," he said. "If you thought the worst of me, why did you allow me to make love to you last night?"

She raised her gaze with defiance. "You used me to gain control of Ash Park. I saw no reason not to use you for my own pleasure."

Her barb hit home. Rage flashed through his eyes, although his tone remained even. "Then, by all means, use me as freely as you wish, wife. I am at your disposal."

"I told you: last night was an exception. Like you, I am not willing to share."

"You are not sharing me with anyone, dammit!"

"That's correct. I am not."

A few angry paces carried him suddenly across the room, where he loomed over her chair like a sinister force.

"What will it take to convince you?" he demanded. "I have not been with another woman since before I asked your father for your hand in marriage! Hell, I haven't even *wanted* another woman since the day I met you! Tell me, Daphne, what will it take for you to believe me?"

Her neck ached as she arched her head back to look up at him.

"It will take trust, Iain. Something we have lost."

He straightened away from her. "Then we must rebuild it."

"You think it so simple?"

He shrugged, walking over to the window. "You tell me. You are the expert in matters of faith."

Daphne threaded her fingers together, squeezing tight. Why was he doing this? she wondered. What could he want from her now? He had Ash Park. Legally, she couldn't take it from him even if she chose to.

"I don't know if it can be rebuilt," she said.

Iain huffed a humorless chuckle. "That doesn't sound like you. The Daphne that I knew would say that there's always hope."

She saw his gaze suddenly swerve to the wall, his attention fixed to the portrait.

"I'd like to propose another trial period," he abruptly said. "Another seven days to earn back your trust."

Daphne could not believe her ears. "Why, Iain? Why not leave well enough alone? I've been in London long enough to see how a modern marriage works. You don't need my trust; you don't need me at all."

"I want a legitimate marriage, just as I told you at Ash Park."

"Because you desire an Ashingford heir?"

"I want a child. Don't you?"

She shook her head in pain-filled wonder. "First, Ash Park. Now a son."

Iain didn't pretend to not understand. "You're wrong, Daphne. I want much more than what you can give me. I want you."

She pushed to her feet. "Don't deceive me again, Iain. If it's a child you desire, say so. You needn't lie to me this time."

"Blast it, why must it be one or the other? Can't you believe that I want you, as well as the estate and an heir? Or are you so much your mother's daughter, you refuse to accept the truth?"

Daphne swayed. It was like hearing an echo of her father's words. *Don't make the same mistake your mother did, Daphne. Don't let pride blind you to the truth.*

And yet, her heart cried out, the truth was that Iain's father had loved her mother. Iain only wanted her.

Then, with sudden awareness, Daphne understood what she'd failed to realize before. Like so many of life's miracles, her husband didn't believe in love. It wasn't that he couldn't love her, a dreamy-eyed plain Jane; he couldn't love anyone, for he didn't know what it meant.

"I *am* my mother's daughter," she answered with dignity. "Mother was proud, but I, too, am fair. What do you expect to gain during these next seven days?"

Iain moved from the window and came to stand before her, taking her hands in his. "I want the opportunity to convince you to return to Ash Park with me."

Daphne tried not to think of what the hands holding hers had done to her last night as she answered, "How?"

"We'll carry on as you've been," he said. "We'll attend the social functions you've agreed to appear at. We will present ourselves as husband and wife to the *ton*.

"I will prove to you, Daphne, once and for all, that you can trust me when I say I have no interest in any woman but you."

"And what of—" Daphne blushed, annoyed she couldn't voice her question.

A finger settled beneath her chin and Iain tilted her face up to his. "That, my dear, I will leave completely up to you. If you think that you can resist me . . ." He shrugged, flashing the devil's own smile.

Daphne wondered if she could.

Chapter
Twenty

"Rotten luck, Cunningham, the cat showing up while you mice were playing."

The name "Cunningham" caught Iain's attention as he was passing behind a column on his way to fetch a refreshment for Daphne. He paused, lingering unseen behind the marble pillar, while the party's din swelled around him.

"I don't know what you're talking about" came the cool reply.

"Come on now," the anonymous voice returned. "You and the Marchioness Lindley were having some fun before her husband came to Town."

Iain's fingers clenched in their fine kid gloves.

"Vellum, I fear that you're sadly mistaken," Cunningham said. "Lady Lindley and I are only good friends. She is delighted that the Marquess has been able to join her."

"Right. And I'll wager you were delighted as well, huh, old man?"

Iain was developing an intense hatred of this Vellum character, and if it hadn't been for the fact he was eavesdropping, he might have called the blighter out.

"Lady Lindley's happiness is my only concern. That and her good reputation," Cunningham added pointedly. "I wouldn't care to learn that rumors were circulating that might prove damaging to either her happiness or her honor. I might be obliged to do something about it."

The warning was subtle yet effective.

"Oh, no! Of course not," Vellum protested. "She's a lovely girl. You won't find me saying otherwise. I say, is that Harold Booking . . . ?"

Vellum's voice trailed off and Iain assumed the man had prudently slipped away rather than face pistols at dawn.

Iain stepped out from behind the pillar and identified the blond head as Roger Cunningham's.

"It seems I owe you, Cunningham."

Startled, the younger man swiveled around. His expression was less than welcoming as recognition narrowed his blue eyes.

"Didn't do it for you, Lindley, surely you know that."

Iain inclined his head. "Nonetheless, your defense of my wife puts me in your debt."

"Forget about it," he said in obvious dismissal, turning to survey the throng of partygoers.

Iain assessed the younger man's open hostility. *Was* Cunningham a displaced lover?

"I understand you were to be Daphne's escort this evening."

"What of it?"

Iain gave him a tight smile. "I merely wished to thank you for your attentiveness to Daphne during my absence. Most considerate of you."

Roger returned his probing gaze with admirable equanimity, no guilty twitches or betraying blushes.

"Daphne is an old and dear friend. I will always be there when she needs me."

Jealousy stabbed into Iain like a thousand needles, but he said with calm, "My wife is fortunate to have such a staunch ally."

"Oh, but she has many more than me. She's won the hearts of half the *ton* since her arrival, don't you know? Daphne is like that. Warm, ingenuous. People cannot help falling in love with her once they meet her."

"Have you?" Iain asked, wondering if he might have to kill the man.

"More to the point, Lindley"—his smile taunted—"have you?"

Iain's stoic facade did not crack. "Good to see you, Cunningham." And he strode off in the direction of the punch bowl.

By the time Iain returned to Daphne's side, he had managed to bring himself back under some semblance of control.

After stalking away from Cunningham, Iain had been ready to ask Daphne flat out if she'd taken the young baronet as a lover. Doubts were eating away at him like a chancre. He had to know. But after their discussion of trust that morning, Iain didn't see how he could possibly question her without causing her to be furious with him.

And thus losing all the ground he had gained.

He tried to tell himself that what was done was done. Whatever sins Daphne might have committed since fleeing Ash Park were partly his as well. He could have gone after her. If he'd followed her and told her the truth straightaway, she might have believed him. Instead he'd been too arrogant to pursue his wounded, fugitive bride and now he was paying the price.

What a price it was, too. His mind's eye persisted in torturing him with visions of Daphne in another man's arms, pictures of her ivory-gold skin sliding across the flesh of a stranger. He knew such jealous torment was mad. That Daphne was not the sort of woman to throw herself into a liaison merely out of spite. She had too much spirit, too much heart.

Or so Iain told himself. Trust was not a virtue he was familiar with.

Returning to Daphne's side, he found his wife in conversation with some regal-looking matron who coincidentally, and irksomely, reminded him of Isadora Harkwell.

He handed Daphne the glass of punch as she politely gestured to the other woman.

"Lady McBride, have you met my husband, Lord Lindley?"

Iain cordially bowed over the grande dame's hand.

"Lady McBride was closely acquainted with my mother," Daphne explained.

"My condolences," he said.

"Oh, not *that* close," Lady McBride protested. "I hadn't seen her in years. Not but once or twice after she moved to the 'Wold, I think."

Daphne shot him a reproving glance. Apparently, she hadn't misunderstood his remark.

"I was just assuring your wife, Lord Lindley, that she'd done the right thing by throwing off her mourning. Anyone who knew Isadora would know that she despised the practice. Death simply held no significance for her, if you know what I mean."

Iain smothered a cough behind his hand. "Uh-hum. Yes, I think I do."

His wife sent him another quelling look.

"And the resemblance. La!" Lady McBride beamed at Daphne. "As soon as I laid eyes on her, I said to myself,

'As sure as I'm standing here, that's Isadora Whiting's daughter.' Why, the likeness is most remarkable." She turned to Iain and gently rapped her fan on his forearm. "Don't tell me you can't see it?"

Iain's upper lip curled as he labored to construct a smile. "I try not to," he answered.

Lady McBride sobered, again misinterpreting. "Too painful for you, is it?"

Daphne abruptly broke in. "Pardon us, my lady, but my husband promised me a moonlit tour of the garden. You will call on me, won't you? I'd so love to hear about you and Mother."

"Nothing would give me greater pleasure, my dear. At my age I get few opportunities to look back fondly on my youth."

With a date for tea set, Daphne allowed Iain to lead her out of the ballroom. As soon as they stepped onto the terrace, she dropped her hand from his arm.

"How dare you?" she burst out.

"How dare I what?" he asked, taken aback.

"Do not patronize me, Iain. You forget that I know all about our families' history. About your father and my mother and her father." Her green eyes sparked indignantly in the light from the garden lanterns.

"Cling to your bitterness if you must," she continued. "'Tis your affair. But I bid you, do not publicly mock my mother's passing as if it were a cause for jest."

Iain was at a momentary loss for words. "I . . . I didn't intend to jest," he said.

"Oh, no? At least Mother was honest about her sentiments. She made no bones about her feelings for you, while you, on the other hand, did a commendable job of masking your contempt. Until she was dead, that is. But, then again, you had a reason for hiding your disdain, didn't you, Iain? You had to claim Ash Park first."

"Now listen here," he said, feeling his own temper start to rise. "If you think your mother was honest about anything, you're deluding yourself. Why do you think she despised me? Because I reminded her of her failings, that's why: her doomed love affair with my father and the fact that *her* father stole Ash Park from us.

"Yet would she admit to it? No. Not once did she contact my father after the accident, not once. And Ash Park? She fought me tooth and nail over that property even though she knew it was mine, by rights."

"You criticize her for being overproud? I invite you to take a look in the mirror, Iain Ashingford. What proof do you have that my grandfather stole Ash Park from yours? And how do you know that Mother didn't secretly mourn your father's infirmity as greatly as you did?"

"Isadora wasn't the type to have regrets," he acidly remarked.

"As if you knew her so well!"

"I knew her better than you think," he retorted. "And I'll tell you the woman was no saint. If she had been, she wouldn't be where she is now."

Daphne gasped and Iain realized how heartless that had sounded.

"What I meant was—" *She wouldn't be condemned to being a ghost,* but he could hardly say that.

"Daphne, I didn't mean—"

"I'll be going home now," she icily informed him. "You may take a hackney." She stalked away from him, her head high.

Iain muttered an oath, watching her disappear into the ballroom.

"Trouble in paradise?" a voice asked from the garden's shadows.

Iain looked around. At the base of the terrace's stairs, a round and generous form emerged from the darkness.

The Comtesse deCheval.

Cursing inwardly, Iain wondered if the evening could possibly yield any further misfortunes. Perhaps he could contract the plague or be crushed by a falling meteor? Either of those possibilities struck him as more appealing than an interview with the Comtesse.

Winnie ascended the few steps to the terrace, grinning like the cat who ate the canary.

"Eavesdropping, Winnifred?" he asked, knowing himself guilty of the same charge.

"I do apologize, Lindley." She shrugged innocently, her gown dipping low enough to reveal the upper crescents of her nipples. "I hadn't intended to, but it was difficult not to overhear you and the Marchioness. Your voices carried into the garden, you know."

Iain's gaze lingered on her swollen breasts and he asked himself what he had ever found attractive about the woman.

She sauntered forward, her cloying perfume an unpleasant reminder of their last encounter.

"How are you and your little bride rubbing along?"

Iain wanted to tell her it was none of her damned business, but settled for a terse, "As well as might be expected."

Winnifred pushed out her lower lip in a sympathetic pout. "Mmm, she does seem to be a high-strung child. I can see now why you reacted the way you did at Ash Park."

Iain lifted a quizzical brow. Winnifred was no doubt referring to how he had tossed her out on her ear once he'd learned Daphne had fled.

Winnifred came closer, trailing her fan across her upper chest in case he'd failed to take note of all that was displayed there.

"I want you to know, Lindley, that I don't bear any hard feelings about what happened at Ash Park. 'Twas evident that you weren't yourself after being caught out like that." She smiled at him conspiratorially, nodding toward the

French doors through which Daphne had just exited. "Under the circumstances, we might consider renewing our acquaintance."

Iain mentally shook his head. Either the Comtesse was painfully obtuse or more seriously in debt than he'd realized. Had not he made clear that he had no interest in pursuing an association with her? He'd been nothing short of rude when he'd sent her from Ash Park. Why, then, did she continue to pursue him with such persistence?

He could think of any number of London gentlemen who would be happy to take the buxom widow under their protection. He had assumed that she might have singled him out because of his sound financial position and his reputation for being discreet and generous with his lady loves. Who was to say if the Comtesse cared about discretion, although her fiscal circumstances were inarguably dubious.

Once flattering, her continued pursuit was beginning to grow bothersome. In truth, more than bothersome. Flat-out irritating. He stepped back a pace and glanced to the patio's French doors.

What if Daphne were to return and find him in conversation with Winnifred? Dear God, he'd never be able to talk himself out of that mess.

"Winnifred, I don't believe—"

Iain was interrupted by laughter as a small group of party guests appeared at the open door behind him. Iain turned toward the interruption, and his gaze clashed with Roger Cunningham's deprecating regard.

Iain silently cursed. Damn him. Cunningham would probably run to Daphne first thing tomorrow with the tale of this tête-à-tête he'd come upon.

Iain didn't even look at Winnifred as he bid her good evening and stalked away.

Chapter
Twenty-one

Daphne awoke the next morning, still furious.

How unfeeling and arrogant could a man be? He wished to earn back her trust, he said, to set their marriage on an even keel, yet he maligned her dead mother to her with all the compassion of a . . . of a . . .

She looked around the room.

Of a bedpost, she decided.

Last night she had been shocked and disappointed by Iain's behavior. Time after time she had found it within herself to forgive him. Forgive him abandoning her, forgive his role in her mother's death, forgive him buying Ash Park with her virginity, forgive him his deception, his intrigue with the Comtesse.

Unfailingly, she had sought to empathize with his motivation, to appreciate his viewpoint. She had understood that he was bitter, that he'd been cheated by fate of both a mother and a father. She realized that his childhood had been without joy or normalcy, that he'd lost faith in everything and everyone.

But how long, she bleakly asked herself, would he remain blind to the beauty of life? Would he never abandon his resentment? Would he be bitter the rest of his days?

Daphne had believed that she could heal him through her love, but now she doubted herself. This wasn't one of her fairy tales where love's true kiss had broken the sorcerer's spell. Roger had been trying to convince her of that all along, but she hadn't wanted to believe him. Perhaps her friend had been right.

Daphne punched at her pillow, unwittingly releasing the lingering scent of clove and lemon.

Blast the man! If only she would stop agreeing to his ludicrous seven-day arrangements!

But how could she say no? To her way of thinking, there was always a kernel of hope in even the bleakest situations.

For instance, she had agreed to Iain's request for an additional week partly because she had known that the Comtesse was in London. The woman had already been in Town when Daphne had arrived with Roger, and at the time when Daphne had first learned of this, she hadn't given it much thought. Aside from a pang of jealousy, she had tried to dismiss the woman from her mind.

But during yesterday's discussion with Iain, Daphne had abruptly recognized that the Comtesse must have left Ash Park immediately after her. There it was, her kernel of hope. Her optimism had leaped to the fore. Maychance Iain *was* telling the truth. It had been an accident that she'd found him in the widow's bedroom; he hadn't been involved with the Comtesse at all. He'd sent her away.

Or, her logic argued, had the Comtesse left of her own accord, embarrassed that their relationship had been exposed?

Daphne sat up with a sigh. The next six days would be futile. She loved Iain, but she seriously doubted whether she could ever trust him. And what was a marriage without trust?

The question continued to plague her both that day, and the following one, as she avoided Iain as best she could. Even as she secretly yearned for his company, she deliberately sought out diversions and entertainments where he could not join her. She accompanied Roger's sister, Deborah, for an afternoon at the mantua makers. Another evening was spent embroidering at Viscountess McBride's town house. She took tea with Lady Cunningham on Wednesday, and attended an exclusively female gathering at Lady Campton's on Thursday.

It was during the second day, at Lady Campton's house, that Daphne learned that she needn't quite yet abandon all hope for her husband.

Lady Campton, a popular hostess, had gathered together approximately two dozen ladies of the *ton* for an afternoon of cucumber sandwiches, lemon tarts, and gossip. Although the group was a lively bunch, Daphne's spirits were low throughout the afternoon. She didn't participate in the discussion of Byron's latest scandal or the question of where one could find the most charming of circular fans. She tried to put on a bright face, but thoughts of Iain continued to haunt her.

As the ladies moved about from circle to circle, Daphne found a moment to slip away to the pianoforte in the corner of the drawing room. She was studying the new Austrian music when a young woman approached her.

"Lady Lindley, my name is Sarah Raymond."

Petite and softly spoken, Sarah, who had to be two or three years older than herself, instantly struck a maternal chord of protectiveness within Daphne. There was something about the plainly dressed girl with the mournful brown eyes that made Daphne's heart go out to her.

"How do you do?" she said. "Please sit down and do call me Daphne. Everyone here is so informal."

"Oh, I don't mean to bother you. I only wanted to ask after Iain."

Iain. The familiar use of his name stilled Daphne's fingers on the sheet music.

"You know my husband?" she politely asked.

"Yes, we grew up neighbors in Sussex. I haven't spoken to him in nearly two years, but I . . . I've thought of him often and prayed he was well."

Daphne fought back a spurt of jealousy. She thought of him often, did she?

"He's very well, thank you for asking."

Sarah lowered her eyes. "I'm glad. After all that he's been through, Iain deserves his happiness. He is the kindest, most selfless man I've ever known."

'Twas a wonder, Daphne thought, that her eyeballs didn't pop from their sockets. If it had been anyone but the gentle Sarah, she might have burst out laughing.

"How generous of you to say so. I presume you refer to the circumstances with his father," she said, cautiously casting about for a reason for this young woman's devotion to her husband.

Sarah looked back to her lap. "Well, yes, that of course. He was so patient with Lord Lindley—his father, I mean. Iain nursed him tirelessly, right up to the very end. It wasn't easy for him to watch the only person he'd ever loved die a slow, painful death."

Daphne frowned. "No, it couldn't have been, could it?"

"Actually, Lady Lindley—"

"Daphne, please."

"I . . . actually, Daphne, I accepted Lady Campton's invitation today only because I knew that you were coming. I don't normally go about much."

Daphne couldn't hide her surprise. "Why did you wish to speak with me, Sarah?"

The girl flushed guiltily. "I know it's none of my concern, but I was anxious about Iain. He has made so many sacrifices, I wanted to know if he was happy at last."

"Sacrifices?"

Sarah bit into her bottom lip. "I am sure he's too honorable to have told you about it," she said, lowering her voice. "But he nearly lost everything he valued in order to save my reputation. I—I was ruined. 'Twas my own foolishness—"

"Sarah, you needn't tell me this," Daphne whispered urgently, covering the woman's hand with hers.

"Yes, I do need to tell you," she persisted, her voice quavering. "You see, the old Marquess had died only a few weeks earlier and he and my papa had been close. Anyway, Papa learned of my . . . my condition and was threatening to throw me out. The babe's father had fled and I—"

"Sarah, don't," Daphne pleaded, seeing how much it cost the young woman to speak of her disgrace.

Sarah raised her eyes, wet with tears. "Papa must have spoken to Iain about my plight, for the next thing I knew Iain had asked for my hand. We'd been nothing more than friends, I swear to you. I was astonished. I refused him, but he wouldn't accept no. Then . . . I lost the baby and it ceased to matter."

Daphne's breath had snagged in her throat. Why had Sarah shared her most secret shame with a woman she did not even know?

"Why are you telling me this?" she finally managed to ask.

"I knew that your family held Ash Park—"

Daphne blanched. Did all of Society know he'd married her for the property?

"And Papa had told me of Iain's vow to his father."

"Vow?"

Sarah looked uncertain. "Perhaps I shouldn't say any more."

"Why? Oh, are you worried that I don't know? It's all right, Sarah, I am well aware that Iain wanted Ash Park and

I was the medium for acquiring it." Daphne hoped she didn't sound too embittered.

"So you do know, then? On his deathbed, the old Marquess made Iain swear he'd get Ash Park back."

"I see," Daphne said softly. "But what does that—"

"Daphne, Sarah," Phoebe Knockerly called. "We're starting up a game of dumb-crambo, and we need another to balance the teams. Come on, one of you must join in."

Daphne looked anxiously to Sarah.

"It's all right," Sarah said. "Go on."

But she didn't want to go. She wanted Sarah to finish her explanation. "But what of—"

"Think about what I've told you, won't you, Daphne?"

"Yes, of course, I will, however—"

"Daphne," Phoebe called. "Are you in, dear?"

Sarah offered her a shy smile and waved her off. "Go on. You understand."

Daphne didn't begin to understand but she was dragged away to dumb-crambo, where she played very poorly. When the game finally ended, Sarah had already departed.

Daphne left Lady Campton's in a daze.

Iain was out when she returned home and she was glad for the time to think. She could not understand what had possessed a painfully shy creature like Sarah to expose her most private humiliation to a stranger.

Daphne climbed the stairs to her room, shaking her head. Sarah's family must have hidden the scandal well in order for Sarah to still be received by Society. Why would the girl have taken the extraordinary step of risking exposure of her shame?

Because Iain deserved his happiness. Because he was the kindest, most selfless man she'd ever known.

Daphne was still going over the conversation in her mind when someone rapped at her bedroom door.

"Yes?"

"It's me, Daphne. May I come in?"

She tensed, Iain's mere voice drawing her nerves to the surface of her skin.

"Yes, come in."

He entered the room in his riding clothes, the smell of earth and leather about him, and Daphne could not help but stare. Ridiculous as it was, she felt as if she were looking upon a stranger. Who was this man who had been an enigma to her from the start? What more from his past had he hidden from her?

"You've been avoiding me," he said.

She didn't bother to deny it.

"I have something for you." He'd been holding his right hand behind his back and he brought it forward.

She hesitated. He didn't think he could buy her trust with an expensive bauble, did he?

She gave in to curiosity and reached out as he placed something fragile and green in her hand. She brought it closer to her face.

"It's a four-leaf clover," he said. "I was out riding and I passed an entire field of it and I thought . . . well, I thought of you."

A picture of Iain on all fours hunting through a field of clover almost made her smile. "Thank you," she said. "I will press it and save it."

His gray eyes warmed with evident pleasure, heating her insides as well as his gaze.

"I was hoping you might accept it as a peace offering," he said. "For I am terribly sorry about the misunderstanding the other night. Our discussion veered into dangerous waters and I should have known better than to discuss Isadora. It might be hard for you to believe, Daphne, but my acquaintance with your mother was . . . closer than you'd think."

She frowned. "You had never even met her until you came to Harkwell House the week before the wedding."

"That's true," he conceded. "But my father had spoken of her and I had looked into your family's background."

"And from this you hated her?"

"Daphne, I did not hate your mother. She was a spirited, intelligent woman, a worthy adversary." He glanced down to his riding boot. "Although I'll confess I thought of her as such. An adversary, the enemy."

"Was I of the enemy camp?"

"No, I never thought so until—" He stopped, running his fingers through his hair. "Until Isadora and I spoke the morning of the wedding."

"And?" Daphne prompted.

"And she reneged on your father's promise. She told me that Ash Park would never be mine. She even hinted that you would never truly be mine since you'd married me only for my title."

Daphne should have been shocked, but she wasn't. She had figured all along that something similar must have taken place.

"So when did you stop thinking of me as your enemy, Iain? Or have you yet?"

"Oh, for God's sake, Daphne, don't be absurd! As soon as you came to Ash Park, I knew that you hadn't meant to betray me."

"I see. But you did believe that you'd been cheated by my mother?"

"Yes."

Daphne smiled faintly. "You know, Iain, 'tis a matter of perspective. To my mind, the crux of the problem was that Mother's notion of honor conflicted with yours."

His forehead creased, his eyes narrowing. "What do you mean?"

"I mean that Mother's sense of honor demanded she protect me from a loveless marriage—from a man marrying not me, but a piece of property. Your sense of honor, on the other hand, required you to fulfill your father's dying wish."

Iain seemed to grow half a yard, his spine going rigid. "Who told you of that?" he gruffly demanded. "Dammit, if it was Dobbs, he's gone too far this time!"

"Dobbs told me nothing of this. I learned of your promise from Sarah Raymond."

"Sarah?" He looked genuinely startled.

"She said she was a neighbor of yours in Sussex?"

"Yes, the Raymonds' property bordered ours," he answered, his expression guarded. "We were friendly as children. She's in London?"

"Yes. Although she's not going about much in Society. No one knows about . . . her misfortune."

"She told you?"

Daphne nodded.

"Why, in God's name?"

Daphne gazed down to the tiny clover, already showing signs of withering. "I do not know."

Iain shifted his weight, looking ill at ease. "Did she speak of me?"

"She asked after you," Daphne replied, giving him but a portion of the truth. "I said you were in good health."

"Ah." Iain thrust out his chin, tapping his boot in an unsure tempo. "About tomorrow night," he abruptly said. "Did you still wish to attend the Archers' masquerade?"

"I'd nearly forgotten about it. Would you care to go?"

"I believe Dobbs picked up a costume for me today."

"Yes, then let's go. I've always loved playing dress-up."

"Good." He half-turned toward the door before looking back at her. "Are you going out this evening?"

His question sounded almost wistful and Daphne suddenly regretted having made plans.

"I'm attending a musicale with Lady Cunningham."

He nodded stiffly. "I'll be at my club."

He left and Daphne sank into a nearby chair. She yanked off her gloves, her thoughts running about in circles.

Iain had seemed relieved when she'd told him Sarah only asked after his health. Did he not want her to know that he'd once offered for the girl? Why not?

It had been a chivalrous gesture, an honorable one.

"Honor," Daphne repeated aloud.

Why hadn't she seen it before? That was what Sarah had meant about Iain's sacrifices. Giving up his youth to care for an invalid father. Practically sacrificing himself to protect a friend in need.

And, because of the vow he'd given his father, he'd forfeited even his right to choose his own bride.

She'd said it herself only a minute ago. For Iain, marrying her had been a question of honor. He had had no other choice, for heaven knows that Isadora would never have sold him Ash Park.

Yet . . .

Daphne sat up in her chair. When Iain had offered to marry the girl, it had been a doubly selfless act. Not only was he wedding a woman, pregnant with another man's child, to protect her name; but he was also surrendering any hope of fulfilling his promise to his father. He was relinquishing his own honor for Sarah's.

That was it. That was what Sarah had wanted to show her. Iain hadn't been completely ruthless, blind to all else, in his quest for Ash Park. He'd nearly given it up. For a friend.

Daphne felt like weeping. Perhaps there was still hope for him yet.

She smiled down at her drooping four-leaf clover.

"Hope."

Chapter
Twenty-two

"How are matters progressing?" Dobbs asked the following evening as Iain prepared for the Archers' masquerade.

"Hmmph," Iain snorted dispiritedly. "I don't know if I could accomplish in three years what I must in the next three days."

"I would imagine that now is not a propitious time to say 'I told you so'?"

Iain launched him a killing look. "You know, old man, the Duke of Cumberland has put it into fashion to do away with disagreeable valets."

Dobbs smiled sweetly. "I fear for my life. Or at least I will when you see which costume you're sporting tonight."

"What have you done?"

"We-e-ll." The valet hunched his shoulders. "I asked her ladyship's maid what the Marchioness would be wearing and then selected your attire to coincide with hers."

"And what is Daphne to be?" Iain asked suspiciously.

"Lady Lindley is the Faerie Queen tonight."

"You didn't."

"Yes, my lord, for this evening, you are Puck."

"That's it, Dobbs, you *are* a dead man." Iain raised his hands, simulating wrapping them about his valet's neck.

"Now, now. Lady Lindley enjoys a touch of whimsy. She'll no doubt appreciate your efforts to be in concert with her disguise."

"Hah, and I shall play the fool all evening."

"It will be a stretch of your thespian skills, my lord, but I daresay you'll manage."

Iain sobered. "You think me a fool, don't you?"

"I think"—Dobbs arched a grayish-white brow—"that you have made some serious errors in your short-lived marriage."

Iain grumbled, hating to hear the truth. "But I've tried to remedy them, you know I have. Even that blasted four-leaf clover didn't advance my cause and I spent all afternoon on my hands and knees, ruining a pair of riding trousers in the bargain."

Dobbs pursed his lips. "You're looking for an answer in the wrong place."

"What's that supposed to mean?" Iain asked, struggling into a pair of forest-green stockings.

"You needn't look in clover. Look in here," the valet suggested, pointing to his chest.

Iain dismissed him with a shake of his head. "You're getting to be a sorry romantic in your old age, Dobbs."

"You'll be the sorry one. I'm beginning to think you're hopeless."

"Hopeless?" Iain echoed as he shrugged into the costume's tunic. "Hopeless, no. But maybe you're right about one thing, Dobbs. I have been looking in the wrong place."

*   *   *

Iain waited until the last possible moment to slip away to the library. He had his doubts about what he was about to do, but he was a desperate man. He was losing Daphne.

He had sensed it ever since they'd argued four nights ago. She didn't look at him the way she used to, her eyes now veiled with, what he thought to be, disappointment. He had hoped that the silly little clover could break down some of the barriers between them. Not bloody likely.

It was going to take more. Something big. Something supernatural.

Iain opened the safe by the light of a single candle, wondering what he would do if Isadora had disappeared. What if she'd left the snuffbox and gone back to ghost land?

His fears were for naught.

"Lindley, I swear by all that is holy—"

"Calm down, Izzy. We haven't time for sparring right now."

"Well, I've had plenty *of time on my hands, you despicable man, and if you think I'm going to tell you what I've discovered—"*

"Can you save the vilification for later? I've a question for you."

He heard her sputter. *"As if I'd give you the time of day!"*

"The other day, when you said you were my only hope, exactly what type of hope were you offering?"

Her response was wary. *"Why do you ask?"*

"I fear I've blundered badly and am in your daughter's black books—"

"Sounds like cause for celebration to me," came the sour reply.

"You would think so, wouldn't you?"

Dejected, Iain lowered his forehead to rest against the wall. What had he been thinking? Isadora would no more be his ally than he would be hers.

"How is Daphne?" Isadora asked. *"Not as blue-deviled as you, I trust?"*

"See for yourself," Iain muttered as Daphne pushed open the library door.

"Here you are," Daphne said, obviously surprised to find him in the dark room. "Have you changed your mind about going?"

"No, not at all. I merely wanted to fetch my favorite snuffbox." Putting action to his words, he scooped up the box and shoved it into the tunic's pocket.

"Well, the carriage is waiting," she said. "Shall we go now?"

"Indeed."

Daphne turned around and Iain hurriedly whispered, "We're going to a masquerade, Isadora, so keep it quiet in there."

"Remember, Lindley, only you can hear me," said the voice from his pocket.

"Oh. Right." He heard her so clearly, he tended to forget that not everyone did. "Very well, but no pinches, no jabs, no ghostly tricks, understood?"

"I understand much more than you think, boy."

"You make a lovely Faerie Queen," Iain said as they settled into the coach for the short ride to the Archers' home.

Daphne fidgeted with the feathered mask she held. "Thank you. And you are a charming Puck."

Isadora laughed. *"Are you 'that shrewd and knavish sprite'?"* she quoted. *"Knavish, yes. Shrewd is yet to be proven, Lindley."*

Iain clasped his hand over his pocket. "Shh."

"Ask her how Percy is faring," Isadora demanded. *"I've worried about him."*

Iain set his teeth together. Perhaps it hadn't been such a good idea to bring Isadora along.

"Daphne, ahem, I've been wondering how your father is getting along. You had said that he'd taken your mother's passing rather poorly."

Daphne raised her gaze to his and Iain caught his breath.

It couldn't have been his imagination, could it? For only a brief moment before she'd lowered her lashes, he thought he'd seen that light in her eyes. The one that had been missing. The luminous look that said he could slay dragons and rescue fair maidens.

Where was the cool disappointment of the last few days? Had she softened toward him? Was it . . . Isadora?

"It's really very sad," she said. "Papa and I had a long talk before I came to London, and though he might be recovering a bit, his mourning has affected his health."

"Oh, dear," Isadora murmured.

"I'm sorry to hear that," Iain said. "Do you think a change of venue might help?"

"I had suggested he accompany me to Town, but he said he wasn't ready yet. He has some ridiculous notion that he was responsible for Mother's death."

"What?" Iain's pocket cried.

"Why is that?" he asked more calmly.

Daphne turned up her palm. "He thinks if he hadn't forced the issue of our marriage, Mother wouldn't have died."

"Why, that's poppycock!"

"You don't agree?" Iain asked, fearing her answer.

Daphne smiled sadly. "No. I don't."

The coach rolled to a stop, their journey already at an end, since the Archers' town house stood only at the opposite side of Grosvenor Square.

Iain and Daphne both donned their masks before stepping down from the coach, hers pink and feathered, his a simple black domino.

For an August party, when so many had yet to return

from their country residences, the Archer masquerade still proved to be a frightful crush. Iain figured that anyone who was anyone in London must have been invited to the affair, for the place was crammed to the rafters with goddesses, devils, harlequins, and gypsies.

Although Iain tried to remain at Daphne's side, it was inevitable that they be separated among such a crowd. The din was enormous, the ballroom stifling hot. The revelers reveled more freely beneath the protection of a disguise and a certain frenzy pervaded the atmosphere.

Glad for his anonymity, Iain circled the ballroom, searching for his wife. A Salome, whom he thought he recognized as a recent widow, was entertaining a group with her own version of the Dance of the Seven Veils.

Iain cocked a sardonic brow as another gauzy scarf flew free. "It's a good thing you can't see this, Izzy," he murmured beneath his breath. "You'd probably drop dead all over again."

"*Hmmph.*" Isadora sniffed. "*I can still hear, you know, and I find this type of revelry completely shameless. We weren't such hedonists in my day, I'll tell you that.*"

Iain smiled while his gaze sought an auburn head. "You forget that I know of your past, Lady Harkwell. By all accounts, you were a spirited young miss."

"*Spirited, but scrupulous,*" she primly countered.

"Hmm-mm." A circuit of the room completed, Iain had yet to locate his wife. "I wonder if Daphne escaped to the courtyard, or the atrium as Archer likes to call it. The man's mad for all things Greek."

"*If I were you, I'd find her straightaway, Lindley. Who knows what debaucheries are taking place this evening.*"

Iain couldn't picture Daphne as party to any debauchery, but nonetheless, he was eager to find her. Encouraged by her demeanor in the coach ride over, he wanted to press his suit while she was still amenable.

Pushing through the throng, he made his way to the courtyard at the center of the house. He had never viewed Lord Archer's vaunted atrium at night and he had to confess that the sight was impressive. Massive Greek statuary surrounded a shallow pool, its waters reflecting both the ivory marble and the soft moonlight.

The absence of lanterns and the refreshing coolness made the courtyard an ideal site for trysts, and Iain stumbled upon more than one clenched couple as he wove his way around the large statues.

Pausing at the far end of the courtyard, he suddenly noticed a shadow flitting behind him. His instincts sounded an alert. He was being followed. Intuitively he knew that his pursuer was not Daphne. Deciding on caution over confrontation, he ducked behind a trident-bearing Poseidon.

The shadow stepped into the moonlight. A shepherdess. A buxom one.

"Winnifred."

"What?" Isadora tersely questioned. *"Whinny is here?"*

"Unfortunately, yes."

Iain cursed the woman's perseverance. After he'd rudely ousted her from Ash Park, he'd have thought she would have given up on him. Perhaps he'd underestimated his appeal, he thought, tongue firmly in cheek.

Damn, all he would need was for Daphne to find him alone in the moonlight with the Comtesse. . . .

"Take me out so I can have a look," Isadora directed.

Iain pulled the snuffbox from his pocket, cradling it in his gloved palm, then peeked around the statue. Winnifred was drawing nearer, obviously hunting for someone.

"Mercy," the snuffbox said. *"Have you seen much of her since you came to London?"*

Iain whispered vehemently back, "Despite what you might believe, there's nothing between the Comtesse and me, nothing! For some reason, though, the woman refuses to accept it. She approached me at the Knockerly party a few nights ago and then *coincidentally* ran into me at the Egyptian Hall yesterday."

"She hasn't given up."

"No, and I must say I find it odd."

"Look, she's passing us by," Isadora said.

Indeed it seemed as if the Comtesse was abandoning her search.

"See here, Lindley, I wasn't going to tell you about it," Isadora reluctantly began, *"but under the circumstances..."*

Her voice faded in apparent indecision.

"Well, what is it?"

She clucked her tongue. *"I don't know,"* she drawled, *"I might not be permitted to—"*

"Fustian, Isadora, just spit it out, won't you?" he growled more loudly than he'd intended.

"Don't take that tone of voice with me, sirrah!"

Iain heaved a deep breath, trying to calm down. He needed her, he mustn't forget. "I swear, Isadora, you would try the patience of a saint."

She sniffed. *"I have."*

Iain considered tossing her and her snuffbox into the reflecting pool but manfully restrained himself. "What were you going to say?" he asked.

"Hmmph. After you locked me away in that dreadful safe, I had some time on my hands. I discovered something. A secret niche. Here."

"In the snuffbox?" Iain raised the lid and peered inside. "A hidden compartment, how interesting."

"Yes and there's something in there. A piece of paper."

"Let us have a look then," he said, poking at the box's bottom.

"Agh!" Isadora gasped. *"You cheeky rascal!"*

Iain pulled his hand back as if burned. "Oh, I say, I'm sorry. Hadn't realized—"

"I should hope not!" Isadora huffed. *"I rarely allowed my husband such liberties."*

Iain had to bite his lips to keep from smiling. "Well, how am I to retrieve the note without compromising you?"

"You cannot. At least, not as long as I'm occupying the snuffbox."

"So the compartment can't be opened until we return to Ash Park?"

"Precisely. Therefore, we should plan to return to the estate posthaste."

Iain wagged his head. "I won't leave London. Not until Daphne agrees to come with me."

"Lindley, this is important," Isadora insisted.

"It couldn't be more important than winning back Daphne's trust."

There was a long silence.

"Very well," she replied evenly. *"But I urge you to return as soon as you can."*

Behind a snake-crowned Medusa, the Comtesse deCheval gleefully rubbed her hands together.

At long last, they had their clue! The clue to the Earl of Whiting's hidden treasures.

She had decided that tonight would be her final attempt at seducing the Marquess Lindley. Her vanity could only withstand so much rejection and she had almost begun to think that he didn't find her attractive.

Luckily, just when she thought she'd lost him among the statuary, his voice had drifted across the darkness to her. She'd dodged behind a marble figurine and listened in on the peculiar tête-à-tête.

Unfortunately she had only been able to make out half of the conversation, for whomever Lindley had been talking to had spoken too quietly for her to hear. Some of it, she simply couldn't make heads nor tails of. Why was it that the snuffbox's hidden niche could only be opened at Ash Park? And why was Lindley concerned about compromising the person—or woman—in question? Not that it mattered, Winnie told herself. Not really.

Lindley possessed a snuffbox with a mysterious piece of paper. A map, most likely. The map to their riches.

The only issue that remained was how they were going to lure Lindley back to the estate.

She twirled her shepherdess's staff idly between her hands. Bertie would arrive at an idea, he always did. She'd send a message to him this very night, letting him know of the developments.

While she'd been in London, Bertie had finished searching the manor's tunnels and had begun digging up the grounds. Oh, wouldn't he be delighted to hear that they were to be saved from debtors' prison? That all their efforts were finally to yield fruit? Well, maybe not fruit. Gold. Silver. Jewels.

Winnie wrapped her arms about her, laughing softly. She could not wait to return to Ash Park.

Chapter
Twenty-three

The note arrived two days after the masquerade ball. Daphne and Iain were sitting down to a late breakfast when the footman brought it in.

"Pardon, my lord, this just arrived by special messenger."

Daphne looked up from her plate, her gaze connecting with Iain's. A frisson of concern raced through her. It couldn't be about Papa or the message would be directed to her.

Iain broke open the wax seal, his features freezing up as he read.

"What is it?" she asked, unable to tolerate the suspense.

Iain's mouth thinned. "The steward says there is an emergency at Ash Park. He bids me to return immediately."

"What kind of emergency?"

"The fool doesn't say. Two brief sentences by special

279

messenger. You'd think he'd have enough sense to be a bit more informative."

Iain turned to the footman attending them. "Leave us and see that we are not disturbed." He dug into his coat pocket and withdrew the enameled snuffbox he'd taken to carrying. "And take this into the library."

The footman reached for the snuffbox.

"Hush!" Iain said.

"Beg pardon, my lord?" The footman's hand hovered irresolutely over the box.

Iain muttered something incomprehensible under his breath before addressing the anxious-looking servant.

"Go on, take it and make certain Lady Lindley and I are not interrupted."

"Yes, my lord."

The servant exited and Daphne twisted her fingers together on her lap.

These past days she and Iain had been performing a cautious dance and she wasn't sure she wished it to come to an end. Iain was courting her, but this courtship was different from their week at Ash Park.

Before, he'd been relentless in his pursuit, overwhelming her with his own potent brand of charisma. Although flattering, his attention had also been exhausting, keeping her wound up tight, her nerves aflame.

Lately, Iain had shown her another facet of himself—the quiet suitor. He could still make her pulse quicken with a look, but his gentle consideration warmed her rather than burning her up.

She met his gaze across the table and gave up any pretense of eating her meal.

"You wished to speak with me?" she asked.

His answering smile was bittersweet. "It seems that my seven days have been cut short. I must go to Ash Park."

She nodded, a knot forming in her throat.

"It might not be fair to ask this of you, Daphne, but I would like you to consider returning with me. You haven't had enough time yet, I know, but we could take as much time as we needed once we were at Ash Park."

She held silent as he arose and began pacing alongside the table. His hands were clenched so tightly behind his back that she could see the tendons straining in his wrists.

"Perhaps I haven't always been completely frank with you," he said, "but I haven't deliberately lied to you, either. I am who I am, Daphne. I am not perfect, I possess many flaws. Unlike you, I do not always see the best in people, the silver lining to every dark cloud. You are unique in that, I think.

"I won't deceive you into believing I can give you more than I can. I want you. I will protect and care for you. Should we have children, I will be a good father to them. But that is all . . . I can offer."

Her heart sank.

She had known, of course. Love was not part of the deal. How could Iain give her something when he had yet to understand what it was?

Her gaze fell to her wedding ring. Many times over the last few months this ring had been on and off her finger. Many times Daphne had made a leap of faith, trusting that her love would be enough for the both of them. That wasn't the case any longer.

"When will you leave?" she asked.

"At first light tomorrow."

She folded her napkin with infinite care and placed it beside her plate. "I will consider your . . . offer."

"I cannot ask for anything more."

Isadora was in a terrific quandary.

On the one hand, she felt she should warn Lindley about the Thompsons before it was too late.

Most obviously, Bertie and Winnie had not yet abandoned their search for whatever it was they were searching for. And the more Isadora thought about it, the more convinced she became that what the Thompsons sought was concealed at the base of her snuffbox.

Lindley would be returning to Ash Park with her and the box. This she was sure of. No matter that he'd told her he would not leave without Daphne, he could not ignore the urgent summons. The property meant too much to him.

If Bertie was to learn of the hidden note upon Iain's return . . . Well, who knew what lengths the corrupt steward might go to in order to get his hands on it?

On the other side of the coin, however, Isadora had been strictly prohibited from interfering in any matter other than Daphne and Iain's reconciliation. The consequences, should she warn Lindley, could be—quite literally—hellish.

As it was, she might already have stepped over the boundaries by telling him about the hidden paper. She hadn't intended to, but once she'd realized that the Comtesse was stalking him, it had occurred to her that the mysterious note could be the object of the Thompsons' search.

Even after Daphne had fled Ash Park and Iain had sent Winnifred away, Isadora had observed Bertie hunting through the manor's tunnels. The steward had forsaken the bogus ghost act and, instead, had taken advantage of the time Iain had spent sketching at the gatekeeper's cottage.

She had followed Bertie for a time, but as his quest continued to prove unproductive, she had grown bored.

Instead she had begun to spend her afternoons at the cottage, observing Iain's artistic endeavors. He was gifted, of that there was no question. However, her fascination with his work rested not so much in his skill as in his subject. Daphne. He drew nothing but her, day after day.

Some of his portraits had been so full of longing that even Isadora had felt her heart pull. And it was during this time that she acknowledged that she might have misjudged him. Somewhat.

He still had to prove himself—she was far from convinced that he was the right man for her daughter—but those sleepy afternoons in the tumbledown cottage had gone a long way to lessening Isadora's aversion for her Ashingford son-in-law.

Thus, her dilemma. Dare she gamble the hope of a celestial resting place against the slight chance the Thompsons learned of the note and menacingly pursued it?

Isadora chose to opt for heaven. Lindley was no fool, despite all her slurs to the contrary, and she decided that it was unlikely he would reveal the note's existence until he knew what it said. He had no reason to confide in the bumbling steward.

Still unresolved, however, was the issue of why she was here in the first place. The star-crossed lovers.

If Iain were to leave London without Daphne, the two might never come together again, and she would be stuck in purgatory until the end of time.

Isadora shuddered.

She couldn't allow Daphne to stay behind. She knew her daughter was wary, but the girl had to be persuaded. But how? Faith, how might she convince her when she, herself, was unsure of Lindley's commitment?

Percy might have been able to influence Daphne, but he was at Harkwell House. And sick with grief.

Isadora's eyes clouded. For the thousandth time she wished she might escape her ghostly bonds and go to him.

Reassure him. If she could only tell him she was getting along all right. That death was not so terrible.

Daphne's appearance at the library door lifted Isadora out of her dismals. Like a ray of summer sunshine, Daphne lit up the room in her yellow gown and matching turban.

Isadora smiled with pride. Even six months ago her daughter wouldn't have been able to wear that turban. It simply would not have suited her. But these last months Daphne had blossomed with a newfound confidence, finally reaching the potential Isadora had always known she possessed.

Daphne would never be an Incomparable, but she was an Original. A woman with spirit and grace and a heart as big as the heavens above.

But what had brought Daphne to Iain's sanctuary? The girl looked troubled, her face too pale. What had that Lindley rascal said to her?

Meandering aimlessly around the room, Daphne pulled a book from the shelf, then replaced it without even glancing at the title. She ran her fingers down the row of leatherbound volumes, her auburn brows knit tightly together. 'Twas evident that something weighed heavily upon her daughter's mind.

Daphne continued to circle the room until she stood behind Iain's desk. Then she raised her gaze to the portrait that shielded the safe and studied the woman in the gilt frame for a very long while.

"I know who you are." Daphne's low whisper was soft as a sigh. "You are Iain's mother."

What's that you say?

Isadora hadn't given the portrait much attention, but suddenly she was riveted.

James's wife.

Fair-haired and doe-eyed, the woman bore only the

smallest resemblance to her dark-haired son. The artist had painted the young Lady Lindley sitting before a pianoforte, and she looked very frail and very small. Although she was smiling in the portrait, her expression was strangely, hauntingly melancholy.

Isadora had never met the girl, had never even known her name.

"Susan Ashingford, the Marchioness Lindley," Daphne said quietly. "No one speaks of you."

Isadora frowned. *No one knew her. She married James, bore him a son, and died before her eighteenth birthday.*

"Your son never knew you, your husband never loved you. Or were you even aware that James loved another when you wed him? Papa, at least, knew that Mother's heart was elsewhere engaged. I wonder if you did."

Isadora soberly studied Susan Ashingford's image. *Yes, Daphne, I think she knew. If she didn't at first, she knew by the time this portrait was done.*

"You look sad," Daphne said, tilting her head to the side. "Did you love him even though he didn't love you?"

Isadora wagged her head. *So that's what this is about.*

Daphne sank into the chair behind the desk, contemplating Susan Ashingford. Her expression was so empty of hope that Isadora was beginning to worry when the footman announced that Sir Roger was calling.

"I'll receive him in here, Thomas," Daphne told the servant, shaking off her reverie as she stood.

Isadora hadn't seen young Cunningham since before he'd gone to Town in the spring. He, too, she noted, had matured. In his London finery the boy now looked a man, a handsome one at that.

"Roger, how good of you to come by," Daphne greeted, her face lighting up with real pleasure.

Roger doffed his beaver. "Mother said you hadn't been

by since Wednesday so I thought I'd drop in to see if you were well."

"You dear, you always show up just when I need you."

"What's wrong?" he asked as he and Daphne both sat down.

Isadora saw her daughter's gaze dart to the closed door, the portrait, then back to Roger.

"Nothing is wrong, necessarily. 'Tis only that . . . Iain has asked me to return to Ash Park with him."

A shadow passed over the young man's face. "I see."

"I don't know, Roger, I just do not know what to do. I'd always hoped that when I married it would be happily ever after, but . . ."

"But you've lost hope?"

Daphne lifted a delicate shoulder. "Iain is a good man, but a cynical one, and his cynicism doesn't come by choice. It simply isn't in him to believe."

Her gaze drifted back to the painting. "He doesn't even think he is capable of love."

Roger said nothing.

"I don't know if I can go with him to Ash Park, uncertain as to whether he'll ever love me."

"And you love him?"

Isadora admired Roger's composure, for if ever there was a man wearing his heart on his sleeve it was Roger Cunningham.

"I do," came Daphne's quiet response.

Only Isadora saw the flash of envy in his eyes.

"Well," he said, clearing his throat. "I might not be as proud as you, but if the woman I loved would consent to have me, I wouldn't even hesitate. I would follow her to the ends of the earth whether she loved me or not."

"Would you rea—" Daphne's voice abruptly died as her eyes met his. A rosy blush washed into her cheeks. "Oh, Roger—"

He jumped to his feet before she could say more. "That's what I would do," he gruffly said. "*If* I were in love."

Grabbing up his hat, he headed for the door. "I must be off. I only wanted to check on you." Then he paused, his hand on the latch. "Good luck, Daphne."

"Thank you, Rog," she whispered.

Poor fellow, he's got it bad, Isadora observed as young Sir Roger let himself out. *Head over heels, he is.*

She clucked her tongue in sympathy, glancing back to her daughter. Daphne still looked undecided.

Are you or are you not going to Ash Park, my girl? she asked, waving her quizzing glass. *You heard Cunningham. Is your love for Lindley so paltry that it pales in comparison to Roger's infatuation?*

Daphne sighed and Isadora could almost read her decision in her expressive face. The girl was going to stay. She wasn't going to risk her heart any longer.

Botheration!

The only other possibility would be to induce Iain to remain in London, but Isadora held out little hope of that. She knew how those Ashingfords felt about that blasted estate.

She was feeling nearly as blue-deviled as her daughter when, from the corner of her eye, she spied it.

A small sketch of Daphne tucked beneath some legal papers.

She knew that she shouldn't. She was only allowed to interact with Lindley. She'd be breaking the rules yet again. But she did it.

Operating from the snuffbox, it took every bit of her ghostly skills and then some, but she managed to slide the sketch out from beneath the documents and send it floating onto the floor as if disturbed by a breeze.

Distracted by the fluttering paper, Daphne turned to look toward the desk, yet did not rise.

Come on, Daphne. Get up and have a look.

She merely gazed at the paper a few feet away.

Faith, girl! Isadora cried. She glanced heavenward. Perhaps no one was watching. She blew gently at the paper until the sketch drifted almost to her daughter's feet.

At last Daphne leaned down and picked up the paper. Her green eyes instantly widened.

Like so many of the others Isadora had seen Iain sketch, the drawing illuminated and brought into focus Daphne's subtle brand of beauty. Here she was the Faerie Queen, ethereal, luminous, and magical. The pencil strokes were airy and soft and it was obvious to anyone that the artist had drawn his subject with a loving hand.

He really is quite talented, Isadora conceded. But had the drawing done the trick?

Daphne's head was bent until she raised it . . . to wipe a tear from her cheek.

Isadora nodded with satisfaction.

I'd say we're all going to Ash Park.

Iain spent the afternoon at Gentleman Jackson's, relieving his frustration.

He had just settled into his curricle, headed to an appointment with his man of affairs, when he spied Roger Cunningham riding up to the house. Iain's first instinct had been to jump out of the carriage, wrench the fellow from his mount, and throw a bunch of fives into his handsome face. Truthfully, that had been his second and third instinct as well.

Fortunately—or perhaps not—the voice of reason had intervened, and he'd decided to leave his man of affairs hanging and go someplace where he could bloody a nose and not have his wife think the worse of him for it.

Even before he'd seen Sir Roger skipping up to his doorstep, Iain had not been in the best of spirits. He kept replaying in his mind his earlier conversation with Daphne, thinking that he ought to have been able to handle the discussion more tactfully than he had.

He didn't want to deceive her. He knew what she wanted from him and he honestly wished he could give it to her. But to his mind, it was like squeezing blood from a turnip. It wasn't in him. The idealistic fantasy of romantic love that Daphne so obviously craved simply was not in him.

So after smashing a few jaws, and acquiring a set of sore ribs for his trouble, Iain dragged himself home early that evening, his mood not much improved. He had detoured through St. James Street for a glass of max at White's, hopeful that a shot of gin might numb the ache in his side— and that other undefined ache in his chest.

One glass had become two and two had become three, so that when he stepped through the door of his town house, Iain knew that he was not a fetching picture. And there stood Daphne in the foyer, waiting for him.

"Oh, dear," she said.

Iain self-consciously straightened his cravat while handing his cape to the footman.

"Good evening," he greeted with as much courtesy as he could muster. His ribs hurt like hell and the gin wasn't settling well on his empty stomach. "Did you wish to speak with me?"

Daphne nodded, still looking at him as if he'd grown a second head.

"Yes?" he drawled.

She blinked. "I merely wanted to inform you that I'll be leaving with you in the morning."

Relief washed through him, a hundred times more potent than the gin. His shoulders sagged and he felt as if he'd been carrying the weight of anxiety with him the entire day.

"I'm pleased," he only said.

She dipped her chin. Her adorable, pointy little chin. "I should see to the packing."

As she headed upstairs Iain lifted his gaze to the ceiling and came the closest to praying that he'd done in two decades.

"Thank you," he whispered.

Chapter
Twenty-four

"I don't wish to trumpet my own horn," Isadora said, sounding as if that was exactly what she planned to do. *"But you should be thanking me that Daphne has agreed to follow you to Ash Park."*

"Hmm?" Iain murmured.

Curled up on the opposite banquette, Daphne had just nodded off to sleep, lulled by the coach's rocking.

"I wasn't supposed to," Isadora went on, *"but I did wield some influence in her decision."*

Iain cast her a wry, sidelong glance.

Isadora had demanded that he lift the snuffbox's lid so that she could stretch her legs—so to speak. He didn't like for her to materialize when other people were present because he found it too disconcerting. Nonetheless, he released her, figuring that he probably owed her a good turn.

"I thought you might have exerted some pull," he said in

a low whisper. "The question is why? You couldn't have done it for me."

She gave him a withering look. *"I must return to Ash Park. Naturally, I want to be with my daughter as long as I can."*

Iain didn't much care for the sound of that. "Just how long do you plan to remain in residence? *My* residence."

"Really, Lindley, I already told you. I must stay until my mission is done." Her ghostly pale brow wrinkled. *"Although I am beginning to wonder how far I must see this thing carried out."*

"And you're not allowed to disclose the nature of your assignment?"

"No," she firmly replied.

Iain crossed his arms over his chest, drumming his fingers thoughtfully. "You know, Isadora, I would be willing to lend my assistance if you'd only tell me what this mission is about. As fond as I am of you—"

"Rubbish!"

He fought back a smile. "—I cannot say I enjoy being haunted."

"Do you think I enjoy haunting you?" she tossed back. *"An arrogant, puffed-up, disrespectful—"*

"I think you love it," he said.

"Hmmph!" She flung her boa over her shoulder.

Iain shook his head, unable to hold back that smile. Damned if the old girl didn't have spirit. Dead or alive.

"See here, Isadora, since we're on the subject, I've been meaning to talk to you about this haunting business. Once we're back at the manor, I don't want you spying on me or anything like that, you understand? Once you're freed from that snuffbox, I expect you to act like a proper guest. No surprises or tricks. No popping in and out."

She arched a haughty brow. *"I'm a ghost, Lindley, not a gremlin. I conduct myself as befits a lady."*

"Hmm-mm. Like that guided tour through the tunnels?" She sniffed. *" 'Twas naught more than a prank."*

"Well, no more pranks," he warned. "I don't want any nonsense. My hands will be full enough as it is, dealing with Thompson's bloody emergency."

Isadora opened her mouth, then clamped it shut.

"You were going to say?"

She jerked her head to the side. *"Nothing. I was going to say nothing."*

"I say, that's a refreshing change."

To his surprise, she didn't return his taunt, but busied herself adjusting a glove button. *"About the snuffbox, Lindley . . ."*

"What about it?"

"Aren't you curious as to what the note contains?"

"Curious enough, I suppose."

She was taking a great deal of care fastening and refastening buttons. *"I wager you didn't know that my father commissioned that snuffbox,"* she said.

Iain stiffened. "I did not know that."

"I didn't think so. You wouldn't have begun carrying it about had you known, would you?"

He met her regard evenly. "Had I known, I would have thrown it into the river."

Her expression was suddenly glacial. *"Oh, you're an obstinate creature. My father did* not *steal Ash Park. Your continued insistence that he did is an affront to the Whiting's good name!"*

"Your father disgraced that good name over fifty years ago, Isadora. You simply refuse to admit it. You never have been able to acknowledge when you were wrong."

She swelled with indignation. *"Because I am never wrong!"* she imperiously declared.

Iain laughed.

"I no longer care for this company," she huffed. With an

angry swish of her skirts, she disappeared back into the snuffbox.

Iain closed the lid with a click.

"Good riddance."

'Twas almost dusk when the Ashingford coach turned into the driveway approaching Ash Park.

The two days of hard travel had been tiring and Daphne was surprised by how glad she was to see the phoenix-embossed flags flying above the manor. She'd left the estate under the unhappiest of circumstances and hadn't expected to feel as if she were coming home to Ash Park. But she did.

The cobblestone bridge, the regal stands of oak, the magnificent fountain. Everything from the color of the grass to the scent of summer lilac called out to her, welcoming her back.

"I'd forgotten how very beautiful it is."

"I can never forget," Iain answered her. "Ash Park is in my blood."

Daphne did not answer, understanding all too well.

The setting sun was washing the house in a rosy glow, and as she gazed out the coach window she remarked how peaceful everything seemed.

"I don't see any evidence of an emergency," she commented. "What do you think it could be?"

Iain's features subtly tightened. "I don't know. Something about this strikes me as odd."

"What do you mean?" she asked with a start of alarm.

"I don't mean anything yet. We will have to see."

The coach pulled up to the front of the house and Wilkinson hurried forward to greet them, abandoning any sense of domestic decorum.

"My lord, my lady, welcome home," he cried, throwing his skinny arms wide. "Ah, Lady Lindley, how the house has seemed empty without you. We are so very pleased to have you back." His composure began to slip and he dabbed at the corner of his eye.

"Thank you, Wilkinson. I'm glad to be home as well."

"We're both glad to be home," Iain said. "Where is Thompson?"

The butler shook his head mournfully. "That Mr. Thompson has been acting passing strange of late. He's been running hither and thither, wandering around the house at night. Then, yesterday, he just up and disappeared."

Daphne drew in a surprised breath but Iain didn't so much as bat an eye.

"Would you have any idea, Wilkinson, as to the emergency he wrote me about?" Iain asked.

"Emergency, my lord?" The butler stuck out his lower lip. "Well, Mrs. Emmitt's gout flared up, but I doubt he'd have written you about that."

"I doubt he would have," Iain dryly agreed.

As they entered the foyer Iain didn't pursue the matter with the butler, instead asking Daphne if she would like to rest before dinner.

She would have refused, curious to learn about the missing steward, but she was, in truth, fatigued.

"Perhaps I will have a short rest," she conceded.

Unfortunately, once she'd gone upstairs and was lying in the luxuriously soft bed, she felt anything but restful. Gazing up at the starry canopy, Daphne could not keep away the memories of the last time she had lain in that bed. Her heart began to pound too fast and she threw off the coverlet, suddenly too warm.

Iain's hands stroking up her sides, his fingers exploring, his tongue plundering . . .

She tossed fitfully onto her other side.

Iain had not even tried to kiss her since that single night

of passion they had shared in London. She knew that he wanted her—she'd caught him more than once staring at her, his gray eyes hot with need—but he'd made no overtures of any kind.

Of course, she had only herself to blame if she lacked for his attentions. The morning after that London interlude, she had virtually banished him from her bed. Iain was not the kind of man who would beg for her favors. Whether or not his pride still stood in the way, she knew that he would wait until she issued an invitation.

Last night he had taken two rooms at the inn without consulting her. This night only a connecting door would be separating them. Was she ready to lower her guard? To throw off her defenses and submit completely to being his wife?

She rolled over and pulled from her reticule the sketch she'd taken from his library.

Her lips curved in a wistful smile.

This sketch was as meaningful as any poetic declaration of love. Iain might not know it, he might not recognize it, but this little drawing told her more clearly than anything else that he cared for her.

Did she really need to hear the words when she could see with her own eyes evidence of his feelings?

She was about to ring for Rose when a maid knocked at her bedroom door.

"Pardon me, your ladyship, but Mr. Wilkinson suggested that you might wish to take dinner in your chambers. His lordship is investigating the steward's whereabouts and won't be dining with you tonight."

Daphne looked with disappointment at the covered tray. She had hoped that she and Iain might be able to talk this evening; there was much they had yet to discuss regarding starting their marriage anew. Again.

"Thank you. You may set the tray down by the fireside table."

The maid retreated and Daphne glanced down at her wrap. No need to change for dinner.

She picked at her meal, then put herself to bed fairly early. She had been feeling especially fatigued of late, most likely, she thought, due to the London hours she'd been keeping this past month.

When next she awoke, her room was lit by the soft glow of a three-quarter moon. Her uneasy sleep had been disturbed by a noise from Iain's adjoining bedroom. She wondered as to the hour.

The moon appeared to be still climbing the sky and she judged it past midnight. Had Iain been searching for the missing overseer this entire time?

She remained in bed, listening to him move about his room. After a few minutes she realized he was not yet retiring. She sat up.

She couldn't sleep, and by the sounds of it, neither could Iain. Why shouldn't she speak to him now? He wasn't likely to enter her bedroom unbidden, so she would probably have to go to him first. Why shouldn't she? They *were* husband and wife.

She climbed out of bed and pulled her wrap on over her nightrail, deciding that she didn't want to give the impression she was throwing herself at him. Going to his bedroom in the middle of the night ought to be sufficiently forward.

"Iain?" She rapped at the connecting door.

It flew open, his dark silhouette immense against the moonlight.

"Daphne."

She tugged at the sash on her wrap.

"I heard you moving about—"

"I apologize. I didn't mean to disturb you."

"Oh, no, you didn't," she lied. "I . . . I thought we might talk."

He hesitated only a fraction of a second. "Certainly."

Stepping aside, he ushered her in.

His room was smaller and more simply furnished than hers, probably at one time an antechamber to her grander apartment. The window coverings hadn't been drawn and the moonlight streamed almost as brightly as sunshine through the leaded glass panes.

Iain made no move to light a candle. He walked away from her to stand before the hearth, his face concealed in the shadows.

"I thought we should discuss our . . . arrangement," she lamely began.

"Very well." His voice resonated from the darkness, its husky timbre sending goose bumps skittling along her flesh.

She wrapped her arms around her waist. "When I agreed to accompany you back to Ash Park, it was left unclear how we were going to proceed."

Iain inclined his head. "I didn't think it wise to press you."

"Yes, um, that's very considerate of you. However, now that I'm here—"

Daphne licked her lips. This was more difficult than she had imagined.

"Now that I'm here," she tried again. "I thought I should tell you that I consider this more than another seven-day agreement."

There was a brief silence.

"You understand what I can offer you?"

A hint of a smile crossed her lips. She understood even if he did not.

"Yes."

"And you are content for our marriage to be a true one in every way?"

She pushed her shoulders back, not shrinking from her response. "More than content, husband. Eager."

The sharp sound of his breath shattered the weighty stillness.

"Release your hair," he unexpectedly asked.

Her pulse doubled its meter. He would waste no time with further talk and she was glad. Fiercely so.

She reached over her shoulder and began untwining the long length of braid that had trailed down her back.

He watched her from the screen of shadows.

When she was done, she ran her fingers through her hair, spreading it across her shoulders, releasing the scent of honeysuckle into the room.

"Now take off your wrap for me," he invited.

Although she could not see his expression, she could feel the fire of his gaze and her breasts swelled in response. She felt deliciously wanton and wicked, disrobing for her mysterious shadow-lover.

With deliberate slowness, she removed the robe, allowing it to fall to the floor.

"Pull your gown off," he bid her, "so that I might see your body in the moonlight."

She shivered and did as he requested.

The jagged cadence of his breath was the only sound.

"Now, Daphne, cup your breasts in your palms and offer them to me."

Heat rushed to the woman's place between her legs. She hesitated, then slid her hands up over her abdomen, wrapping her fingers boldly around the soft mounds.

"Oh, Iain," she breathed, and closed her eyes against her own brazenness.

Her body was throbbing with remembered need.

Suddenly a head was at her breast and Iain was suckling

her, pulling at her nipple with his tongue and teeth. She would have fallen from the sheer bliss of it, but he took hold of her, bending her back over his arm as he claimed her.

She moaned his name again and again.

She wanted it to go on forever. But, abruptly, it stopped.

"Hush," he whispered at her ear.

She quivered in his embrace, confused. Was this another part of his game? she wondered.

He reached down and, still supporting her, grabbed hold of her nightwrap.

"Put this on," he said, his voice pitched low.

"Wh-what—"

"Shh." He placed a finger over her lips.

Flustered and inflamed, Daphne wasn't sure she cared for this type of play anymore. She needed him. She needed fulfillment—

And then she heard what he must have already.

Footsteps. Quiet, yet audible, they were in the corridor, coming nearer.

She obediently slipped into the wrap as Iain held her, his whole being projecting wariness.

"Daphne," he whispered. "I want you to go back to your room."

Dazed, she was just beginning to sense the menace surrounding them. The frantic message from the steward, his mysterious disappearance, prowlers in the middle of the night.

"No." She couldn't leave Iain to whatever danger lurked in the hallway.

"Daphne, listen to me, I want—"

She clung to him. She wouldn't leave him.

"Daphne, please—"

Then the door to his chamber slowly began to creep open and her heart leaped into her throat.

It was too late.

*   *   *

Isadora was seething as she followed Bertie and Winnie into Iain's bedroom.

This was precisely what she had feared.

When she had first learned of the steward's unexplained absence, she had been somewhat apprehensive. Where could he have gone? And for what purpose?

Then again, she had reasoned, maybe Bertie had already found what he had been searching for and had fled. Maybe she had leaped to conclusions in thinking he had sought the snuffbox's hidden document.

Then, shortly after midnight, she had spied Winnie and Bertie sneaking into the manor. She'd trailed after them as they had headed directly for Iain's study, their whispered conversation confirming that the snuffbox was indeed their mark.

While they had prowled through the study Isadora had battled herself not to employ her powers against them. The unprincipled scoundrels.

An andiron accidentally dropped on Bertie's head . . . Winnie rolled up in the carpet like a plump sausage . . . She had barely restrained herself.

Her fury had yielded to trepidation, however, when the Thompsons' search had come up empty and they had proceeded upstairs. Their daring, she'd thought, could only bode ill.

Now, hovering outside Iain's bedroom, Isadora knew real dread.

Bertie had yet to push all the way into the room and the light from Winnie's candle spilled through the crack of the half-open doorway.

All was dark inside. And very quiet.

Despite everything she'd been warned about, Isadora could not stand idly by and watch.

She rushed into Iain's room ahead of Winnie and Bertie, her gaze darting to the bed. Empty.

Then she looked from the bed to—

Dear heavens!

Along the far wall stood Iain, a silver candle stand clutched in his fist. And, at his back, stood Daphne. Her Daphne, her precious daughter—

Isadora labored to keep calm. She momentarily considered revealing herself to Iain, but she feared that her appearance might distract him.

Before she could decide what to do, however, Bertie pushed the door open and stepped inside.

Isadora clutched at her heart.

Bertie was wielding a pistol.

From behind him, Winnie's candle glinted off the barrel of the gun and illuminated Iain and Daphne at the opposite side of the room.

Daphne gasped and Isadora saw Iain push her behind him.

"Ah, Lord and Lady Lindley." Bertie grinned unctuously. "What a pleasure to see you both again."

"I'm afraid I cannot return the sentiment," Iain coolly replied. "Not for you or for your devious companion there."

"Devious, my darling Winnie?" Bertie laughed, a thin, ugly sound. "It runs in the family, don't you know?"

In the faint light, Iain's eyes narrowed with sudden awareness. "What do you want, Thompson?"

"You know what I want."

"Can't say that I do," Iain easily answered as if a gun weren't pointed at his head. "You'll have to oblige me."

"Don't toy with me, Lindley. I want Whiting's treasure, dammit!"

"Treasure?"

"Come on now. I've worked hard for it and I want it! It's a map, isn't it? The snuffbox hides a map."

Isadora knew that Iain hadn't yet checked the hidden compartment, for he'd been too occupied searching for Bertie.

"Sorry. I haven't any idea what you're talking about."

Bertie's hand began to tremble as his frustration mounted.

"Whiting told me you'd come after it. He told me he'd hidden something valuable here at Ash Park. Jewels, money, something. Anyway, I want it! I'll shoot you if I must but I will have that snuffbox one way or the other."

Iain held up his hand in a placating gesture. "Calm down, Thompson. You may have the snuffbox if you want." He tipped his chin to the back of the room. "It's on the mantel."

"Get it for me," Bertie demanded, waving the pistol.

Iain glanced over his shoulder at Daphne, then retrieved the snuffbox from above the fireplace.

"Bring it here."

Iain complied, dropping it directly into the steward's hand.

Bertie tucked the pistol under his arm and snatched open the box. He fidgeted with it for a moment before he pulled out a yellow scrap of foolscap. "I've got it," he cried.

Winnie stepped forward, licking her lips in anticipation. "What is it, Bertie? What is it?"

Isadora saw Iain start to inch slowly backward to where Daphne stood.

"This is a hoax!" Bertie suddenly cried, crumpling the paper in his fist. "Why, this is nothing more than a confession. A worthless confession." He tossed the paper to the ground and pulled the gun out from under his arm. "What have you done with the map, Lindley?"

Iain stilled. "What type of confession, Thompson? Perhaps it's more useful than you believe."

Bertie grimaced. "It's nothing. Whiting begs forgiveness

for cheating the Marquess Lindley at cards. I see no value in that."

Isadora clapped her hand over her mouth, stunned.

"Does it say nothing else?" Iain persisted. "Perhaps there's a hidden clue."

The steward gestured wildly with the gun. "There are no clues, dammit! Whiting asks for the property to be returned to the Ashingfords so that his soul may rest in peace." He sneered. "Ironic, isn't it?"

His fingers were shaking convulsively now. "I'm going to have to shoot you, aren't I, Lindley? It's the only way. I cannot play games with you all night."

"Now, Bertie—" Winnie tried to interject.

"Shut up, Winnie." He leveled the gun.

Isadora felt in a daze.

Soul at peace. Begs forgiveness.

Bertie was going to shoot Iain.

It all happened so fast.

Isadora had no time to think about anything, no time to tell herself that her interference would cost her a heavenly berth. She simply threw herself at Bertie the same second that his finger pulled at the trigger.

The gun jerked to the side and exploded in a brilliant flash of light, freezing an image in that flash: Iain's face, contorted with fear, as he lunged toward Daphne.

And then the flash dissipated and Isadora gazed in horror at her bloodied daughter, fallen in Iain's arms.

Chapter
Twenty-five

"Faith, what's keeping him? He's been in there for over an hour!"

Although Percival Harkwell's observation was no different from his own, Iain wished his father-in-law would keep his tongue between his teeth.

He nearly told him so, but checked his surliness before the words could escape him. He had no patience for anyone right now. Not even a grieving father.

The last twenty-four hours had strained Iain's nerves to the absolute breaking point. He'd neither slept nor eaten and he'd washed his hands over a dozen times, vainly trying to wash away the blood he was convinced yet clung to his hands. Pacing back and forth the length of the drawing room, he knew that he was not entirely in his right mind.

As he paced he passed by Lord Harkwell, deliberately avoiding his father-in-law's tormented gaze. Guilt gnawed at him that he couldn't offer the man some comfort, but Iain feared that if he dared speak, he might shatter into pieces, losing his tenuous grip on his sanity.

"My lord?"

Iain's heart leaped into treble meter before he realized that 'twas only Wilkinson standing at the door. Not the doctor.

"Your solicitor, Mr. Kane, is here," Wilkinson said.

Iain closed his eyes. *Blast*. Walter must be reporting back to him about the filing of the charges. Dammit, for all Iain cared Bertie and Winnie could burn together in hell. Miserably. Eternally. The only thing that mattered now was Daphne.

He would have liked to have sent Walter Kane away, but Iain felt he owed it to the man to be civil. The solicitor had been extremely helpful in the wake of the shooting.

"All right. Send him in."

With his head cradled in his hands, Lord Harkwell did not even look up from his seat on the divan.

Walter entered, still wearing his overcoat and carrying his hat. It didn't look as if he planned to stay long.

"I'm sorry to intrude, Lindley, during this very difficult time," the solicitor said. "But I wanted you to rest easy at least on one score."

Iain could offer him no more than a brusque nod.

"You'll be glad to know, that is . . . your sworn statement was more than sufficient for the local magistrate. Enough that you will probably not be required to testify against the Thompsons. You were right, too, about the Comtesse being a half sister to your steward. From what I've learned she clawed her way up from the lower classes, keeping her background hidden. Eviden—"

Walter abruptly cut himself off, apparently reading Iain's expression. The solicitor cleared his throat. "At any rate, you needn't be concerned about either of those two. Justice will be served, I assure you."

Justice? Iain wanted to shout back at him. How could he speak of justice when Daphne lay upstairs, her destiny as uncertain—

"Lord Lindley?"

Iain swung about.

The physician, Swinton, stood in the doorway, his expression grave.

"I'd best be going," Walter Kane murmured, stepping around the doctor as he hastily took his leave.

Iain followed after him, crossing the room to Swinton in three heart-stopping strides.

Images instantly branded themselves into Iain's memory. Images that would last forever. The mockingly cheerful chime of a clock. A tiny crescent-shaped scar at the corner of the doctor's grimly set mouth. The lingering smell of vinegar and camphor that made Iain want to gag.

"Yes?" he questioned, wondering if it was the vinegar or his own heart in his throat that threatened to choke him.

Sad, pale blue eyes looked back at him. "I wish I had better news for you, Lord Lindley. The bullet did not penetrate, only scoring her skull, but she's very weak. Very weak, indeed. I fear 'tis only a question of time."

The suspended moment crashed around Iain like the roar of thunder. Blood pounded through his temples. Never had he known such a murderous rage. He wanted to kill someone, but the Thompsons were safely behind bars.

"You don't understand," he quietly gritted out so that Lord Harkwell could not overhear. "She cannot die. You *cannot* let her die. You are said to be the best damned physician in the country, for God's sake. Do something."

Swinton laid a hand on Iain's shoulder and it was all he could manage not to shake it off.

"I know it's hard, son. Who can explain the vagaries of

fate? It's never easy losing a loved one, but to lose both her and the babe at once—"

Iain jerked his head up, his gaze slicing through the doctor like a blade.

"You didn't know of the child?" Swinton rubbed his chin. "Well, she is fairly early along, she might not have realized it yet herself."

Iain wrenched away from him, feeling as if he could not breathe, as if the life were being crushed from his chest.

"I'm sorry to have broken it to you like this," the man was saying. "It might have been better for you not to have known—"

Iain cut him off with a sharp movement of his hand.

"Not to have known what?" Percival Harkwell shakily demanded, rising to his feet.

Swinton looked to the Baron and back to Iain. Iain shook his head slightly. He couldn't share this. He couldn't.

"Your daughter's prognosis is not good," was all Swinton told him.

But it was enough.

Lord Harkwell swayed on his feet, the color draining from his face. The doctor rushed to him and helped him back to the divan as Iain watched it all with a vague sense of detachment.

No one should have to feel such pain, he thought to himself. He wouldn't. If he held fast to the demonic fury that was eating away at his insides, he would feel none of it. Only the rage.

Swinton settled Lord Harkwell, then approached Iain again.

"I'm sorry, Lord Lindley," he said quietly. "I've done all I can for your wife. You might consider sending for a cleric."

Iain had to dig his nails into his palms to keep from leaping at him. "Stop talking like that," he hissed. "There must be something that can be done for her."

The physician pursed his lips. "At this point, my lord, nothing short of a miracle could save her."

A miracle.

Iain seized onto that word like a lifeline.

"I may see her?" he asked.

Swinton nodded. "I would advise you to go straight up." His gaze softened with apology. "And send for the priest."

Ignoring the second half of the physician's counsel, Iain rushed from the room. He took the stairs two at a time, his heart thudding in his chest.

A miracle, he kept repeating to himself. A miracle.

"Isadora," he called as he ran up the staircase. "Isadora!"

Although he'd not seen her since before Daphne had been shot, he knew she was still at Ash Park. Her sorrow had been a tangible thing in the hours following the accident, her keening cries, which only he could hear, echoing throughout the mansion.

"Isadora! Answer me, dammit, answer me!"

As Iain reached the top of the landing a hand suddenly grabbed at his arm and he spun around in relief.

"Where have you—" It was only Dobbs.

"My lord, are you . . . all right?"

Iain yanked away from him, livid. "Leave me be," he bit out.

"But, Iain—"

"No!" Iain turned from him and began to sprint down the corridor to Daphne's chamber. "She's probably with Daphne. Of course she is. Yes. Where else would she be?"

He was gasping for breath when he came to the end of the hallway and shoved open the door to Daphne's bedroom with a bang. Mrs. Emmitt was seated beside the bed.

"Lord Lindley, you shouldn't—"

"Get out," he ordered.

"My lord—"

"Get out!" He pointed to the door behind him.

Mrs. Emmitt's departure must have registered somewhere at the back of his mind, but he couldn't be certain. He was consciously aware of only one thing—the pale figure resting on the bed.

"My God," he whispered. His hand fell weakly to his side.

She lay there so very still, ashen, and frail. Even the bandage circling her head was not as white as her bloodless complexion.

He knelt beside the bed and took her hand in his, gently running his thumb over the fragile pulse beating at her wrist.

He remembered with painful clarity sitting at his father's bed like this, holding a hand, struggling to keep the specter of death at bay with only his force of will. He had not succeeded then, but he would this time. He must.

Each shallow breath she took he followed with his gaze, trying to imprint her face forever into his memory. The slope of her forehead, the straight, proud nose, the overly wide and generous mouth.

"And to think I had once not thought you beautiful," he said softly.

When was that time? He could barely remember. Sometime before he had discovered the luminosity of her spirit; before he had understood that she was his light, a beacon that could reach into the darkness of his soul.

What would he do without that light? What would become of him?

"Daphne," he whispered, leaning closer to her ear. "You cannot leave me. You cannot. There can be no one else. You are my life. You are everything." His voice cracked. "Everything."

She did not stir.

He lowered his head to the counterpane, swallowing hard over the knot of tears that threatened to unman him.

His thumb suddenly twitched. He lifted his head, panic strangling him. He'd lost the faint pulse beneath his fingers. He pressed harder against her wrist.

Nothing.

He looked to her chest.

It was still.

"No!"

He leaped to his feet. "No-o!"

A roar of anguish tore from his throat, resonating into the corners of the chamber.

"You've taken her, haven't you, Isadora? You've taken her from me!"

He spun around, frantically gazing about the room. "This was it, wasn't it? This was your mission. Your revenge! You swore I wouldn't have her, didn't you?"

He clutched at his hair with both hands, knowing that he teetered on the brink of madness.

"Damn you, Isadora, do you hear me?" he bellowed. "I won't let you cheat me again. I'll follow you to hell and back if I must, but I'm coming after you, do you hear?"

He turned to look down at Daphne's peaceful form, then lifted his face to the ceiling.

"By God, Isadora, I won't let you do this," he whispered brokenly. "I know I don't deserve her, you were right, but I love her so damn much."

He crumpled to his knees beside the bed and laid his cheek against Daphne's hand, squeezing his eyes shut as the rage slowly drained away from him.

"Please give her back," he pleaded. "Bring her back to me and all will be forgiven. Please."

Against his fevered cheek, Daphne's fingers were cool. So cool.

Then they fluttered.

He raised his head. Her fingers were moving.

He looked up. Her face was still pale, but . . .

He placed his hand over her chest and felt a shuddering breath work its way through her lungs.

It was a miracle. By God, a miracle.

And he wept.

Throughout that night and the following day, Dr. Swinton continually cautioned Iain against getting his hopes up. She was still unconscious, he said. She was too weak.

But Iain never doubted. He would never doubt again.

His confidence rubbed off on Lord Harkwell, who seemed to make a recovery of his own. He and Iain kept a vigil at Daphne's bedside throughout that long night, and Iain knew that they were not alone.

He had thanked Isadora time and time again, never asking how or why. Although she did not reveal herself to him, he knew that she was there and that she had heard him.

Late the next afternoon, as the sun began to surrender to the gold-green horizon, Daphne opened her eyes.

"Iain?"

He smiled. "Welcome back, my love."

"Daphne?"

She turned her head to the other side of the bed.

"Papa, what are you doing here?"

Her father's eyes brimmed. "Trying not to blubber like a babe," he answered.

"What's happened?" she asked. "You both look so sober."

Iain squeezed her fingers. "Don't you recall being shot?"

A small frown arced between her brows. "No. Was I?"

"Indeed you were," her father answered.

Daphne's gaze clouded as she glanced to her father. "Papa, I cannot quite believe you are here, because I had the very strangest dream and—I know it sounds silly—but Mother came to see me and she wanted me to give you a message. Isn't that odd? That you should be here and I'd have such a dream? And the funny thing was it all seemed most real."

"What was the message, Daphne?" Iain prompted.

She smiled uncertainly as if embarrassed. "Well, I know 'twas only a dream, but Mother was quite adamant. You know how she was."

Iain nodded, his lips quirking. "I do."

"At any rate, she said I was to tell you, Papa, to quit blaming yourself, that she was responsible. And"—Daphne's smile softened—"that she'd loved you all along and wished she'd told you sooner."

Lord Harkwell had to stand up and walk away for a moment, hiding behind his handkerchief.

Daphne turned to Iain. "I know you don't believe in any of that nonsense, Iain—"

"Oh, no, Daphne, you're wrong. I believe in everything."

She dipped her chin, giving him a quizzical look. "What do you mean?"

He twined his fingers through hers. "I believe in it all, Daphne, everything you've tried to teach me. Stars, clover, angels, miracles. But, especially . . . I believe in love."

Her moss-green eyes widened until Iain could see his reflection in their depths.

"You do?" she asked breathlessly.

"I do," he answered with all his heart.

Far above the clouds in a place filled with light and joy, Isadora tossed her boa over her shoulder, hooking it on a newly acquired gossamer wing.

She looked down on the trio standing together in Daphne's room and sniffed. It wasn't an earthly Isadora sniff, full of disdain, but rather an angelic kind of sniff, laden with happy tears. And above her turbaned head a gold-rimmed halo began to glow.

Epilogue

Iain and his month-old daughter, Isadora Faith Ashingford, were waiting in the study as Daphne made final preparations for the christening to take place that afternoon. Guests had been arriving since yesterday, all eager to see the baby, and Iain was glad to finally have some time alone with his carrot-topped daughter.

For a man who'd never believed in miracles, Iain had seen his share over the last few months. Daphne's recovery had been the first, eclipsed only by the wondrous experience of witnessing his child's entrance to the world.

As she slept, tucked into the crook of his arm, Iain walked over to his desk and removed an object from the bottom drawer. A snuffbox.

He held it before the babe and whispered, "This is my

christening gift to you, little one. This was your great-grandfather's snuffbox and it's very, very special. Magical, even."

His daughter snuffled softly, her tiny fist clenched against her mouth.

Iain smiled. Lord, if she didn't look exactly like her namesake. She even sounded like her, the feisty little baggage. She had a cry that made her demands known from one end of Ash Park to the other. Daphne couldn't understand where it came from, but Iain knew. And he loved it.

He glanced to the snuffbox in one hand and his daughter in the other. Dear God, he missed her. And if that wasn't a miracle, he didn't know what was.

It had been nearly nine months since he'd last seen Isadora, and he hadn't felt her presence since the day that Daphne had awakened from her injury. He'd spoken to her often but had never sensed a response, was not even certain that she could still communicate with him.

Nonetheless, he clutched the snuffbox in his palm and looked heavenward. "Isadora, I hope you can see your granddaughter here. She's a beauty, let me tell you. A spirited miss in the true Whiting tradition. You'd be proud."

He smiled down at the sleeping baby. "I was even thinking for her first birthday, I'd buy her a quizzing glass, what do you think of that?" He laughed softly, his expression sobering. "I can never thank you enough, Izzy, and I hope you're happy where you are. We miss you here."

"Who are you talking to?"

Iain spun around. Frowning and smiling at the same time, his wife stood inside the doorway.

"I was talking to Isadora," he answered.

"How is my angel?" Daphne asked, coming close to peer at the bundle in his arms.

Iain glanced up. "I hope she's well."

"Of course she is," Daphne answered. "Her papa takes such good care of her."

She touched the baby's cheek. "We should probably be leaving for the chapel. Sarah and Roger arrived and are eager to become godparents. You know, they didn't say so but I believe they cut their honeymoon short to be here."

Iain gave her a mock scowl. "Naturally. What could be more important than our daughter's christening?"

Daphne wrapped her arms around his waist and lifted her face. "Isn't it wonderful that they found each other? They seem very happy, don't you think?"

Iain gazed down at her. "They couldn't be as happy as we are, my love."

She sighed. "Who would have thought it? We began so wretchedly, who would have believed we stood a chance?"

Iain looked over Daphne's head to the suddenly glowing snuffbox he held, and smiled. "I wouldn't have even said we stood a ghost of a chance."

And now for a preview of the next
Haunting Hearts romance

Heaven Above

Coming in October 1996 from Jove

"Blake! Our baby just moved. It was just the tiniest little flutter, but I felt him."

Glenna Tanner wanted to jump up and scream out her elation, but she settled for calmly announcing the news to her husband, who had paused from doing laps at the shallow end of the pool to ask how she was feeling. She watched his expression soften as he pushed himself up and out of the pool and headed for her shaded resting place in the gazebo.

God, how I love this man, she thought, enjoying watching the sun reflect off crystalline rivulets of water as they caressed the planes of Blake's long, muscular body. He was sexier now at thirty-seven than he'd been as a college boy, with muscles finely honed and defined with maturity. Glenna stretched sensually, wishing the difficulties of this high-risk pregnancy hadn't dictated that they abstain from the joys of sex.

"This time everything is going to be just perfect," she told him when he knelt beside her lounge chair. "Here, give me your hand. See if you can feel him, too."

"I'll get you all wet, honey." But he let her place his wet, cool palm on her still-flat stomach and indulgently tried to feel motion that even to Glenna had been so fleeting it had barely registered in her conscious mind. "Do you feel all right?" Blake asked, concern evident in his warm, loving gaze.

"Never better. There! He moved again. Did you feel him?"

"I don't know. Maybe. Isn't it a little soon?"

"We're nearly halfway there. Blake, I just know that this time, we're going to have our baby. I've already carried this baby a month longer than I ever have before." Glenna sensed Blake's reserve, his fear of hoping too much that after so many years and two heartbreaking miscarriages, they were finally going to have a child.

"Sweetheart," he said softly, "I'm hoping as much as you are that everything will turn out right. I just don't want anything to happen to you."

Glenna knew the warnings they had received from Greg Halpern, her obstetrician and Blake's longtime friend, were never far from Blake's mind. She realized her longstanding endometriosis and history of placenta previa made the chance of this pregnancy being a success remote. Still, she refused to let worries infringe on her joy. She and Blake were finally going to have the baby she had wanted every day of the fourteen years they had been married.

This time she had known she was pregnant practically from the moment of conception. She was following Greg's instructions to the letter, hardly ever finding herself bored by the long hours of bed rest. And now she was nearly four and a half months along—and she had felt her baby move!

"Would you like to have lunch out here?" Blake asked, unfolding his big body from its crouched position and slinging a beach towel around his shoulders.

Glenna smiled. "It would be nice, unless you think it's too hot." The latticework of the gazebo shaded them nicely from a sultry July sun, and a fan turned lazily from the ceiling, cooling the air and shooing away the occasional moth and butterfly. "I feel lazy today," she added.

"Me, too. I'll ask Mary to bring out the food."

Glenna thought Blake looked more at ease when he lifted her from the padded turquoise chaise lounge and set her onto one of the chairs that ringed a small, glass-topped table. Ordinarily she would balk at being treated as if she were made of glass—but not now, while the little life inside her was so tenuous.

"Your son or daughter and I thank you," she quipped, leaning back and resting her head against Blake's hard, flat belly.

"You're both welcome," Blake replied as he leaned down and brushed a gentle kiss across her lips.

They spent the afternoon outside. Even as restricted as her activities were because of the baby, Glenna liked just sitting, relaxing with Blake and enjoying his company this beautiful summer day. She sighed, regretting that the day was almost over, as she watched a bright orange Texas sun begin to disappear in the western sky.

Suddenly chilled despite the heat, Glenna shivered. "I'm cold," she told Blake, who sprang up from the lounge chair where he had been snoozing and hurried to her side.

"Let's go inside," he suggested, concern evident in his solemn gaze.

"All right." With more effort than the simple action should have required, she sat up and slid her legs to the floor. "I think you'd better carry me," she told him quietly, not wanting to alarm him by admitting just how weak and dizzy she felt.

His strong arms enveloped her, and she felt safe, until she glanced down at the chaise where she had been resting and saw the dark, red pool of blood.

"I'm bleeding," she said, unable to keep fear and hopelessness from showing in her weakening voice. "You'd better get me to the hospital."

Blake stopped pacing the length of a sterile-looking waiting room and sank down onto an overstuffed sofa.

What in hell is taking them so long?

He propped his elbows on his knees, bringing his head down to rest on his hands. With every noisy tick of that clock on the wall, his panic escalated. He shivered. They kept this room about as cold as a refrigerator, but he knew the chill in his body owed more to fear than to the hospital's air conditioning system.

Had it been just hours ago that he and Glenna had laughed in the gazebo by the pool? Had it been today that she had held his hand to her abdomen and challenged him to feel their baby's faint, fluttering movement? Right now, Blake thought dismally, those warm, happy moments seemed light years away. For the hundredth time, he glanced at the thin, gold Rolex Glenna had given him last Christmas. Then he clenched his fists with helpless fury.

Three hours. It's been three hours. She may be dying in there and there's not a goddamn thing I can do to help her.

Blake got up and strode to the windows, staring out into bleak darkness punctuated with bright lights of downtown Dallas that winked in the distance. The cheerful kaleidoscope of color somehow seemed obscene.

"Blake?"

He spun around at the sound of Greg Halpern's voice.

Greg looked as bad as Blake felt, and Blake's hope for a happy ending died before it had a chance to materialize.

Wearily Greg tugged off the paper surgical cap that covered his hair and stuffed it into a pocket of blood-spattered green scrubs. He looked as if he'd been through a war, Blake thought as he tried to find his voice to speak.

Greg apparently noticed Blake's loss of words. "I couldn't save the baby. It was a little girl. I'm sorry." He met Blake's gaze with sad, dark eyes.

"Glenna?" The question came out in a husky croak.

"She's in recovery."

"And . . ."

"And she's all right. We got the bleeding stopped—at least for now."

Blake finally took in a breath of air. "What happened? Not an hour before the bleeding started, Glenna was the happiest I've ever seen her. This morning she felt the baby moving for the first time. Greg, I'm afraid this is going to push her over the edge."

Greg sank into a chair and rubbed a hand across his stubbled chin. "You want a technical explanation?"

Blake nodded.

"The placenta separated. Remember I showed you on the ultrasound last week how low the placenta was attached? Quite simply, the growing baby put enough pressure on it to make it come loose. When this happened, Glenna started to hemorrhage."

"You mean this is the same thing that happened the last time Glenna miscarried?"

"Yes, except that this time she was farther along. That made the situation worse." Greg rubbed the bridge of his nose, as if to ease the strain of bright lights on his eyes.

"Did you have to . . ." Blake's words trailed off. He couldn't voice what he half hoped, half feared.

"I should have, but I didn't. Glenna refused permission

for a hysterectomy unless it was the only way to save her life. I'll take you to see her now. Blake, tonight is not the time, but very soon we three are going to have to have a serious talk," Greg said as they walked together to the recovery room.

Stiffly Glenna made her way to the breakfast room to "visit" with Greg and Blake. She had been home three days now, and it felt good to get out of the bedroom for a change.

Glenna had worked hard to shelve the deep sadness she felt when Blake had told her they had lost their little girl. Still, they had each other. And she had made up her mind that they *would* have their baby, next time.

"You said we needed to talk," she told Greg after joining Blake on the sofa. "I'm ready."

Glenna watched Greg looked pointedly at Blake. Then she felt Blake's hand enfold hers in a reassuring way, and her determined optimism began to erode.

"It would be tantamount to suicide for you to risk another pregnancy. For the sake of your present and future health, Glenna, you should have a hysterectomy as soon as I can schedule it."

Shocked, Glenna jerked her hand from Blake's and stared out the window at the spot she had planned for her children's playhouse. "I thought your specialty was helping couples who have problem pregnancies, Greg, not taking away their chances of ever having a baby," she snapped, knowing she was being rude as well as unfair, but unable at the moment to do more than lash out at the bearer of bad tidings.

"Glenna. Honey, let's listen to Greg." That was Blake, ever the conciliator, Glenna thought with a good deal of malice.

Still, she murmured, "Sorry," to Greg and sat back down to hear him out.

Greg sighed. "I know how much you want a child. And if I thought you could survive it, Glenna, I would be the first to suggest another try. It's my business to deliver healthy babies no one else thought had a snowball's chance in hell. I don't think you'll listen to me if I try to soft-pedal the facts, and you're both my friends as well as Glenna being my patient, so here it is, straight out.

"*You* have one of the worst cases of endometriosis I've ever tried to treat. I've operated three times, trying to correct it, but it just keeps coming back. On top of that, you have had three miscarriages despite our taking every precaution we could devise. Two of those pregnancies ended because of the placenta breaking away from the lining of the uterus and causing hemorrhage—and *placenta previa* is a condition that tends to recur. You're thirty-seven years old. Any of those factors alone would be sufficient for most obstetricians to caution you against trying again to have a baby." Greg paused, taking a sip from his drink before continuing.

"Before this last miscarriage, I had hoped you could carry the baby long enough to deliver a preemie that might have a chance for survival. Glenna, I'm sorry, but I don't believe you have a chance now of having a viable child. It is my opinion that the pregnancy itself could easily kill you. And, if you don't have the hysterectomy, your health is going to keep deteriorating until you won't be able to enjoy living."

Glenna felt herself shivering in spite of the sunny warmth of the glass-walled breakfast room. Blake's arm encircled her shoulders, and he pulled her against him for comfort, but the chill in Glenna's soul would not subside.

"You mentioned something at the hospital about options?" Blake said quietly to Greg. Suddenly Glenna felt a ray of hope.

Greg stretched out his legs in front of the glass-topped cocktail table. "Both of you want a baby. I see no reason why you wouldn't be able to adopt one or more."

"No!" Glenna sat up straighter and raked Greg with a furious gaze. "I want *our* baby."

"Glenna, that's not possible, honey," Blake said, stroking her shoulder as he spoke. "I want *you*, alive and well, as I believe I've said a thousand times. I'm willing to adopt—or simply to stay as we are, just the two of us."

"What about *in vitro* fertilization?" Glenna asked, suddenly recalling Greg's highly publicized successes with helping make "test tube" babies.

Greg smiled slightly. "That's not an option for you. *In vitro*'s for ladies who can't get pregnant in the usual way, not ones who can't carry a baby to term. If you don't want to adopt, exactly, you could hire a surrogate mother," he added. "That was the other option I had in mind."

A surrogate. "Then the baby would be Blake's," Glenna said excitedly. "How do we do it?"

"Hey, wait just a minute here," Blake interjected. "I don't like that idea one damn bit. Forget it."

"No! I won't just forget it. Greg, tell us how it's done." In her mind, Glenna was already picturing a plump, dark-haired newborn nestling snugly in her arms.

Greg shot a helpless look toward Blake. "The procedure itself is simple. You hire a healthy woman, I determine when she's ovulating; and when the time is right, I do an artificial insemination in the office, using fresh semen Blake has collected and delivered to me. Then we cross our fingers, and if we're lucky, nine months later you bring your baby home."

Glenna could almost feel Blake's mind formulating a scathing retort. "Why don't you explain the part that's everything but simple, Greg?" he finally asked, before entering into a recital of the myriad legal woes that could arise from entering into an agreement with a surrogate mother.

I'm finally going to have Blake's baby.

Glenna pushed her husband's arguments firmly from her mind. Not even his closing statement, a flat-out, adamant refusal to consider letting a stranger carry and bear his child for pay, diminished her resolve.

Presenting all-new romances— featuring ghostly heroes and heroines and the passions they inspire.

♥ *Haunting Hearts* ♥

__*STARDUST OF YESTERDAY*
by Lynn Kurland   0-515-11839-7/$5.99
A young woman inherits a castle—along with a ghost who tries to scare her away. Her biggest fear, however, is falling in love with him...

__*SPRING ENCHANTMENT*
by Christina Cordaire   0-515-11876-1/$5.99
A castle spirit must convince two mortals to believe in love— for only then will he be reunited with his own ghostly beloved...

__*GHOST OF A CHANCE*
by Casey Claybourne   0-515-11857-5/$5.99
Life can be a challenge for young newlyweds—especially when the family estate is haunted by a meddling mother-in-law...

__**HEAVEN ABOVE**   *(10/96)*
by Sara Jarrod   0-515-11954-7/$5.99
When Blake Turner's wife passes away, her ghost wants Blake to begin a family—with the surrogate mother of their child.